THE END OF IT ALL

A WEIRD WORLD SAGA BOOK

CAI FEASBY

CAT READS FICTION

For Mom

Who filled my childhood with music, cats, crazy trips and experiences. Who kept the doors to creativity, wonder and dreams firmly open when others wanted to slam them shut.

ONE

When the end of the world comes, what the fuck do you do?

Would you cry or maybe scream and shout, cursing the heavens at whatever god you pray to? Would you drop to your knees and simply give in to the sheer desperation of the situation? Maybe you'd run from your home and your crappy life, kiss a random stranger or throw rocks at your insufferable neighbours' windows. Maybe, just maybe, you'd end it all. Maybe even take a few others with you, willingly or not.

In the end, everyone did this and much more and, even surprisingly, much less. When the announcement had come I, like most of the populace, was numb-struck. When it happened it was the last in a line of negative events spun, seemingly, out of control by a dying mainstream media, desperate for views, clicks and attention.

'What's this?' I thought as I looked at my TV, 'What is this bullshit?'

The picture had changed to a rainbow of vertical bars. The text "Emergency Broadcast System" displayed in text made from rectangles, it seemed, against a black bar in the middle of the screen, doubling as a background for the half-friendly, slightly monotone voice of a mysterious, unseen broadcaster. Probably not even real. The voice calmly repeated the following message:

"Attention, a national terrorist event is underway. Stay calm and remain in your homes. Do not attempt to travel. Communications and broadcast services are experiencing temporary disruption. Normal services will resume. Please await further instructions."

My phone rumbled. I wrestled it out of the pocket of my jeans. The screen was already glowing, demanding attention. Several texts from colleagues. All saying the same sort of thing:

Have you seen the TV?

Is this for reals?!?

Wots goin' on?

I picked up the remote and thumbed through several channels. All were displaying the same message, the same voice repeating the same message.

'...Normal services will resume..."

My mind fumbled and grasped at the idea that this was some kind of elaborate prank. I looked over the TV, checking for any weird USB devices or anything else that could be interfering with it. If this was a prank, it was a good one. I reached for my silver laptop, unfolded it, and the screen flickered into life. Password entered. Ladybird was already running. I typed 'emergency broadcast system prank' into the address bar and hit return, which would normally start a search. But surprisingly enough, the internet didn't appear to be there.

No Internet
Try Checking the network cables, modem and router
Reconnecting to Wi-Fi
ERR_INTERNET_DISCONNECTED

Strange.

I checked the wifi connection on the laptop and then the router. Everything seemed fine. I glanced at the phone socket; the dirty white rectangle attached to the wall had the cable firmly fixed and in place. I rebooted the laptop and went to my phone's browser.

The same. Zero connection.

It's about this time I heard raised voices outside. I didn't pay too much attention, at least I usually didn't. Every now and then the neighbours would get a little excited and start shouting at each other, their kids or just generally anyone who was walking by. At first I thought it was the usual, but after a quick peek around the curtains to see what was going on (don't judge me, you've done it too), I saw the guy from across the road, not usually the shouty sort, quite the opposite, he looked fairly agitated and was pointing and looking like he was trying to get his three kids and wife into their estate car. His attention was divided between throwing coats and the odd bag into the rear of the car and coaching and urging their younger children into the car. The wife carried a large box of something and placed it in the trunk and guided one of the younger children into the vehicle and secured her with the seat belt. They didn't look happy. He pointed, looking a little red in the face; even being slightly overweight meant that the several trips to and from the house to the car meant he looked tired and sweaty.

The whole thing looked curious, and an alarm bell rang at the back of my head. I realised I'd furrowed my brow and was idly itching my cheek.

I turned my attention away from the outside world and back to my phone. I thumbed through my contacts and found Charlie and pressed the mobile icon to start a call.

After a few seconds I got a busy tone. I disconnected and tried Jenny. Again, busy.

Three more contacts, and it was all the same. Even good old dependable Dad was busy.

The TV was still displaying its cheerful rainbow image with its less than cheerful content.

I left it on and walked to the kitchen and turned on a small radio which lived on the window sill over the kitchen sink. Maybe it wasn't the best place to keep a radio, but it was a gamble I was happy to take. I switched it on; the small power button made a satisfying click. I waited a few moments and was greeted with silence. I checked the Channel; "Absolute 80's". Maybe something a little more informative was available. I pressed the channel selection button until I found BBC Radio 4. I got a small pulsing, beeping sound. I moved to Radio 5. Again, nothing.

Maybe going a tad old school would help, I thought as I changed from DAB to FM.

The regional BBC station was already programmed in and surprisingly was functional, although I'd joined in mid-section.

'...the terrorist attack on the capital not seen since 9/11. We're receiving further reports that Westminster has been devastated, too. The House of Commons is largely destroyed, with further reports of severe damage to the MI5 building and the surrounding areas. Internet and other broadcast services have been affected. The government is urging people to remain calm and has advised against travelling unless the journey is absolutely necessary. We'll update you as soon as we have more'

I changed the channels and found a local radio station closer to home.

The signal was garbled; the radio emitted strange pops, beeps and squeaks, but behind it was a female voice, sort of authoritative in the way the BBC seems to breed its presenters. The voice seemed to pop in and out of existence. I could make out a few words here and there.

"....disaster.....London....ingham....sion.....manch....ed mist....survivors"

It was sort of frustrating, but I got the gist. This definitely wasn't a prank or joke.

Like everyone else, I would have to wait for more details later.

You'd think that there would be blind panic, but there wasn't. There was perhaps more malaise to the world. I felt nothing, but then life had a certain capacity to enable a disconnect.

I turned off the radio, filled the kettle halfway, clicked it on and waited for the water to boil. The faint sound of the neighbours' car, finally pulling away, echoed in the background.

I checked my phone again; no new calls, no texts, no service.

It was sort of refreshing in a way, the silence, the disconnection.

The kettle bubbled, boiled and finally clicked off. I hastily dumped instant coffee in my favourite mug and poured in the hot water and stirred a few times. I tapped the spoon on the edge of the mug, which clinked pleasantly. I tossed it into the sink and paced into the living room and slumped onto the sofa.

I sighed and took a tentative sip of the hot beverage.

"Well," I announced to no one but the four walls. "I suppose this makes for a different Saturday than usual."

TWO

By Saturday night the TV and radio had returned. The emergency broadcast was replaced by almost constant news. Although the signal remained erratic, with periods of seemingly random downtime or moments when the image would glitch out and distort. Scheduled programmes were interrupted, shifted and even cancelled. Breaking news and pictures of the event were being broadcast to all and sundry at all hours. Explosions had been reported in London, Manchester and Birmingham, although the broadcast only showed smoke and out-of-focus images from Birmingham and Manchester. Central London had been isolated and seemingly cordoned off after a larger explosion, although the extent of the damage wasn't widely known at the time.

The news was morose, and after a day of constant doom and gloom, I turned off the TV and tried to find something else to focus on.

There had been an upside; the government had announced a day of mourning in honour of our first responders, many of whom had perished on that first day, and this coming Monday already being a bank holiday meant that Tuesday would be a public holiday for this purpose. Which suited me just fine. I didn't mind work, it wasn't my dream career, but it did pay the bills. Any day off is a good day.

I checked my phone again; according to the latest reports, there was limited service on most networks. However, I hadn't seen anything anywhere approaching 3G for days, and the little icon at the top of my phone told me there was little to no chance of any connection. 5G was a pipe dream at this stage.

A dull roar echoed through the sky outside. Somewhere a fighter jet, or maybe several, was doing manoeuvres or whatever it was they were tasked with. The noise of military jets and helicopters was starting to become normal. At any point in the day you could go outside and watch them flitting back and forth over the sky. Sometimes you could only hear the faintest of jet engines or the glimpse of something dark dashing between clouds. Other times you could see the slow meandering of a large helicopter in drab olive green against the blue of the sky.

The initial excitement was dying down, at least in our area. The tense air of panic that had weaved its way into our collective minds had now been replaced with complaints and frustration at what we didn't have. The lack of internet annoyed more than a few and seemed to take greater precedence than the lack of groceries at the local supermarket. I braved the annoyed crowds, well the more annoyed crowds than usual, and picked out a few things in my weekly shop. I was expecting bare shelves, but the store seemed fairly well stocked, although the fruit and vegetable section was now a desert; lonely, battered and bruised apples languished along with the odd misshapen potato. I grabbed a large bottle of cola, a few cans of "cat piss" energy drink and a few assorted bottles of beers and sugary drinks. I shuffled my way around the aisles with various goodies, picking up a decent selection of biscuits. The next aisle over was home to savoury snacks: chips, or crisps as I was constantly told, and other salty biscuits. I grabbed a random few packs and threw them onto their sugary counterparts. Done. Even in the midst of whatever this was, the world still plodded on, and life with it. Which meant it was my turn to host game day. Which was why I was stocking up on less than healthy options for my food and drink.

The biweekly get-together had become something of a high point in our, for want of a better word, normal and uneventful lives. My two friends, Charlie and Josh, and I had found ourselves somewhat rudderless of late. Josh had abandoned hopes of being a pilot after he ran out of money and shortly found work as a forklift operator. Charlie settled into life as a truck driver, which kept him away from people and office work. And me? I'd fallen into working on a tech support help desk, answering phones and redirecting calls to other, more technical, departments. It was a job that was uninspiring and, dare I say it, boring. But it afforded me something most precious, which I clung to: time. The time to do something else. I'd been trying to motivate myself and find some other career, something more meaningful, but somehow it eluded me. I'd taken the job five years ago to fill a gap, to pay bills and figure out my next move. After the third year I realised that I wasn't going to make a move. Somehow, I made it work, but there was always that nagging feeling that I could be doing something more, hell, I wanted to be doing something more. But what? Forever the eternal question.

Game day had become the thing which brought us together, kept us together, and kept us strong and sane. Well, as sane as we could be at any rate. Game day would also translate into movie day, depending on the mood, but this week would most definitely be a game day; Josh had been raving about a new fighting game that had been released the week before, and this would be our introduction. In preparation we'd each agreed to purchase a copy and not play the main story mode, which we'd experience together, electing instead to practise in Gym mode, which was a glorified training section. Naturally I'd put in a good few hours, and I assumed everyone else was doing the same. I was looking forward to it; it would be a small diversion, something different for everyone to talk about. To relax for a few hours and forget about attacks, wars, politics and what would happen next and where.

I felt strangely at ease and quite happy as I walked home, groceries half stuffed into a backpack and the rest in a canvas carrier bag. Just three friends and some graphic video game violence until the early hours of the morning.

THREE

"You know that's what they want you to think, right?"

"No, I didn't, Charlie, Tell me again." said Josh, a smirk spreading across his face

"What?" said Charlie, continuing regardless of Josh's sarcasm. "So the internet just stopped working on its own, a network designed to withstand multiple nuclear attacks."

"I only have to see how bad the service I get with BT is to realise that it's no surprise and certainly not a deliberate effort to stop people communicating." Josh countered

"Not not communicating. Sharing information," corrected Charlie

"Same difference," said Josh absently, waving a bottle of cola in the air, as if to punctuate the point.

I could see Charlie gearing up for another salvo and decided to interject.

"How about you two quit bitching at each other long enough to clear this fight?" I said, gesturing to the TV, "I'm still waiting to kick whoever's ass is going to win this round!"

Charlie looked annoyed, but he eyed the TV, the paused image waiting to lurch back into life when someone was ready to select 'Resume' from the options displayed in the center of the screen.

"Anyone want anything else?" I offered

Josh was straight in with a request; as always, the lure of food and drink was a primary driver.

"Feel free to surprise me. I iz hungry!"

Despite the amount he ate, he was remarkably trim. It was Charlie who, strangely enough for someone who claimed to always be on the move, was on the dumpy side. Although I wasn't one to judge, as I'd put on a few extra pounds over the last few years.

I wandered back into the kitchen and found the second pack of Wagon Wheels, the best kind, with a jammie middle. I also found they had been compromised, the top of the pack seemingly torn open by some ravenous beast.

"I see you already found the second pack."

"I have no idea what you're talking about." Replied Josh

"Oh, what the fuck was that, you cheating fuck!" complained Charlie; well, it was more shouted.

After playing through a good amount of story mode, we'd turned our attention to versus mode, in earnest. Charlie had a thing for fighting games; in fact, he and Josh were pretty good. At times they'd beat each other to a standstill if they had a decent amount of experience of the game they were playing. This was not one of those times. Charlie had won three rounds in quick succession, he seemed to have got to grips with one of the characters called Rhona, a fairly muscular female fighter who seemed to have some good punches but had several moves which threw opponents to the ground and submitted them in short order. Josh had shouted "cheese" a number of times after failing to counter these moves when he clearly had enough and unleashed his secret weapon; his character, despite the game being marketed as a realistic fighting game, had a secret ability to change into some kind of ninja and throw some kind of acidic blast which quickly ended Charlie's streak.

"Welcome to cheese-land," retorted Josh. "How do you like my Gouda?"

I laughed as I watched.

"How the hell did you do that? And what the fuck?"

Josh blew out a sharp "Hah"

He smirked as his character, called Eric Mac of all things, fired another burst of energy and won the match, breaking Charlie's winning streak.

"A grandmaster never tells his secrets," said Josh, triumph blazing in his eyes

"Oh fuck right off" said Charlie, digging into his pocket and pulling out his phone "I'm getting some...oh."

In the moment he'd forgotten about the lack of internet; in fact, we all had. Game night was doing what it did best, providing an escape from our humdrum reality, from our humdrum lives, maybe a little too well!

"You want in?" asked josh, extending the controller in my general direction.

Charlie protested, "You can't just walk away from this, Josh, bloody cheat!"

"It's not cheating if it's part of the game."

"How the hell is a ninja spitting acid part of the game?"

Josh laughed

"Guess you'll have to play through single player to find out."

"Cypher!" Shouted Charlie, "Turncoat! We agreed, "No play-throughs."

Josh shrugged

"Sounds like you girls have business to attend to." I said, "I need a coffee. Anyone else want one?"

"Sure."

"Sounds good, thanks."

I heard Josh speaking but couldn't make out exactly what he said as I filled the kettle with water.

"Oh fuck you," came the louder reply from Charlie. Which I heard just fine.

I smiled to myself as I dumped instant coffee into three mugs and waited for the, now rumbling, electric kettle to boil.

———

A handful of hours passed. Many cups of hot and cold drinks had been consumed, the entirety of the biscuits I had bought had been decimated, and the remnants of packaging were now stuffed into a nearly full bin in the kitchen. Controllers were finally being put down. Josh rubbed his face, a sure sign he was tired. Charlie seemed to stare off into the distance. After so much sweet stuff, I craved something hot and savoury. My stomach gurgled at the thought.

"Pizza before we call an end to this?" I suggested

Charlie broke from his staring competition with the wall. "I'm there; I'm voting no mushrooms if we're sharing."

"Pizza!" said Josh, "No sweetcorn for me. Tastes like spots."

I grimaced at the description and instinctively picked up my phone and opened my favourite food ordering app. No connection.

Even after a few days of no internet, we all hadn't yet adapted. We had clung to the idea that somehow it would be okay and everything would work again, just as it had done in the days and eventually weeks previously. I pulled open a drawer in the kitchen. It was stuffed with all manner of bits and pieces. Batteries that may, or may not, work. All of varying types and sizes. Old headphones and older charging cables for a phone I hadn't owned in years and probably would never own. I rummaged around and disturbed more of the contents. A plastic fork, no, a spork. Bits of paper with hastily scribbled notes, now mystery hieroglyphs of unrecognisable scrawl. The large majority were leaflets for local and not-so-local takeaways. I pulled a few out and flicked through them looking for the menu for Pizza Dude. I knew I had one somewhere. Technology had largely replaced menus, and there was a real risk that I'd thrown it out. But who was I kidding? This drawer existed as a testament to the fact that old and useless shit has a place to sit and, maybe one day, be useful again. I rummaged deeper, trying to find more menus to look through. I pulled a Magic Troll from the depths of the drawer and held it up; its cheeky grin and bright magenta hair dominated my focus. I tossed it on the counter, half wondering where the hell it had come from, and returned to my hunt.

After the third dive I found my quarry. Why was it that you always found what you were looking for last out of everything? I swept most of what I'd pulled from the drawer back where it came from, leaving a few items rolling around on the countertop. I figured I'd tidy up later. The troll almost glared at me in defiance with its cute yet chubby face. I pushed the derpy-looking toy into the drawer and closed it; it was an abrupt slam.

I turned my attention to the leaflet, which I unfolded.

Pizza Dude was one of our favourite spots; hell, it was our only favourite spot. Sure, we indulged in the chain pizza and burgers that you see everywhere. But Pizza Dude was something special. The pizza was fresh and made by hand, not mass-produced in a factory somewhere. I looked down the menu and made a decision for everyone before pressing the contact name I had stored in my phone.

After several attempts I finally managed to get through and place an order, although it would appear everyone else had the same idea. Our pizza would take an hour to make. I volunteered everyone for a walk down to the shop for a pickup, which was met with various amounts of disapproval.

I left Josh and Charlie engaging in verbal battle about the game and possibly pizza while I went to the toilet to empty an overly full bladder. I returned to more bitching, although of a different kind.

"You gotta be prepared." Charlie was saying

Josh was saying not much, which was something. He seemed to shrug, as if giving up.

He sauntered past me and into the kitchen.

"Whatever! I need a slash."

Charlie looked at me with calculating eyes.

"Here." He stepped forward, pulling a small brown envelope from somewhere I don't remember.

"What's this?" I said, flipping the envelope in my hands, it had my name written on it.

"It's a plan," responded Charlie. "If things get really bad, we need a plan."

I sighed and looked at him, trying to gauge his intent; he seemed genuine

"So what is it, really?" I went to thumb the envelope open but Charlie interrupted

"Don't open it now; it's for when things get real bad, like world-ending bad. It's a plan of action to make sure we're all on the same page."

"And I can't open it now?"

"No"

"You realise that makes no sense." I said. I looked at the envelope again "it's a note which says 'go fuck yourself', isn't it?"

"Fine, be like Josh."

"Sensible?"

"Close-minded and untrusting"

I shrugged, and Josh appeared, looking very pleased with himself.

"The toilet is now out of order," he said, "for the next fifty years."

"For fuck's sake, Josh, did you at least spray?" I barked

"Mmmaybe" he replied

"Great, I guess I'm braving whatever infection Josh has," grumbled Charlie as he head off towards the toilet; at least I assume that's where he was heading

I turned to Josh, envelope in hand.

"You get one of these?"

Josh smirked. "Yeah, I opened it."

"Oh?" I said.

"It's just a list of shit and some directions."

"Oh my god!" came the slightly manic voice of Charlie from upstairs. "What the hell is this SMELL?"

I looked at the envelope and walked into the kitchen and tossed it into the garbage.

"We'll be outside," I yelled to Charlie

I heard a muffled reply of some kind, which I assumed was an acknowledgement.

I grabbed my coat from the back of a chair and waited outside with Josh. The cold air of the night instantly prickled and pinched my exposed skin. Our breath billowed into the new night sky. The dull orange glow of light pollution emanating from Leeds in the distance.

The two of us stood, waiting like lemons, for Charlie. We talked about nothing in particular, and we were discussing the under appreciated merits of Terminator Salvation when Charlie appeared.

"Ready." he smiled

I closed and locked the door, and we set off on foot. Driving was an option, but sometimes a walk can make you feel like you've earned your pizza treat. The walk to Pizza Dude was a good two to three miles, and we were there in what felt like no time, having pulled apart all the movie remakes that we had seen in the last few years and discussed the continued downturn of our favourite franchises.

We arrived at Pizza Dude, and our pizza was pretty much ready when we stepped through the door. The temperature outside was getting colder and fast, so we decided to take our box and sit on one of the tables in the shop itself. Pizza was eagerly devoured as we continued to forget about the problems of the real world for a while. I glanced towards the counter every now and then. A small TV flashed images in the back of the kitchen, entertainment for whoever was on shift. I could see that the news was constantly being watched. A few employees would idly look at the screen and listen to whatever was being said. The noise of cooking and customers ordering and talking loudly drowned out the sound.

I noticed the TV would flicker and the picture would halt. Strange colours would creep over the screen; the perfect image was now blocky and hardly recognisable. Within an instant it would correct itself, and the broadcast would resume. It seems to do this quite a bit.

"You okay?" I heard a familiar voice say, I felt a prod on my shoulder and my attention snapped back to my friends at the opposite side of the table, the pizza box in front of me now empty.

"Sorry, just zoned out there for a second."

Josh drummed loudly on the table. "I think I'm going to call it a night, ladies."

He stretched his arms up and rubbed his face.

"I think I've had enough victory for one day," he added

"Cheating does make you tired." Charlie chimed in, "So I've been told."

"Superior knowledge and experience isn't cheating."

Charlie huffed and opened his mouth to say something.

"Geez, girls," I interjected, "why don't you two get a room?"

They both looked at me like I'd sprouted a second or maybe third head.

I ignored them, extracted myself from the table, picked up the empty pizza box and relocated them to the nearest bin. As I walked back to the table, where Charlie was now wrestling with his coat to get an arm through a sleeve that appeared to have folded back in on itself. I glanced at the counter; several kitchen staff members glanced up at seemingly random intervals while they prepped food and moved between different workstations.

Carlo, the owner, sat just behind the counter, glancing

back at the TV. He turned back towards the shop door and saw me walking past and smiled.

"Crazy night, huh?"

"I guess everyone wants pizza, non?"

"No, not pizza," he said and nodded towards the TV. "The London cordon has been increased, and some sort of emergency meeting is going on."

"Must be bad."

Carlo shrugged. "Just what they're saying on TV. Apparently all trains to and from London have been cancelled. People stuck at train station, but good for business."

A wide grin creeping across his face.

"Well", I said, walking by, "at least business is good in a crisis."

Charlie had managed to get his coat under control by the time I returned to the table. We said our goodbyes and filed out of the warm, almost claustrophobic, shop and into the cold night.

"Fuck, it's cold," said Josh. "Right, I'm going to get going. Good day, chaps."

"Yeah," Charlie agreed and I nodded

"Let's do this again. Charlie, you're it." I said

"Sweet," he replied, "and I'll give you a good shoeing for sure."

Josh tutted and turned to walk away. "I'm out," he shouted and strode off

I waved goodbye to Charlie and watched him run a few steps to catch up to Josh. I turned around and started to walk in the opposite direction, towards home.

The streets were more alive than I expected. A few people staggered here and there, probably drunk. I made sure to avoid them as best as possible; trouble sometimes followed them closer than I was comfortable with. Several shouted and jeered in my general direction. I felt a sort of nervous tension. I balled my fists into my pockets and walked on, the shouting and laughing dying slowly into the background as the main street gave way to the quieter residential streets. Sirens wailed in the distance.

The silence was somewhat unnerving. I quickened my pace. Home beckoned. I looked forward to making a coffee, collapsing on the couch and maybe watching something on YouTube. I silently cursed myself for forgetting about the lack of internet. It occurred to me that we had been, in a very short amount of time, pre-programmed to accept that the internet would always be there.

Maybe it would be back up and running by the time I got back. Maybe I could finally watch the end of Season 5 of Z Nation?

I shoved my hands deeper into my jacket pockets, hiding them from the ever chillier cold air.

Maybe I'd upgrade that coffee to a hot chocolate.

I hunkered down; I could feel my muscles tighten and bunch up as the cold needled at them, trying to drain the warmth from them. I turned another corner and onto the long street which led to home. A few cats darted here and there, enjoying the cooler air and another chance to catch an unsuspecting critter. Houses slowly scrolled by as my mind drifted. I thought of nothing in particular, although my thoughts kept coming back to a warm bed and a hot drink. It felt a little more tired with each step towards home.

As my feet started to get numb, I turned the final corner and saw my front door not more than fifty feet away. I felt like running the last few feet. I fumbled with my keys as my fingers refused to work as normal. I finally managed to insert the small key into the lock, turn and give the door a push. I was treated to a wall of warm air as I stepped inside.

I hastily closed the door and kicked off my cold shoes. I headed to the kitchen and clicked the kettle on. I turned to the cupboards to find a mug when I noticed something on the counter opposite. The kettle started making a noise like a small jet engine as it began heating the water inside. I walked over and saw the small, brown envelope I'd thrown into the trash earlier. The envelope was marked with little stains from whatever was in the bin. A small yellow Post-it note was stuck to the envelope. A handwritten note of a single word was written in neat, precise handwriting.

'Bitch!'

I laughed aloud and pushed the envelope into the allotted 'stuff' drawer where, no doubt, it would remain unforgotten. Almost the next best thing to throwing it away. The warmth of the house was comforting, and I found myself feeling more tired than ever.

I thought about watching TV, but I doubted there was anything on, aside from the current news cycle of constant doom soothing. I continued to watch the kettle boil until it clicked itself off. I poured a half-and-half mixture of hot and cold water and gulped the warm coffee down in short order. I picked a few biscuits from the cupboard and slowly munched on them as I leaned on the counter, thinking generally about nothing.

The coffee warmed my stomach. My eyes felt itchy and tired.

I almost stumbled up the stairs and managed to brush my teeth, change out of my clothes and crawl into bed. Sometimes I wished I didn't have to sleep. But today I was glad to close my eyes and let the darkness take me.

FOUR

The sound of thunder woke me up with a start. A shuddering boom which jolted me awake. Tired and confused, I listened for several fleeting moments before I realised it was the sound of a jet engine. Whatever was up there was very low and thus very loud. I rolled onto my back and rubbed my eyes. What time was it? The sky looked dark from within my bedroom, but there was a dull orange flicker that seemed to light up the room in a strange moving texture.

I swung my legs out of bed and cradled my head in my hands and yawned. I rubbed my head and pushed up from the bed as another massive roar echoed throughout the sky. The faint throbbing sounds of helicopter rotors in the distance joined the cacophony of noise. I pulled the curtains just enough to peek at what was going on outside.

A few people were milling around the street, chatting to each other and pointing up at the sky, which seemed to bathe the whole street in a soft orange colour. The sky itself was a glorious pattern of flickering orange. I couldn't quite see the source, which was obscured by my neighbours' roofs. Several black angular shapes moved quickly in front of the dancing orange spectacle; more planes. Some moving silently, their engines masked by altitude and distance. Several were closer and possibly the same that roused me from my slumber. I looked back down the street and saw more people joining the impromptu meeting outside; doors cracked open, and more people ventured outside to watch the show. I checked the clock on my nightstand: two thirty. This was altogether too early. I yawned involuntarily and let the curtain collapse back against the window. I felt both tired and awake, if that's possible, and decided the best course of action would be to make some coffee. I have no idea where the idea of coffee as a pick-me-up came from; for me, coffee has always been somewhat of a soothing friend. It's that warm morning hug that you need from a drink. I slobbed my way towards the kitchen, feet shuffling against the hardwood of the landing, the ever-constant creaking of wooden stairs as I made my way to the kitchen. The tiles of the kitchen were cold and familiar as I walked over to the counter and flicked on the kettle. I pattered into the lounge while it did its thing, a watched pot and all that.

I slumped down onto the couch and pulled the remote from a crevasse of soft fabric and thumbed the power button. The small red light on the corner of the set blinked off, and the screen flicked on. The single image of the emergency broadcast system stared back at me. I flicked through the channels as a monotonous buzzing alert demanded my attention. The same image playing on all channels. The only information presented was a single one-line message.

'Please stand by.'

I had thought we had got past this and were heading back to some kind of normality, but it appeared not. Services were up and down like a yo-yo, as I've heard people say.

I flipped the remote back onto the sofa and shuffled back into the kitchen to make my coffee, leaving the TV to its own devices.

I set about preparing coffee, the kettle now appearing to reach a crescendo. I dumped a good heaped teaspoon of coffee into my favourite, still unwashed, mug. I reached for the kettle when

BOOM

I didn't so much hear the sound as feel it. It sounded like the sky had split in two. The windows of the house seemed to shake and rattle in protest; I jumped and knocked over the small jar, spilling coffee over the counter. Car alarms screeched and cried out as if in response. Hurried, urgent voices and the odd scream came from the street outside. I hurriedly went to the downstairs window and drew the curtains. The sky was now a deep red; a thick black cloud of smoke appeared to be climbing into the sky. It seemed like almost everyone was in the street. Some people were running; who could tell where, but they seemed to run down the street, maybe to a neighbour's house or maybe just back into their own. It occurred to me that even though I shared the street with these people, I hardly knew any of them. They were almost total strangers. I felt a weird sense of disconnection. Some of them stood and watched the sky. Watching the tiny jets peel away into the distance. It almost looked like daytime. The sky itself seemed like it was on fire. I peered both ways to get more of a glimpse of what was going on, but there was too much movement. I found myself venturing to the door, unlocking it and stepping outside. The cold of the night hit me, but the brilliant orange of the sky, even though it was marred by the steady plume of smoke, held my gaze and seemed to push the cold away. I was entranced; I'd never seen anything like it. I snapped out of the trance and looked around. People were seemingly everywhere. The large majority were watching, pointing, commenting, and talking amongst themselves. I noticed a few were hurriedly throwing bags and other assorted items into their cars. Some were half dressed in their night clothes. Loud voices, wild gestures, and a few children laughing and running around, if you can believe it. Their parents too involved in their own worries to care about a little hyperactivity at this hour.

I got the overwhelming sense of not really knowing what to do. Knowing what to do involved actually knowing what was going on. I felt the raw fingers of panic start to claw at the edge of my consciousness; maybe I was finally waking up, or maybe I was just realising that maybe things weren't ever going to be the same again. At the time it seemed such a silly thought. I figured things might settle down, panic would subside and people would return to whatever their normal lives were. I ventured back into my house and closed the door, shutting everyone out, literally and figuratively. I slumped on the couch and tried to rouse something from the TV; there had to be some service. I flicked through multiple channels. Nothing, just the standard emergency broadcast image, and even now it was glitching and flickering in and out of existence. I checked my phone; no bars showed, just the small 'no signal' message at the top of the screen. I sat and stared at the silent TV and felt lost, disconnected. I hadn't a clue as to what to do, where to go or what was even the right thing to do. Should I just stay put and hope something happens, that somehow word arrives to tell us that everything is okay, or until the TV and mobile phones come back online? I pushed myself up from the sofa and pattered into the kitchen and flicked the kettle back on to reboil the water. The kettle roared again, and within half a minute steam was pouring out of the top of the spout, and the thermostat inside clicked itself off. I stirred the coffee and hot water together and added some cold water to top it off. I took a small sip and almost recoiled; it was still too hot. I placed the mug on the counter and felt my gaze turn to the drawer at the end of the far worktop. My eyes settled on it, and I let the world wash over me, the sounds of excited and aggravated people still managing to be heard through closed doors and windows. To my surprise I found my hands shaking. I pushed myself away from the counter and walked to the drawer and opened it. Charlie's envelope, with the Post-it note still stuck to the front of it, sat on top of the pile of takeaway menus and random junk the drawer seemed to collect.

I lifted the envelope out, flipped it over and ran my finger through the back of it, tearing it open. I pulled out a single, neatly folded piece of paper. I opened it up and saw that it had writing on both sides. One side appeared to be several lists; a small number two circled was at the top of the page. I flipped it over. At the top of this page was a one in a circle. This side appeared to be a letter, of sorts, composed by Charlie, and printed this out as follows...

> Dear [my name had been scribbled out and 'pain in the arse' substituted],
> If you're reading this, then we're all fucked. And in these final hours I wanted to make sure that you understood my need to make sure, as a friend, you knew exactly how I felt, even if I couldn't say it in person.
>
> I WAS FUCKING RIGHT!
>
> I'm not 100% sure what's happening or what will happen, but I figure we need to stick together no matter what.
> First, cobble together as many of the supplies listed overleaf as possible, and then we'll mobilise.
> Josh and I will make our way to YOUR house. This means stay put and don't go anywhere.
> From your house we can figure things out and get a proper idea of where to go and what to do next. And yes, I have ideas.
> The most important thing is not to panic and keep to the plan.
> Also, water. Water is important. Fill as many containers with water as you can.
>
> Signed Charlie [scrawled]

I flipped the letter over, and there was an extensive list of all manner of food items as well as what looked to be medical and hygiene-related bits and pieces. I glanced through and tossed the letter onto the counter. This felt ridiculous; this felt like an elaborate prank. Would Derren Brown be turning up anytime soon? Would there be a knock on the door and a camera be there? I looked out my kitchen window; the night sky was alive with the deep, flickering oranges, reds and yellows. The faint outline of aircraft continued to be manoeuvring in the distance. I looked back at the letter and picked up my cup of coffee and made my way in the lounge and sat down on the sofa and found some music to listen to and wondered if and when Charlie and Josh would turn up.

FIVE

And turn up they did, three hours later, several cups of coffee and a good way through an old science fiction novel I'd been meaning to read for a while. The neighbours had continued in the street until they got bored, returning inside, hiding behind closed doors. Lights had slowly been extinguished. Lit windows disappeared and plunged the houses in darkness as silence slowly claimed the street; just the distant sounds of sirens and the dull rumbles of aircraft charging through the sky disrupted the calm. The glorious silence was disturbed by an urgent banging at the door, and I knew it was Charlie, or at least assumed it was, given his irrational disdain for doorbells. I settled the cold remnants of my most recent cup of coffee onto the small wooden side table and took my time opening the door. As I opened it, I was greeted with the sight of Charlie and Josh looking cold. Charlie had his hand held up as if he were about to pound on the front door again.

"What's up, turds?" I said and opened the door fully to let my two friends in.

They scurried through, huffing and puffing.

"Fucking freezing," grumbled Josh to no one but the universe.

Charlie settled himself onto the sofa and glimpsed into the

mug to see what I was drinking. Satisfied, or disappointed, with the contents, he settled back and looked at me and Josh, who was loitering in the general area.

"So then," he said gleefully. "End of the world anyone?"

"Not the end of the world," said Josh, pushing past me and slumping onto a vacant chair.

"The fucking sky looks like it's on fire," retorted Charlie, stretching out an arm, gesturing to the window. "What do you make of that?"

Josh shrugged. "Fire in Leeds?"

"It does look like most of Leeds is on fire from here," I said

"Thank you," said Charlie

"But that's just a fire, not anything else" I added

Josh smiled smugly and looked at Charlie and gave him the finger.

"This isn't normal. Everything about this isn't normal. No internet, no TV, and mobiles and phones are up and down like a yoyo. Plus the sky and the jets."

"Fair point," said Josh. "But you're not going to have roaming gangs of zombies in the streets, mark my words."

"I'm not saying that, you vast slug!"

Josh snorted a laugh at Charlie's insult.

"So what are you two doing then? Besides inviting yourself over?"

"I think," said Charlie with a gleam in his eye, "we should check it out."

"What?" I found myself saying

"We should check it out and see what's going on. Leeds is just down the road; let's go see what's up."

I looked at both of them, who looked at me. Ideas of sitting, drinking coffee and letting everything settle down and return to normal seemed to have vanished.

"Well, I've got nothing better to do and I'm awake now," said Josh

"Are you fucking mad?" I asked

"C'mon, where's your sense of adventure? Besides, we're

just going for a look," explained Charlie. "It's not like we're going to try and do anything."

I thought for a moment and felt the pressure of two sets of eyes gazing at me. I let out an audible sigh.

"Fine." I said, "Give me five minutes to get changed, and we can go and see this is nothing like you think this is."

SIX

"I didn't think it would be like this," I said, eyeing the traffic jammed in around us.

We'd taken my car and driven away from our small little town just beyond Selby and headed through backroads and eventually joined the A63, which would take us towards Leeds, avoiding anything that might be super congested. Our plan was sound, but the traffic had got busier rapidly, and soon we found ourselves stopped and, within several minutes, hemmed in from all sides as other traffic joined, obviously thinking the same as we were. The single carriageway was now chewed with cars all going the same way, towards Leeds. I looked around for some kind of way out, some way to turn around, but there was none. The grassy verge to the side was thick and muddy. Up ahead I could see several cars, stuck fast. One car was still, valiantly, battling the elements, wheels spinning and engine revving, but only getting more and more mired in the filthy, sticky ground.

I could hear Charlie drumming his fingers on the door in the back of the car. I glanced in the rearview mirror and saw him intently looking over the sprawling fields, now illuminated by the orange sky, itself now a dying light. Now obscured by several plumes of dirty black smoke.

There was a big sigh from the passenger seat.

"This isn't quite the adventure that was advertised," said Josh

We were now only a few miles or so from Leeds, and the A63 wasn't a large road, not like the multi-lane motorways of the A1M or the M62. I wondered what they would look like, how many cars would be jammed and trapped on these arterial roads which had served the UK for so long. I heard a familiar click, and a blast of chilled air filled the car as Charlie opened the door.

"Wait," I said. "Where are you..."

"Just wanna check it out," he said, leaning down into the car before slamming the door closed.

Josh and I sat tight; we watched Charlie walk down the queue of traffic. Other people were also out and about, looking, wandering around. Some talking to each other. It would appear as though Britain was doing what Britain does best: queue and gossip.

Josh shifted in his seat as we watched Charlie tramp out of our immediate view.

"Don't tell him this," he said, glancing my way. "But I'm starting to believe."

I looked at Josh, eyebrow involuntarily raised.

Josh laughed.

"It's crazy to think, but this isn't normal. I've never seen it like this."

"Could be an accident." I said

"No", said Josh, his gaze returning to beyond the car. "This feels like something else."

I sat and gripped the steering wheel. A nervous knot in my stomach twisted and flipped.

Truth be told, I wanted it to be nothing. Wanted it to be just something else. But even I was feeling on edge as something tugged at my psyche, some unknown force. Some whisper in my ear, letting me know that nothing would be the same again.

My knuckles were going white, and I slowly released my grip on the wheel.

I said nothing, but both Josh and I heard everything in the silence of the car.

Charlie returned thirty or so minutes later. Josh and I had elected to step out of the car to stretch and generally people-watch.

Charlie half bounded up to us, red-faced and slightly out of breath.

"It's jammed all the way up to the A1 by the looks of it."

"You look far too excited," said Josh, flatly.

"The roads blocked," said Charlie enthusiastically

"We can see that," I said, motioning to all the cars in front and behind us

"No. I mean, the road has been sealed off at the junction. Someone dropped concrete barriers on the slip-roads to the motorway."

"What?" Said Josh, "There's no way that's true."

"Go check it out for yourself," replied Charlie. "This is big. I can feel it."

"You look way too excited for this," I said, the lack of sleep starting to catch up with me.

"So now what?" Asked Josh

"Well," said Charlie, "let's press on; we can't drive beyond here, but we can walk."

"Are you for real?" Asked Josh

Charlie considered the question for a moment. I stifled a yawn while they argued amongst themselves. More recently I had been finding myself staying quiet, almost apart from them when they get like this, I find it's easier than pushing my own oar in, as it were.

"I am, indeed, for real." Charlie postured

"For fuck's sake. Fine."

Josh relented

Charlie strode off, walking a few steps before turning back to us.

"C'mon," he gestured. "Let's go; you'll not believe it until you see it for yourself."

Josh grumbled something but followed Charlie. I brought up the rear, stuffing my hands into the pockets of my jacket and hunching forward against the cold of the day, and wondered, to myself, what the hell I was doing.

Twenty minutes later I was unzipping my jacket as we approached the roundabout that linked the A63 with the A1. Cars were jammed almost against each other. A bunch of people were wandering about, but there weren't many people in or around the multitude of cars which were stacked haphazardly across the carriageway. The whole situation felt strange, unreal. The sun had risen, and the colour of the sky was changing. A cloud-heavy sky, illuminated by the flames which were enveloping the center of Leeds. As we reached the roundabout, we could see the motorway below, which was strangely deserted. I peered southbound and couldn't make out a single vehicle. I looked around amidst the chaos of cars and could see large blocks of pre-formed concrete, stacked three deep, blocking each of the on and off-ramps that would lead to the motorway below.

Charlie noticed what must've looked like a confused look on my face.

"See?" He said, nudging Josh, "The blocks are keeping everyone off the motorway."

Josh said nothing. He just looked around and confirmed what I'd already seen. We calmly walked over to the north end of the roundabout and peered over the metal railings.

He walked back and rubbed his head as he approached us.

"Doesn't make any sense." He said, "Unless they don't want people to use the motorways."

"Who's 'they?" I asked

"Pffft," shrugged Josh. "Ask the key master there," he said, nodding towards Charlie

I looked back to see Charlie leaning over the edge of the bridge, looking down at something on the motorway below.

"If he's the key master, does that make you the gatekeeper?" I ventured

"I think that's a role you're more suited for, non?"

I fake gasped "such a biiiiitch" I whispered

We laughed. But not for long. Someone yelled from the far end of the overpass. Instinctively almost everyone looked over and saw one of the onlookers, a man, pointing towards the northbound carriageway. I followed his gesture and looked at the motorway and saw several shapes appearing around the corner of the motorway. They were boxy, and it wasn't until they drew closer that I could see that they were dull green 4x4s. There were four or five of them. As they came closer, I started to pick up the engine noise; the drivers were obviously thrashing them quite hard, to who-knows-where. The small convoy raced below us. People ran from one side of the overpass to the other, like some weird game of pooh-sticks. Already the small 4x4's were starting to disappear around the slight bend a half mile or so away up the road.

Charlie turned around, an excited smile on his face, and opened his mouth to say something but was interrupted by a colossal bang which seemed to shake the ground. A wave of screams and shouts rippled throughout the crowd standing on the overpass as everyone turned to face the city, and in the distance a large plume of thick black smoke rolled up into the sky and obscured most of the view.

"Holy shit," shouted Charlie. "What was that?"

Josh was standing watching the fire as it licked up the side of a large oval lid-shaped building, his hands on his head.

"This is getting way out of hand," he said

I stood and stared, mostly in shock. It's one thing to see this kind of thing on TV or on videos online, but it's quite a different thing to see it in person.

For a moment or two everyone on the bridge seemed to be caught in the same hypnotic state as we stared at the fire consuming the building, watching the thick black smoke contaminate the sky. The group mesmerisation was broken by another explosion, this time a little further off in the distance. There was a palpable recoil for everyone as another plume of black smoke snaked its way into the sky. Several people on the bridge hurriedly walked away; some ran to cars. Others, like us, continued to watch. A few seconds stretched on before Charlie turned to me and Josh, an excited look on his face.

"Let's get closer!"

"Are you fucking crazy?" Asked Josh

"C'mon, don't you want to know what's going on?"

"I know what's going on," said Josh pointing to the thick black smoke in the sky

"Let's just check it out. We'll head, what, a mile down the road and see what's happening, if anything."

I said nothing, even though they both looked to me expectantly.

I stared back, giving them my best dead eye. Which turned out to be not so good.

"What?" I barked

"Deciding vote," said Charlie

Oh, Jesus!

"Fine. Let's go for a walk, but not far."

"Fucking yes," said Charlie, with the same excitement children reserved for Christmas morning. He almost skipped off ahead of me and Josh, who stoically watched and sighed deeply and loudly before looking at me with questioning eyes.

"For a start, don't look at me like that; you guys deferred. Secondly, you know what he'll be like if he doesn't get his way."

Josh grunted.

"Let's just get this done as quickly as possible, and then we can go back home to coffee."

"I think I could use something stronger."

We walked in silence; even Charlie seemed a little more subdued after a while. Even though we were walking down a main road, it was eerily quiet. Cars were parked, or abandoned, everywhere: on the road, on driveways and on the verge. There was something desolate, something eerie about it. The houses were empty and foreboding. We couldn't see any activity. As we continued down the road, the queue of cars and vans ahead snaked ahead. As we proceeded, we saw that doors had been left open on several of them. One car had its hazard lights on, the intermittent dull orange flashing pulling the eye towards it.

It was like something from a movie; the cars appeared to have been abandoned. The queue stretched on towards the roundabout just up ahead. I wondered why they'd been left here.

"Fuck me," said Josh. "This is getting weirder."

Charlie was enthusiastically walking around the cars, looking inside each one.

"He's enjoying himself way too much," I said

"I wonder how many other conspiracy theory nuts are jizzing in their pants right now?"

I laughed just as Charlie ducked inside a car. A few seconds later he popped out, just as we came to him.

"I found a bag of cookies," he said, brandishing a small paper bag

He looked at the label.

"Double chocolate, too."

"They're not yours."

"The door was open, and I think this could be the apocalypse, so I'm calling finders keepers."

"That's not how finders keepers works."

Charlie seemed to consider it for a full half second.

"Not anymore," he said and ripped open the top of the bag and dove in.

He pulled a dark circle of chocolate baked goods out of the bag and bit into it.

"Mmmmm," he said, "Ill-gotten cookies taste the best."

"You're a monster." I said

Ten seconds passed before Josh turned around and snatched the bag from Charlie

"Fuck it, I guess a cookie is a cookie."

"You want one?" Offered Josh

"Sure," I said, taking one from the bag. The soft chocolatey cookie did taste good, better even.

"I guess we're all monsters now," said Charlie, grinning like a fool.

We approached the roundabout and saw that it was jammed with more abandoned cars. The scene looked strange. Everyone seemed to just disappear, and we didn't even notice it. We could see that one of the exits had been blocked with more concrete blocks. Traffic looked as though it was being guided towards the city center.

The road towards the city center was heaving with traffic but devoid of anyone.

"This is creepy as fuck," said Josh. "Where the hell is everyone?"

In the distance there was another dull boom, followed by the closer sounds of alarms ringing.

We all looked towards the sound, but there was nothing to see. What we did notice was the roar of low-flying aircraft.

Josh squinted at the formation of two jets in the distance.

"Weird," he said

"What's weird?" I asked

"I swear those are hawks."

I looked at Charlie, and he just shrugged as he pushed the last of his cookie into his mouth.

"And?"

"And", said Josh, "they're a training aircraft; it's what the RAF uses to train fighter pilots. They don't see active duty."

"Maybe this is just a training exercise?" I offered

Even Josh looked at me funny, and I admit it was a bit of a stretch.

I only answered with a shrug.

"Well," I said, "we've come a mile or so."

"Maybe we should press on a little bit more?" Said Charlie hopefully

"What?" Exclaimed Josh, "You mean towards the explosions?"

"Yeah." I said, "Nah. We're going back. There has to be some news or something by now."

Charlie pulled out his phone and held it up to us, not that we could see anything meaningful.

"Still no service," he said

At that moment another explosion echoed throughout the sky. This time it came from behind us and seemed very close. We could see a large plume rising into the sky just beyond the crest of the hill in front of us as we turned towards the source of the sound.

"Okay." I said, "Let's go. Now"

For once Charlie didn't protest, and we all hurried away from the roundabout and retraced our steps back to the car.

As we got near to where we left the car, we could see that the situation hadn't improved. In fact, we could see that more traffic had joined the queue, filling the road up behind us, meaning we couldn't liberate the car. The majority of the vehicles had been abandoned. A few people were wandering around, but there wasn't the same throng as before. I figured that they had the right idea. Get inside and keep your head down.

As we got to the car, we could see the front passenger window had been smashed; a few other cars looked to have been vandalised, too.

"Great," I said

Charlie looked in.

"Shit." He shouted, "My iPad is gone. Fucking thieving bastards."

"Finders keepers," said Josh with a smirk

"The car was locked!"

"Semantics," said Josh, quietly

"Let's keep going." I said, "I want to get home before things get any worse."

I started walking, and the other two caught up quickly. We walked in silence for a while. I mulled things over, replaying the things I had seen. It still didn't seem real. There was a dreamlike quality to it, yet I knew that this wasn't a dream.

We walked for maybe 20 mins before we came to a roundabout. More cars were abandoned, although the roundabout was largely clear aside from a large articulated lorry blocking the junction so no one could get in or out.

"That's weird," said Charlie

"Stand by your beds," said Josh to anyone listening

"All the tyres are flat."

Charlie quickened his pace, overtook us and began looking over the truck.

Josh started to say something before I cut him off with a gesture.

"Let him have it."

"Oh, I'll let him have it," said Josh with a smile

"That's not what I meant, and you know it."

Charlie had disappeared around the other side of the truck. We heard a dull banging sound before Charlie stepped out from behind the truck.

"They look like they've been blown on purpose."

"It's been a while since you've been blown on purpose," said Josh

I stifled a laugh as Charlie looked unamused

"The cabs locked, too" he continued, trying to ignore Josh

Without saying anything more, he turned to the back of the trailer and started opening it up. The large door swung open with a dull squeal.

"Holy shit," said Charlie before he grabbed one side of the remaining closed door and the other side of the trailer and pulled himself up and into the back.

Josh and I walked over and looked inside to see Charlie peering over the large wooden crates.

"Fuck," said Charlie, turning towards us. "They're filled with rock. I bet this rig is easily over+ 40 tonnes."

Charlie jumped down from the trailer and closed the door, the catches snapping shut with a click.

"This thing is a portable roadblock."

"Not so portable now," said Josh as he kicked one of the flat tyres

"Let's just keep moving." I said, "There's a coffee with my name on it at home."

The walk home was long and uneventful. The three of us shambled down the backcountry roads. The world in front of us looked like any other day, but a quick glance behind painted another, very different picture. The smoke from Leeds snaked up into the sky like some great black demon. Flames lit the root of the thick tower as it threatened to block out the entire vista with its dark corruption. More than a few times we looked back and watched for a moment or two before turning back, putting one foot in front of the other. We said little to nothing; even Charlie's enthusiasm and gleeful abandon for the situation at hand had been quashed. An hour or so had passed, an hour which felt much longer, and we arrived at the first roundabout at the edge of town. We wended our way to my house, slowly following the ring road over several roundabouts, crossing a bridge before coming to the final junction that would lead us towards home. The odd car passed by, but the air was still and eerily quiet.

"Thank fuck," said Josh. "We're almost there."

The excitement of the day and the long, somewhat arduous, walk back had stoked a need for coffee and something to eat.

Our pace quickened as we picked our way through the streets heading towards my house. There was hardly a soul around. We saw one person walking at the top of the street, heading to some unknown destination before they shuffled out of view. Some houses looked cold and closed. Others had their curtains drawn. Cars that were usually tightly parked together had disappeared, and only a few vehicles languished in the street. We turned the final corner and almost sprinted to my front door.

The three of us burst in.

"Bagsy toilet," shouted Josh, storming into the kitchen before thudding heavily up the wooden stairs. The door to the bathroom closed with a bang.

Charlie dropped onto the couch with a large exhale of breath.

I sat down on the nearest chair. Tired, I closed my eyes for a minute or two.

I heard the toilet flush, and my eyes flicked open. I wasn't aware of time passing, at least not a significant portion. Even so, Charlie's head was tilted back against the couch, a soft gurgling coming from his parted lips.

Josh stomped down the uncarpeted stairs, each heavy footstep seemingly reverberating throughout the kitchen. He skulked into the living room and slumped into a nearby armchair.

"Anything?" He asked, nodding towards the TV

"Haven't checked."

I didn't have anything to add, and to be honest, I was tired and a little bit irritable, so I idly tossed the remote control for the TV his way. It landed with a dull thump on his chest.

Surprisingly, he made a small squeaking sound as it landed.

"I so need food," I said. And pushed myself up from the chair and headed towards the kitchen.

I lifted the kettle, and, happy with the amount of water contained, I flicked it on. A small blue glow emanated from within, letting me know that it was heating the water. I opened the nearest cupboard and looked for something quick and easy to eat. The kettle started to rumble, a sound like a small jet engine, as the element worked to boil the water within. The sound almost drowned out background noise, but I could just about hear the TV in the background. I found a random, half-eaten pack of dark chocolate digestive biscuits. I wondered how long they'd been hiding at the back of the cupboard. I took a tentative bite from one, and it seemed fairly fresh, although I could tell it had been sitting for a while.

I heard a series of three tones, from low to high, from the living room and then a long pause.

"Hey, the TVs got something" shouted Josh

I broke a small piece of a digestive off, pushed it into my mouth and wandered towards the lounge and leaned against the doorway. The TV showed the same test card as before, the emergency broadcast page, only this time the announcer was relaying what sounded like instructions.

"...Indoors at this time."

I obviously had come in at the tail end of the announcement.

"What gives?" I asked

"Give it a second; it'll play again."

I waited, finishing the small piece of chocolate goodness, half considering reaching for another morsel. I was just about to turn around when the tones sounded again, which pulled my attention back to the TV.

"This is a regional broadcast message. The public is advised that all public travel has been suspended at this time while the authorities assess the current situation and devise further strategies accordingly. Please do not attempt to travel, and only travel for necessities, such as food and essential items. Please stay in your homes and await further instructions. Seek shelter and stay indoors at this time."

"Well, fuck," said Charlie. "I guess it's all gone to pot."

"It'll be fiiine," said Josh settling into the couch

"Just how deluded are you?" said Charlie

Josh closed his eyes and shrugged.

"What about you?" Said Charlie, turning his gaze to me

"What about me?"

"Opinion?"

"I have no idea what the fuck is going on or what we should do!"

There was a long pause before Charlie spoke, like either he was weighing his options or waiting a suitable or maybe dramatic amount of time.

"I do," he said, somewhat quietly

I noticed Josh opened a single eyelid.

"We get the fuck out of here."

"What are you talking about?" said Josh

"We leave," answered Charlie. "Get out of Dodge while we can."

"Crazy talk", said Josh, "doesn't make sense. You heard the TV; we should stay here!"

"It makes perfect sense; things aren't getting better. Just look at what we've seen today. Fucking explosions galore just a few miles down the road. Roads are being blocked. No more communication or information. We need to get away from big cities and we're just down the road from 800,000 people."

Josh opened his mouth and unleashed a bass-heavy belch.

"That's my vote right there," he said

Charlie again turned his attention my way

"Is this a vote? Are we voting?" I asked

"Looks that way," said Josh, both eyes now closed

"What is it that we're voting on?"

"Leaving," said Charlie, with a seriousness I rarely had seen in him. "Going north, away from larger cities."

"And then what?"

There was a pause.

"My sister's house! We go to hers. We ride this out! Whatever this is, we're safer away from it all."

And then there was silence. I could feel a strange kind of tension as the future of what would happen apparently rested with me. This wasn't a situation I thought I'd ever find myself in or even would've wanted. Right now all I wanted was a biscuit, maybe several, and some coffee and maybe a little bit of peace and quiet.

"I vote," bracing myself from whatever barrage would come my way. "We stay."

In one fluid moment Josh opened his eyes and stood up, arms in the air and shouted at Charlie

"Yes. Suck it, fatty."

"Rude," retorted Charlie, far calmer than I expected

I waited for Josh to calm down before adding.

"Let's give it a day or so, maybe even a few. We can see what happens, maybe form a better plan or whatever and just be more prepared."

Charlie's brow furrowed, seemingly deep in thought.

"Deal," he said and nodded

"Rude boy," he added, looking at Josh. "Let's get out of here; drive me home."

In a rare moment Josh said nothing but just smiled. He walked past me, still smiling, and headed to the door.

"We'll be back," said Charlie in his best, or worst, Arnold impression.

I laughed and ushered them out the door and closed it behind them. From the living room I could hear muffled arguing and what would amount to a relentless barrage of insults from both of them.

I was left, as the car drove off, with quiet. I remembered my coffee, which was still idly steaming on the kitchen work surface. I took a long sip before taking a substantial bite from another biscuit.

I gathered up the coffee and remaining packet of biscuits and settled down on the couch. I quickly drank most of the coffee and ate all the biscuits before the highs and lows of the day came home to roost. I hadn't realised I'd dozed off until I awoke in what appeared to be the dead of night. I fumbled for my phone to see that it was 2am. This was turning into a pattern. I shuffled upstairs, quickly cleaned my teeth, undressed and scootched into bed and returned to the not-life of no dreams.

SEVEN

I had hoped to sleep more, to sleep through whatever calamity had befallen our lives. To wake up and have everything just be a strange dream. I don't remember waking up, just being awake, the dim pre-glow of the slowly breaking morning sun illuminating the sky weakly. As my exhausted eyes focused, I could see that it looked foggy outside. I crawled out of bed and sat for a moment before getting up and looking out the window. The street was quiet, and a light mist seemed to be already subsiding; the slight wind appeared to be blowing it away. Even in the dull light the colours seemed off, otherworldly; a pale green tinge seemed to have descended on everything.

Tired and somewhat achy from the long walk and excitement of the previous day, I shuffled down to the kitchen and proceeded to boil the kettle for coffee. I stared out the window in the receding darkness of the garden as wisps of greenish-tinged fog rose into the air and were pushed and pulled by the gentle breeze. The events of yesterday seemed farther away, less real, and more dreamlike.

I heard a click, which brought me back into the here and now, and realised the kettle had boiled. I quickly dumped instant coffee into the mug, followed by hot water, and stirred it with the nearest implement I could put a hand on, in this case a clean knife from the drying rack. I tossed it into the sink and skulked into the lounge and found a place on the couch.

I briefly switched on the TV, only to discover the same message that was playing the day before, or at least a variant. I idly picked up my phone, my timepiece of choice.

05:50. I had no idea why my body woke me up at these hours. I was about to flip the phone back onto the couch when I realised something. I had an unread text message.

If my phone were working, surely this would be a sign that things were returning to normal. I hastily unlocked the device and opened the messaging app. One message, and before I could see who it was from, a slight surge of relaxation and happiness flowed throughout my body. All this rash talk of running and the sight of explosions and roadblocks had put me on edge. And then I saw the sender, "Gov_uk". The body of the text offered little to no meaningful information either:

> GOV.UK CRISIS ALERT. New rules in force now: you must stay at home. Military operating in your area. More info pending. Stay at home. Save lives. Be vigilant.

I tried texting Charlie but was met with a message sending failure alert. I noticed that there appeared to be no cellular connection again.

I huffed and dropped the phone back onto the couch. I took a swig of coffee and decided that the best course of action would be to watch a movie. I switched on the TV and my games console and looked down the list of movies I had stored on a separate storage drive. I found the one I wanted and pressed play. I took another sip of coffee and set the mug down onto the small coffee table and eased back onto the super comfy couch to watch the best film ever made: RobotJox.

I was woken by banging, a loud knocking sound coming from just outside the room. I noticed the TV was still on, and the banging seemed to mingle with what looked to be the end of the movie I was watching before I fell asleep, or so it would seem.

"I'm gonna get in this thing and KICK. YOUR. ASS!" said the voice on the TV

More loud banging.

I felt my brow furrow as I got up from the couch and started for the front door, where the sound emanated from.

My hand was on the handle when another three loud bangs echoed throughout the hallway.

"Jesus Christ, enough with the banging," I said, opening the door to find Charlie and Josh both outside in the bright light of the morning.

I looked at them, and they both looked back.

"Fuck" was all I could manage to say.

"All I'm saying is we should talk about it."

Charlie was arguing his point well, but my only interest was for a quiet life.

"Why is it that you guys are arguing here and not elsewhere?" I said

The chatter between them instantly died, and they looked at me expectantly.

"What?" I said, looking at both of them in turn, expecting something but seemingly getting nothing but blank stares.

And so it had come to this: another peaceful morning disturbed with me standing, metaphorically, between my two best friends about to make a decision that, unbeknownst to any of us at the time, would change the course of all our lives.

The tug of war between Charlie and Josh was thus: Charlie was adamant that we go. We run and hide far away from large cities and away from possible meddling of a government or worse, the military, that would easily bend our will to whatever task, order or desire they wish. Josh's assertion was that we should stay within our local community and near larger cities where help and support would most likely be directed. Both had fair points, and Josh directed a better and more logical argument against Charlie's passionate stance. Ultimately, however, there was an impasse, and it seemed that the final decision would rest at my feet. Which is now where I found myself: a lukewarm cup of coffee in hand, two arguing friends, a slowly building headache and no real sign of any sort of peace and quiet in my life for the foreseeable future.

I stood there, aching, tired and exasperated from dealing with them in greater frequency than I was used to. And I made a decision. Something I'd wrestle with for a good while in the future. Part of me wonders what would've happened if I'd made a different decision. How different would things be? Would it be better or worse? It doesn't do to dwell on the past too much, but even so, even today. I remember that event so well, sometimes more vividly than what came next. I've often wondered if it was guilt that kept the events of that day fresh in my mind while other, more recent events seemed to have drifted away.

EIGHT

The road ahead was clear; I found myself making steady pace, my car loaded with whatever I had packed for a short trip. I'd wound down the window and let the wind rush in. The day was bright and warm, the sun high in the sky. It felt like any other summer day, except there was something else, maybe something sinister. I glanced behind and saw the front of Charlie's car in my rearview mirror. Both he and Josh were sharing, which gave me enough time and space to think. The roads were strangely empty; normally you'd see several cars and trucks making their way to or from Goole, but today there was nothing. Just us. No bikes, no walkers. Just us. We passed through several villages and by several houses set back from the road. Most stood silently; lots of houses had curtains drawn over windows. There was something strangely eerie about it all. I wanted to think of it as just another trip out, but there was a niggling sensation at the back of my mind which resisted the illusion.

We decided to keep to the back roads to keep a lower profile from the authorities that were telling us to stay inside and also out of necessity, as it appeared, from our adventure the previous day, access to larger roads had been barricaded off. The plan was to pick our way north and hopefully pick up a major road that wasn't blocked off and make our way to Northumbria, where Charlie's sister lived. Josh hadn't been happy with the plan up until that point; Josh always had a soft spot for Charlie's sister, and who could blame him? She was smart, funny, knew how to snowboard and could kick ass. She was a super tough cookie, and it didn't hurt that she was super pretty, too. Not my type, obviously, but definitely Joshes. We'd joked about Charlie or his sister being adopted, as they seemed so different, and Charlie had responded by saying that Josh would never be allowed to touch his sister unless she was breaking something off him. I refocused on the winding road ahead, which was now taking us through a wooded area. We were making good progress; we kept our speed around fifty miles per hour, as both cars weren't full of fuel. What we'd lose in speed we'd gain in overall progress; at least, that was the plan.

There was a crackle and a beep from the passenger seat, and I jumped a little. I looked over and saw the walkie-talkie that Charlie had given me before we set off.

I picked it up and held it to my mouth and pressed the transmit button.

"What's up?"

"Nothing," said the crackly voice of Charlie. "Just wanted to see how things were up ahead."

"Quiet until you bipped the ripper," I replied

"Also, when you get to the next junction, just up ahead, go straight over and don't turn right. We thought we could check out York and see if the sixty-four is clear."

"Cool, will do," I said and tossed the black device back onto the passenger seat

A few moments later and we passed over the junction and headed north towards York.

The back roads wound their way lazily by fields and through woods. More small villages came and went, each one just as quiet as the next. Our little convoy of two plodded on for several miles before passing an old airfield and eventually coming to a large intersection marked with traffic lights that appeared to be still working. I pulled up. Charlie and Josh were still close behind in their vehicle and immediately saw several articulated lorries parked across the carriageway, blocking our way towards the city. I pulled forward and parked alongside the nearest truck. Charlie pulled alongside me, and we rolled down windows.

"What now?" I asked

"We can still get around the edge of the city. Follow us."

Charlie immediately pulled forward and turned right, heading away from the city. I followed, trusting that between him and Josh they knew where they were going.

A handful of metres down the road, Charlie turned left down what appeared to be a small back road. As I turned, I noticed a large house with massive gardens on the right.

The road was small and seemed to be heading to another main road that was running almost adjacent to the one we just left. The road ended in a junction with signs telling us we could only turn left, which would take us back towards the junction we left. We turned right anyway and merged onto the small main road which headed back out and away from the city.

Almost immediately there were fields on either side of the road; a few sheep were gambolling around, unaware of any change in their daily lives. In fact, their lives weren't seemingly impacted, as I saw them munching away on grass and lazing in the midday sun.

I followed blindly down the road for a few miles before the turn signals on Charlie's car started to indicate that we would be turning left. We headed into a small village by the main road and struggled to see any major turning. We slowed down and went past a petrol station, very much firmly shut. After we passed the station, Charlie veered left up a small ramp which turned out to be a small side road leading down the back of the village. We slowly made our way through the little hamlet. To my surprise there were a few people out and about, gardening or doing other chores outside. The sun is luring people from inside. As we passed, we were met with scowls, no doubt for choosing to ignore instructions to stay home.

We carried on and soon found our way to another junction; turning left, we headed onto smaller backroads, lined with tall hedges. We made several turns, pulling onto small unmarked roads until we arrived at a larger junction. A large signpost pointed to the right, towards Scarborough, the road clearly marked A64. I pulled up next to Charlie at the junction – no cars, nothing. The carriageway was clear on both sides. Charlie pointed towards the road ahead, and I nodded in reply. I paused a few seconds longer and watched a small plume of dark smoke bubble up from what looked to be the city center of York before pulling forward and over the roadway to join the road which would take us towards Easingwold, a small village sitting on the northern side of the city. Although the roads were free of any other traffic, we plodded along at a steady pace. We picked through the small roads, the skyline of the city suddenly peeking through breaks in the trees and when passing open fields. Soon enough we arrived at another main road. The signpost told us this was the A19. Left would take us towards York, and right would take us towards Thirsk.

As I pulled alongside Charlie's car, I noticed that Josh and Charlie were looking towards York. As I came to a stop, I could see a bank of cars sprawled over both sides of the road. I got out of the car to better survey the situation and to stretch my legs. We'd not really come that far but I felt quite tired. I stretched and looked at the mess of cars. Someone had even left their hazard lights on.

I heard Charlie and Josh get out of the car. Various sounds of stretching and yawning came from them both, which sounded more like an animal being tortured than anything else.

I heard feet shuffling up behind me.

“Weird, no?” said Charlie “I thought we’d see more people out and about.”

“Weird” was the only reply I offered, if parroting was a reply.

“Everyone’s in-fucking-side, where we should be.”

Charlie turned to argue his point, but I intervened.

“No. Stop.” I said, “You two quit it with that shit. We voted; job done.”

Josh said nothing, although I could feel the weight of his disapproving scowl.

Charlie had a big smile on his face and turned back towards the cars.

“I guess the city is pretty much cut off but we’re on the right side. We can head up the nineteen, head to Thirsk, and hopefully pick up the A1 and with any luck it’ll be smooth sailing all the way to Jessica’s.”

“I hope it’ll be that simple.”

Another pair of footsteps, almost dragging against the tarmac, meant that Josh was joining the conversation.

“Has he told you yet?”

“Told me what?” I asked, looking at Charlie; I felt my eyebrows furrow.

“I was just about to mention it before you charged in!” he complained.

“Tell me what, exactly?”

“Are you sure you were going to mention it?” Smiled Josh

“YES,” said Charlie, not able to hide his frustration

I was still as lost as ever

“Tell me what?” I shouted

“My car is almost out of petrol,” Said Charlie

“Wait a minute,” I said. “Did the preppier not prepare?”

I felt a smile spread across my face which felt like it matched the insanely wide grin also set in Josh's face.

“I’m not a fucking prepper,” he said, maybe a bit too defensively, “and besides, I have a plan.”

There was a pause as no one said anything

"So, what's the plan?" I asked

"It's a surprise," grinned Charlie

"Is this really the time for surprises?" I asked

"It's always a good time for good surprises," he replied before heading back to his car.

Josh looked at me, said nothing, shrugged his shoulders and followed Charlie to his car.

I shook my head, let out a deep sigh and headed back to my vehicle.

As I started her up, Charlie was already pulling onto the main road and turning right.

Over the next few miles Charlie seemed to lead us on a strange winding adventure through main roads. It felt like we weren't actually moving too far north but picking our way in a westerly direction.

At one point I picked up the radio and clicked the transmit button.

"Do you know where the hell you're going?"

After a few seconds I heard Josh come crackling through the small speaker

"Apparently so."

"Although he doesn't seem happy about it, methinks he's offended," he added a few seconds later

"Bite me," I replied and settled back into following Charlie's car in front.

I dropped the radio back onto the passenger seat and noticed that, somehow, the small purple troll had joined me and was now bouncing around with the radio. The small figure seemed to glare at me, almost mockingly.

"Fuck you," I said to the small, magical creature.

I was already struggling to know where I was, and after another ten or so minutes, I was completely baffled. I swear we passed the same pub twice, and things were looking familiar until Charlie pulled a sharp left and disappeared down a ratty-looking road. The surface was uneven and potholed and had generally fallen into a state of disrepair. There was evidence that the road had been fixed with tarmac, concrete and even bricks, but I couldn't tell you what the original surface might have been. As we progressed, our vehicles kicked up dust which billowed in the air. The road was short and seemed to dip down and led to a large gate that was closed and no doubt locked. Large trees and bushes hid anything but the gate itself, although I could see what looked to be a largish warehouse through the tops of the trees.

I pulled up behind Charlie and came to a stop; the dust continued to swirl around the cars as we got out.

Charlie pretty much hopped out of his car, spread his arms high and wide and shouted

"TA DAAAA"

Josh looked as confused as I did.

"We're here." beamed Charlie

"Where the hell are we?" Asked Josh, beating me to the punch

Charlie walked over to what looked like an intercom system and withdrew a small card from his pocket.

"BEHOLD," he said, waving the card over the small box.

There was a beep, and the gate shuddered and groaned and started to slowly open.

Charlie, looking pleased with himself, sauntered to his car.

"What?" He said, "Nothing?"

I continued to say nothing and shrugged. Josh looked at me and then at Charlie.

"I'm coming with you," he said, walking towards my car

"Fair enough." I said, "No farting."

Josh said nothing and climbed into my car; he slammed the door a little harder than I would like, which he knew irritated me.

"Thanks for making sure the door is closed," I said, hoping that he heard the sarcasm in my voice

"No problem," he replied, flatly

Charlie started forwards, and I followed him in past the fence. As we cleared trees and bushes, we could see the warehouse was old and had seen better days.

"This place is a total shithole," said Josh

I looked at the side of the warehouse; several window ledges were stained with a strange mixture of that green algae-like substance and a large helping of pigeon shit.

"Yeeeaaahh," I said, taking it all in. "Not exactly upscale."

As we turned around the corner of the old warehouse, the small lane opened up into a huge yard area. The concrete was old but in fairly good condition. There were signs that it had been patched with newer concrete over the years, but strangely enough the rest of the yard was clean and tidy and seemingly at odds with what we'd just seen. This end of the warehouse seemed to be in better condition and was strangely newer in construction; a dozen or so empty truck loading bays presented themselves.

To the right were rows and rows of trucks, sans trailers, huddled together three rows deep. There looked to be twenty or so trucks to each row.

Charlie had put his foot down and zoomed past the trucks and made for a newly constructed office which had been added to the warehouse at the far end of the building. He pulled in front of the entrance and almost tipped out of his car as he got out, clearly excited.

I parked behind him, looked at Josh, and wondered if my expression seemed as confused as his. I got out of the car.

"Let me guess," I said, looking around. "In fact, no, I can't guess. What gives, fatty?"

"Fuel problem solved," grinned Charlie

Before he could explain further, he darted off towards the office, leaving Josh and me staring blankly at each other.

"Obviously he has a plan," I said

"I'm not sure if we should be relieved or terrified," said Josh

. . .

Five, maybe ten, minutes passed before Charlie came bounding out of the office and towards us, a plastic bag in hand. The bag swung and bunched up under the weight of its contents.

"Brace yourself," said Josh

"Problem solved," said Charlie, shaking the bag, which jangled strangely.

Without offering an explanation, Charlie dove into the bag and pulled out a small bunch of what looked like keys and thrust them into Josh's hands. A few seconds later and I had my own collection, which turned out to be several sets of keys, each with a large rectangular fob which was old and very worn.

"What am I doing with these?" I asked

"These", said Charlie, "are for some of those."

He gestured towards the parked trucks.

"I need one of the tractor units on the front row, but there's not much organisation around here. Just press the button on the right, and it should turn on the lights."

"Hold on." I said, "I can't drive a truck."

"Sure you can," said Charlie, "but I'm not asking you to. You and Josh can take your car, but I'll transfer everything from mine to one of these."

Josh laughed and walked towards the group of trucks. There was a beeping sound, and the lights of one of the trucks on the farthest row illuminated.

Charlie followed, and I brought up the rear.

It didn't take us long to find a truck at the front; in fact, both Josh and I had the keys to trucks in the front line. Charlie gleefully plucked the two sets of keys from us and hurried towards the first truck. I noticed a slight change in Charlie's demeanour as he walked around the first vehicle, pulling on this, tugging on that. He inspected under everything and looked at everything he could put a hand on. Josh and I just observed, keeping mostly out of the way.

"You forget," said Josh, "that this is what he does for a living."

"I guess."

"I mean," he continued, "other people see Charlie the trucker, and all we see if Charlie the fuck-up."

I laughed.

"Go fuck yourselves," shouted Charlie, now leaning out of the passenger side of the truck.

"What?" I said

"I don't know what you said, but I know it wasn't all happy thoughts and rainbows!" he continued

I threw my hands up in the air, mostly for comedy purposes. Charlie gave us the finger and continued his inspection.

A few minutes later and the engine to one of the trucks started up; you'd expect to hear some kind of massive roar, but for a big vehicle it made surprisingly very little noise. The truck slowly pulled forward, and Charlie brought the vehicle around, passed us, and parked it next to his car. The engine died, and the truck made a distinct hissing sound. Charlie clambered down and stretched.

"This is the one," he said. "That other unit, H5877, smells like ass. The guy who uses it is a complete scrubber."

"Takes..." Josh started to say before Charlie cut him off.

"SILENCE!" He said, raising a finger to the air.

"Okay, girls," I said, "readjust your tampons. We should get cracking before it gets dark."

"My thoughts exactly," said Charlie as he pulled open the rear door of his car and pulled out the first of many boxes.

It was amazing just how much Charlie had managed to fit in his fairly small vehicle; you'd have thought that by the sheer quantity of what we pulled out that it would've been stored in a van. Almost every nook and cranny had something stashed in it. And it was with equal skill that the entire contents fitted into the cab of the truck. It helped that there were storage compartments everywhere, even a small locker in the side of the truck which, Charlie told me, was usually where load-securing straps were stored or general truck bits and pieces. Now it stored a varied selection of canned goods and water bottles.

After the last of the boxes and random shopping bags of stuff had been packed into the cab, Charlie climbed down from the driver's side and looked, sort of sadly I thought, at his car and then gently tossed the keys onto the driver's seat and closed the door.

"Maybe someone else can use this." He said, "Maybe if they have fuel."

"And a lack of taste," said Josh

"And a death wish," I added

Charlie blew a raspberry in response

"The truck has diesel, but I'll stop by the fuel stand and grab some extra."

"Wait," I said as he turned to climb back up into the cab. "Will this make it to Northumberland?"

"Oh, for sure," said Charlie, now halfway up the truck. "She'll do about 500 miles like this, but it doesn't hurt to have a little extra. Especially while we have the opportunity now."

"I guess I can't argue with that," I said

"I'm sure I could," added Josh

By the time I turned back to see what Charlie would say, he was already in the cab and starting up the gruff-sounding engine of the truck. He pulled the tall unit around in a tight circle before it sped to the far end of the yard, back towards where we came in. We could see that he was making a bee-line for the dirty, filthy storage containers we passed on the way in.

"C'mon," I said, "before we get left behind."

Josh grunted, and I heard him following me as I walked to my car.

By the time we pulled up behind the truck, Charlie appeared to have finished filling the tanks for the truck and was busy filling up what looked to be a metal fuel contrainer.

Charlie filled four of these and lugged them up onto the

metal walkway around the back of the vehicle. .He used what he called a ratchet strap, a long length of thick material with a strange buckle in the middle and two hooks at each end. Charlie threaded these through the handles of the containers and then affixed the hooks, one at each side, of the truck. He then folded the buckle out and pulled the strap tight and then used it like a lever to tighten the whole thing tight. Even though my window was closed, I could hear the rapid click of the ratchet from the passenger window, which Josh had opened. Charlie locked the buckle back in place and then used another strap around the ends of the containers to keep them in place. Once he was finished, he looked at us and gave us a thumbs up before jumping down from the back of the truck and heading to the driver's side door.

"Health and safety!" shouted Josh

I didn't catch the reply, but I can only assume it was insult laden.

As Charlie put a hand on the truck's door, a scream filled the air; it was more of a shrill shout, but it struck through to my core like a sharp knife. I looked at Josh with worried eyes, and he shrugged. Charlie looked around, seemingly trying to get a fix on where the sound was coming from. There was a dull sound of banging in the distance, somewhere beyond the trees. I opened my window with a press of a button on the armrest and could hear the rhythmical banging of a heavy object on metal. More shouts echoed through the landscape. I saw Charlie's eyes getting wider, he raised a finger to the air and made a circular motion before clambering up the side of the truck and vanishing into the cab.

The truck started with a rumble of the engine and a slight shudder on the chassis. The unit lurched forward, wheels slipped on the dusty concrete before gaining traction. Charlie led us out of the compound with little effort. As we approached the entrance, an invisible sensor opened the gate for us. Dust and debris kicked up in the wake of the truck as we pulled out onto the side street. As we turned left onto the main road, dust rolled and billowed after us, as if giving chase, our vehicles leaving tell-tale dirt tracks on the main road betraying our movement.

Our bizarre mini convoy of a massive truck and a small car pressed on for a fair few miles. The going was slow with Charlie setting the pace in the truck. We navigated several small roads before we found a larger main road again. By the time we saw the sign pointing north, the light was fading fast. I pulled up behind Charlie's truck as it came to a stop, giving an audible hiss that I could hear from within the car. The radio beeped and crackled.

"What do you guys think about finding somewhere to stop for the night?"

"You didn't want to press on?"

"I'm not entirely sure it's best to travel at night; our lights are a dead giveaway."

I looked at Josh, who simply shrugged.

"Sure, can we press on a little more? I'd like a bit more distance between us at whatever we heard back there."

Charlie didn't reply; there was a blip in the radio, and within seconds the truck engine fired back up, and he was pulling onto the main road heading north.

The main road was a dream to drive on, compared to the smaller backroads we had been using. Plenty of room and a smooth surface, at least smooth for what passed as English roads. Charlie was able to get a good lick of speed from the truck, as I noticed the speedo reading around fifty-five miles per hour.

A few more miles and we reached a small village. Charlie indicated to turn left at a small roundabout which appeared almost out of nowhere. We all turned left, and immediately the road was smaller and slowly wound its way through a picturesque hamlet. We followed the road until the small, bunched-up houses gave way to larger houses, each with a reasonable square of garden and a driveway to a garage. We could see the black expanse of night expanding outwards into the unknown as we reached the edge of this small outpost of civilisation. Brake lights illuminated the road below, and the left indicator flashed dull yellow, and again the truck turned. I noticed a small sign, black on white, with an image of a lorry on it, pointing the way down another small road. The edges clearly expanded to take larger vehicles. Charlie sped off, and I had to aggressively push the throttle of the car to keep up. The road was smooth and well maintained. Charlie pulled another left into a large concrete yard. There was a large gate which was propped open, allowing us access. Charlie slowly pulled in and drove into the yard and down a small access road that seemed to lead around a large, modern warehouse.

This building was in stark contrast to where we picked up the truck. It was sleek and seemingly well maintained. It only looked a few years old, although it was hard to judge the age of buildings. I followed Charlie closely on the small road that wound its way around the periphery of the gigantic warehouse. We turned right, and a wide yard extended along the front, or maybe it was the back, of the building. Rows of bays, some already with trailers attached to them. Small red and green lights illuminating the trailer and walls on which they sat. Charlie sped off and then right, parking by a set of stairs leading to what I assume was the entrance to the building. I pulled the car next to the truck and killed the engine.

I got out and instinctively stretched. Josh yawned loudly and gave a weird, almost frustrated, shout while stretching.

"Goddamn," he said, "what is this shithole?"

Charlie, looking unimpressed walked over to us

"This is one of our newest warehouses; we store customer stock here. Although it's just for one customer right now," he said, "we can camp out in the lounge."

"Lounge?" I said

"Don't expect too much, but it'll be better than sleeping in the car."

I looked up at the building, which extended up about fifty feet and was constructed in modern aluminium. A designer had desperately tried to make a boring box look less boring, but on a budget.

Charlie led us up a set of metal stairs which clanged with every step. Josh made a point of putting extra force with each step, the sound echoing throughout the area and the vibrations rattling down the structure.

"Child", I said, scolding him

He said nothing and managed to stomp a little bit harder up the remaining stairs.

Thankfully it was a short set. At the top Charlie pulled the door, and it opened.

We stepped through into what Charlie called "the lounge", but what was really a large open area with rows of seats, a few vending machines and several doors. One of which appeared to be signed as a toilet. There was a tall counter, and behind it various workstations with computers, all of which had blank screens, silently waiting for their operators to return.

Charlie saw the disappointment on my face.

"It's not much, I know. But the seats are quite comfy, and there's a toilet and snacks."

"I guess," I replied, trying very hard to be positive.

I heard movement behind us and saw Josh taking a seat. He looked at the seat next to him.

"There's a stain here which looked like someone died on this one."

"Don't be a drama queen," said Charlie. "It's probably just coffee. Probably."

Charlie wandered off through one of the doors signed "no entry, authorised personnel only".

He came back a few minutes later.

"You can access the warehouse from the back, but I've locked that door, so we're all good."

I stood and watched Charlie as he flipped up a portion of the counter and swung open the small door it rested on. He busied himself opening each drawer in turn and rummaging around for something. After several failed attempts, he finally withdrew something excitedly from one drawer with an "Aha".

I watched intently as he approached the counter and held up several small coins.

"Coffee? Something to eat?"

"Hey, if you're buying, I'll have a coffee" I replied

Charlie walked over to the nearest vending machine, a large monolith-like unit with dimly lit rectangles, each displaying the name of a hot drink with a generic photo of the beverage in question. Some of the buttons were marred and faded from use. It appears as though tea and white coffee were the most popular choices.

"Black?" He asked, a finger hovering over the button

"Yah." I said "please"

Charlie pressed the button and inserted the coin. The machine buzzed and whined before dispensing a cup. Hot water slowly flowed into the cup, the machine continuing with its strange mechanical song.

Charlie handed me the hot beverage in a thin plastic cup. I could barely hold onto the drink, and so I set it down on a low table next to the machine while Charlie selected hot chocolate.

The machine spat out several coins, and Charlie looked at the jumble of odds and ends.

He went to the next machine, which vended a variety of seemingly overpriced chocolate bars and other assorted snacks.

"Wouldn't it be easier to just use what we have in the car?" I asked, referring to the boxes of supplies we had gathered for our trip from our respective houses.

Charlie shrugged in response

"Might as well use everything else until we really need to use our stuff," he said

I nodded in reply and picked up the hot coffee and took a small sip. The coffee was hot, too hot to enjoy. I licked my lips to ease the tingling sensation and returned the cup to the table. In the meantime Charlie had wrestled a chocolate-covered peanut bar from the machine and was eagerly unwrapping it.

"Halfsies?"

"No thanks. Not that hungry."

"I know what you mean," he said, stuffing one end into his mouth and wrenching a chunk off before chewing heartily.

From across the room I heard snoring. We turned to see Josh sat, slumped really, in one of the chairs by the entrance, stretched out, arms folded and head nodded forward.

"Been a weird day."

"Mmm-hmmm," mumbled Charlie, chewing a fresh chunk of chocolate and caramel.

"I might grab something warm from the car and settle down," I said

Charlie nodded, struggling with swallowing a piece of the bar.

"I'll have a poke round in a bit, but I might get some shut-eye, too."

I left Charlie to assault the rest of the chocolate bar and headed outside, pushing through the glass and metal door with a creak. The heat of the day was dissipating quickly. Already there was a chill in the air. The sun was slowly disappearing below the horizon, and the moon had emerged, high in the sky.

I made my way down the stairs and opened the back door of my car. I fished out a jacket and a random hoody. I pushed the door closed, which made a dull thunk which seemed to echo between the car and the building. I slowly mounted the stairs towards the lounge and at the top turned to see a set of stars glittering in the night sky. The last few gasps of light from the sun were struggling to prevent the ever-advancing darkness. The air was cooler now, and there was an eerie silence.

I took a deep breath, the frigid air shocking my lungs. I immediately felt more tired than I had in a while. I looked up at the sky again and gazed up at the moon and saw the dark grey continents etched in the dry surface. I wondered just how complacent we'd gotten with viewing that dark orb over the years, and I had similar thoughts as to how complacent we'd gotten with life in general. I hoped and looked forward to a sense of normality and wondered how soon it would be until we'd all be back at my house, playing video games and generally having a good time.

I didn't realise just how naïve those thoughts were. I wondered what the next few days would bring and what Northumbria would be like and how good it would be to see Charlie's sister again. I smiled to myself and told myself this would be a grand adventure or at least a folly to tell the grandkids one day. I idly scratched my neck, feeling the jittery feeling of tiredness pressing at the edge of my consciousness. I pulled the door to the drivers' lounge open and stepped into the surprising warmth of the area and found a suitable set of seats together on which to bed down for the night and resume our adventure, or folly, in the morning.

NINE

I was dragged from sleep by the sound of shouting and screaming. The screaming was male, and more like a deep rage rather than someone terrified or in pain. I bolted upright and tried to take in my surroundings. Confused, a surge of adrenaline had me throwing off the jacket I'd brought with me that I was using for a blanket and looking around the room. Charlie was crouched by a window, and Josh looked to be in just as much shock as I felt. We looked at each other for a split second before we raced next to Charlie to see what the noise was about. More shouting, somewhat intelligible, but it was definitely sounding angry. Harsh. Threatening.

"What's going on?" said Josh as we joined Charlie

"I don't know," he said. "I just heard shouting. Maybe they came from over there."

Charlie nodded to the large expanse of farmland, which seemed to go on as far as we could see. Small houses of a village dotted the horizon, and there were a few larger farm-houses nearby.

I peeked out the window, staying low with the others, not wanting to draw any unwanted attention to us. Outside, in the middle of the expansive yard, was a small group: six, maybe seven men. They were tall and lanky. They appeared to be pushing and jostling each other; one man was on his knees, having stumbled to the ground, one hand was on the floor steadying himself, and the other clutched to his head. He appeared to be the source of the screaming. The other men were shouting, mostly at each other. I picked out the odd profanity and insult, but it seemed to be just a babble of angry shouting. One man tried to pull the other from the ground up; the grounded man tried to get his legs under him, but he stumbled forward and ended up sprawled on the ground, sending the other man stumbling over the yard. Several other men laughed, and more angry words were exchanged.

One of the men from the back stepped forward; he was bald and stocky. He kicked the man on the ground and shouted at the rest. He glanced towards the office or maybe towards the truck parked in front of the office and pointed. The men started to walk forwards, towards my car, towards the truck, towards where we were skulking.

"Oh shit," I whispered

"Fuck me," said Josh. "I don't fancy our chances."

Charlie took a deep breath.

"I'll create a diversion."

Charlie started to get up, but I grabbed his arm and pulled him back down.

"Are you mad?" I asked

"I can do this," he said. "I can get to the truck from the passenger side; they'll not see me until I'm in, and then I'll be in an eight-tonne tank."

"And then what? Run everyone over."

"No," said Charlie, and then he saw how serious I was. "No. I can drive around pretty quickly, and while they're paying attention to me, you and Josh can grab the car and drive around the far side of the warehouse. Once you're clear, I can follow."

"This sounds insane," I said

"They're getting closer," said Josh from behind me. "It seems like they've left their friend behind with another dude."

Charlie stole a quick peek from the window.

"Can we go through the warehouse?" I asked

"And leave our stuff behind?" Asked Charlie, "No fucking way. Plus there could be more of them elsewhere."

"It's just stuff." I said, "We can get more."

"You're kidding, right?" Asked Charlie, "Now more than ever we can't just get more stuff."

"This place is full of it."

"This place is full of empty cans," said Charlie. "It's a storage unit for Blue Cow energy drinks. And there's no guarantee that anywhere else won't be either ransacked or taken over. Plus there's the vehicles."

"Fuck," I said

"Charlie's right," said Josh. "If we don't make a move, things might get worse quick. These dudes don't look like they want to give us friendship bracelets and plait our hair."

"Fuck," I said, pausing for a second to quickly think, "OK."

"When I get in the truck, wait for me to pull around into the yard before you get to the car. Drive down the yard away from where we came in, follow the road around, and it'll take you to the entrance and out. Once you're at the entrance, radio me and I'll follow as soon as you're clear of the yard."

"Don't do anything moronic," I said

I was expecting a sarcastic reply or something quick-witted and semi-abusive from Josh, but I only heard the ruffle of clothing, the slight squeak of shoes on hard flooring and the dull clank of the heavy metal and glass door opening.

I spied through the window and saw Charlie quickly descending the metal stairs; he ducked around my car and climbed into the passenger side of the truck.

"Let's go," said Josh, surprisingly assertive and reassuring. We exited through the same door as Charlie and descended the same stairs. As my foot hit the concrete floor, the truck engine burst to life, and with a hiss of air, the giant unit rolled away and turned towards the group of men.

As the truck pulled away I could already hear shouting. I got to the back

of my car and slowed my pace to see Charlie driving around the group of men who were shouting. Several had makeshift weapons in the form of poles and short pieces of wood. One man had a large crowbar, and another had a house brick, which he elected to throw at Charlie's truck. The brick hit the side of the cab with a thud and dropped to the ground, splitting in two.

Unaffected Charlie pulled the truck around and slowly drove down the yard away from us. The men followed, blind with rage. The brick man picked up one of the broken pieces now on the floor and hurled it back at the truck. It bounced, again harmlessly, off the back of the truck and fell onto the rear end, seemingly settling near the gaggle of hoses which snaked out the vehicle.

I was at the driver's side door, and I felt the car tilt as Josh jumped in; a dull thud, and I knew he had closed the door and was ready to go. I found myself unable to look away as Charlie drove around the men in circles, just slow enough to keep them occupied. He got close to a few, close enough that they swung and hit the truck's bodywork with their improvised weapons. One strike with a large wood pole hit the driver's side window. The truck's engine grew louder, and its wheels spun on the concrete, losing traction, and Charlie turned it harder. The truck swung wildly to the side, hitting one of the men who had stayed at the outset edge of the calamity and who now had been drawn into the thick of it. There was a dull, strangely hollow thud, and the man was flung over the concrete surface like a rag doll. The truck roared again and sped off, this time in a straight line, heading back towards the top corner towards the main entrance. Time seemed to slow in an instant as Charlie turned the truck to swing around again; a large tractor emerged from the side. It had a loading bucket attached, and as it swung into the yard, the driver seemed to acknowledge Charlie's truck and raised its bucket.

The tractor barged into Charlie's truck, blindsiding him and pushing the large vehicle to the side. I stepped forward trying to see what was going on. Willing Charlie to put his foot down and get out of there. But the tractor kept on pushing, relentlessly. The trucks' tyres shuddered and squealed on the concrete surface, leaving thick black marks behind them. Dark smoke ejected from the tractor's exhaust and billowed away, caught by the wind as the tractor pushed the truck against the back wall with a crash. Metal crumbled and glass shattered. The door window erupted in a shower of glass as the tractor pushed the truck onto two wheels and came to a stop. A man jumped out of the tractor with something in his hands; he appeared to fumble with it and then he threw it towards the exposed window of the truck's cab. I caught the barest glimpse of an orange flash as the object sailed towards the window and clipped the metal side of the door and exploded in a ball of flame. Another object followed directly into the cab through the flames which licked the side of the truck door. A roar of approval came from the group of men clustered nearby, and suddenly my whole world fell strangely silent. I heard nothing. I found myself walking forward, away from the car, shouting as loud as I could, but no sound seemingly came. I had a vague recollection from behind me, maybe banging and shouting from Josh, but it didn't register. All I could focus on was the now flame-engulfed cab, knowing my best friend was inside. Anger billowed up and focused my gaze on one thing, the truck and the tractor. Black smoke and flames poured out of the truck cab. My presence, it seemed, hadn't gone undetected. Several men turned their attention to me and began walking towards me. I could see them laughing and joking. I felt my face wrinkle in revulsion. I shouted and screamed in defiance. They swung their weapons at the ready as they steadily walked towards me. I felt something grab me. No. Someone grab me. A hard hand pulled me back, and I realised it was Josh, shouting something. I never knew how strong he was. I fought desperately to get away, to fight. to kick, punch, gouge and spit on whoever these people were. Josh's arm was around me, pulling me away. He shoved me to the car and pushed me into the rear passenger seat. I fell unceremoniously into the car. I saw the door slam closed as I struggled to right myself. I looked out the window just in time to see the truck explode in a massive fireball. The car pulled away with a screech. I banged on the glass and screamed again as hope for Charlie faded. The men broke into a run, finally seeing our method of escape, but Josh had buried the throttle to the floor, and the car took off down the remaining expanse of concrete. I looked back through the rear window at the smoking hulk of Charlie's truck.

The car seemed to slowly turn into the side road which, as Charlie said, stretched the entire length of the warehouse. Time seemed to slow down, like I was experiencing everything through thick treacle. I was aware of Josh shouting something. I had a final glimpse of the scene in front of me, or rather the chaos. Flames were fast consuming the cab of the truck. A few of the men in the larger gang were still shouting and trying to pursue our car. Others had turned back and were running towards the tractor. My last few images were of the tractor backing away from the truck and the unit settling back onto all of its wheels before a massive explosion ripped the cab up from the middle of the truck with a dull thump.

The car gathered speed down the concrete road. Josh's lips were moving, but I couldn't hear anything. The side of the warehouse seemed to move by in a sort of slow-motion blur; the car lurched to the right. I felt myself lose balance and sprawled out over the back seat. Another expanse of warehouse, but this time shorter; the car bounced over several speed bumps, another right turn, and we were heading towards the entrance gate. I could already see the tractor, now coming back up the side road it had driven down. Thick black smoke jetted into the air, and my anger resurged. I think Josh swore, although I can't be sure, but his knuckles were white, locked onto the steering wheel. I saw a few of the men running towards us as we turned out of the entrance and onto the side road. I banged at the window; I'm not sure what I said or shouted. Anger or frustration had taken hold of me. Josh turned the car down the main road and started to retrace our steps, but to where? Ultimately, I had no clue. In minutes our plan was in tatters, and we'd lost a friend. And for what? I sat in the back, motionless, gripped in a strange trance of sorts. Replaying that horrible scene in my mind: the truck lurching, the flames erupting and taking hold, and the final explosion which rocked the truck, and even now, some miles from the warehouse, its remnants could be seen in the air via the thick black cloud reaching into the sky.

I felt like crying, but I was numb. I let the feeling wash over me and let Josh drive. I don't know how long we were driving and which direction we went, but I was suddenly aware that the car had stopped. I blinked and felt like I'd just woken up, tired and confused. I looked around and saw that Josh had pulled the car into a small lay-by on the side of the road. A bin stood, crumpled and overflowing with garbage at the side. The surface looked depressed and damaged; clearly maintenance wasn't a concern. Oil and small puddles of watery strangeness that seemed to smell a little too much of urine gently wafted through the open driver's door. Josh had exited and was looking up and down the road. I fumbled with the door handle; the simplest of tasks seemed to take me far longer than I wanted. But eventually the door opened, and I stepped, or maybe tipped, out of the car and into the warmth of the new day. I looked down the road from the direction we'd seemingly come in. The plume of dark smoke was snaking higher into the sky, although it was a fair distance away, at least several miles.

"We need to go back," I said

"Back?" Josh asked, "What do you mean, 'back?"

"We need to go back for Charlie!"

Somewhere in my unconscious I realised the futility of my desire; I recognised the truth. But I wasn't thinking clearly.

"What the fuck are you on about?" Retorted Josh, angrily. "There's no going back for Charlie."

"He's gone." He added, "He's dead."

"Fuck you." I shouted back. "We don't know that."

"Did you not see the truck go boom?"

Josh paced around, running his hands through his hair, obviously frustrated and very much scared. And to be honest, so was I.

"We're not going back," he added, "certainly not with those cunts there."

He paused, looking back to where we had come from, and continued his pacing.

"FUCK," he shouted into the air. "I fucking knew this was a mistake. All this talk of travel, getting somewhere else. We should've stayed put. Stayed at home."

"Charlie..." I started to say, but I was cut off as soon as the words were out of my mouth.

"Fuck Charlie," said Josh, obviously angry. "We voted on it, and you went with Charlie. If you'd just seen reason and gone with me, he'd be here right now."

"What the fuck, Josh? If you weren't such a massive pussy, we could've helped him."

"Do what?" shouted Josh. "Did you see how many of them there were? We'd end up like Charlie or worse."

"But you were happy to send Charlie out there on his own."

"I didn't say fuck all."

"Exactly. You only say something when it gives you the upper hand or when you're right. Well, congratulations, you were right. And now Charlie's dead. And that's not just on you; it's on both of us."

I stood in front of Josh, almost breathless. We stared at each other for a few seconds before Josh, looking defeated, walked around me and went to the car and reached into the back and pulled out two cans of coke. He walked back, handing me a can before slumping down on the kerb. He looked at the can and pulled the metal tab on top. It opened with a slight fizz. He sighed and took a sip.

I looked up and down the road, aware of how exposed we were. I sat next to Josh. We sat and said nothing, exhausted. I took small sips of warm cola until the can was empty, save for a small drop at the bottom of the can which stubbornly refused to come out.

Josh just sat, probably feeling the same as I was. My thoughts were sharp, and a feeling of despair was eating at my consciousness. After some time Josh broke the silence first.

"I'm sorry," he said quietly. "I didn't mean to; I just"

"I know," I replied

There was a long pause, a justifiably uncomfortably long time, before I asked the obvious.

"What do we do now?"

I heard, rather than saw, as we sat side by side, him take a long swing of his cola.

"I want to go home," he said, finally.

I finally stood up and stretched. My legs and butt ached from sitting on the edge of the kerb. I looked around, surveying our surroundings, before finally coming round to face a still-sitting Josh.

"C'mon." I offered, "I'll drive."

TEN

I drove around the small village we'd left hours ago, following my sat nav, which amazingly worked. The same couldn't be said for mobile phones. Josh was juggling mine and his, trying to get through to the police.

"How can there be nothing?" he said, frustrated

"Maybe we'll get a signal when we're closer to civilisation."

"Maybe," he said, although he didn't sound sure. Truth be told, neither was I. It wasn't like we were in the wilds of nowhere. I didn't want to say anything, but I suspected that for the time being our phones would be useless.

Josh seemed to give up the dialling frenzy for a while. The sat nav instructed me to take a left turn, which I did. Looking at the small electronic map, that route we planned would bring us out just beyond the village, which meant we'd keep a wide berth of the warehouse we'd just run from, or rather, the group of angry douchebags that probably wouldn't be too happy to see us again. Given the rowdy send-off.

I kept checking my rearview mirror, expecting to see Charlie's truck looming behind us. I knew Charlie wouldn't be catching up anytime soon. I took a deep breath and tried not to strangle the steering wheel and just to concentrate on navigating the road ahead.

The small road eventually brought us out at a larger road that I'd recognised from the day before. I pulled up to the junction and was looking left and right down a deserted road; we hadn't seen anyone, friendly or otherwise, since we'd left the warehouse.

I eased the car forward, turning left, which would only be a few miles from a roundabout which would take us south back towards home.

We drove down the road and after only a few miles arrived at another village. A few shops were dotted amongst the largely residential area. The houses seem old, almost ornate in their design. Flowers bloomed and seemed to glow in the sun. Residential abodes gave way to more commercial buildings as we navigated through the village center.

"Look," said Josh, pointing down the road

I couldn't see what he was gesturing towards. My eyes slowly focused ahead, and then I saw it. A small police car parked in the road.

I pulled up in front of the car, and we saw that it was parked in front of a modern building, at least modern in the sense that it had been built many decades after the houses around it. The woodwork was painted blue, and it had a more modern sign which simply read 'Police'. We got out and looked around; I felt a sense of cautiousness, almost an air of tension. We approached the building and could see a few laminated information sheets that had been adhered to the inside of the window, informing whoever might read them to secure their cars and keep valuables out of sight. Another poster advertised a number for something called Crimestoppers. Josh pushed the door, and it opened. He looked at me. Visibly happy and walked in. I followed, and we found ourselves in a small reception area. It was plain; a few chairs were set against the far wall. The window to the outside world was on the right and let in all the light for the room. To the left was what looked to be a partition wall with a small window and a ledge that might pass as a counter. A door that looked fairly solid was closed, which I assumed gave access to the office space behind it.

We approached the small counter and could see into the office via the glass. A small buzzer was mounted to the left and a small sign read 'Press for attention'

I pressed the button and instantly heard a deep, dull buzzing sound elsewhere, but close, in the building. Seconds passed, and I looked at Josh; he shrugged, and I pressed again. The same drab sound permeated through the building.

A minute or so passed before Josh reached across me and pressed the buzzer button and held it down for an uncomfortable amount of time. Still no one came.

Josh finally released the button, looking frustrated.

"Where is everyone?"

"Pass"

Josh peered around the glass trying to see if anyone was back there and was simply ignoring us.

He muttered something under his breath and then pressed his hands against the glass and pawed at it. The glass slowly slid back with a strange rasping sound.

"Hello?" He shouted through the hole, "HELLO?"

He paused before shouting again. I sniffed, and the air smelt strange.

"Do you smell that?" I asked

"Yeah, smells like an old wet carpet."

I didn't reply, but there was something familiar about the smell. It almost smelt like tea or cut grass that was several days old. It wasn't pleasant, but not entirely unpleasant either.

Josh tried the buzzer again; this time it sounded louder now that the glass wasn't slid in place.

Josh tapped the small counter and took a step back, like he was surveying the entire area. He looked around the reception area before heading to the closed door and giving it a try. He turned the handle and pushed, but it was locked. He jiggled the handle and shook the door, but it still stayed closed.

"Where the fuck is everyone?" He finally said,

The strange smell had panicked me somewhat. I felt confused, angry and afraid at the same time. I was aware that I was clenching and unclenching my hands.

Josh rubbed his head before suddenly lurching at the door. He thudded against the solid surface, making a large bang. He almost bounced off it and immediately grabbed his arm.

"Fuck that's tough" he said

"Let's get out of here," I said, my voice strained with an edge of panic.

"Fuck," he said. "How come when you don't need the police, they're everywhere?"

I led the way back out of the office, and we hurried out and onto the street.

"Maybe we should try the phones again."

"Already ahead of you," he said, waving a phone. "But there's still no service."

We walked back to the car and climbed in. I slid my seatbelt on, started up the vehicle and pulled away from the kerb. I could feel my heart beating in my chest like I'd just run for ten minutes. We slowly made our way through the village, windows now down and letting the cooler afternoon air into the car. I took several deep breaths, steadying my nerves. The sat nav gave instructions to drive over another small roundabout, leading us out of the small town. I could already see the junction ahead where we'd need to turn.

As we drew closer, I noticed something wasn't quite right.

"Shit," I said, pulling up to the roundabout and looking right, toward where the exit should be that led back to the highway. I'm sure we'd come in this way, but at some point since last night someone or someone's had dumped what I can only describe as a shit tonne of rubble and assorted garbage over not only the exit but also the entire verge, creating a huge pile which blocked the entire road. The only way we'd be getting through it would be to get out and scramble over it.

Clearly this wasn't going to happen; there was no way I was leaving the car.

Our options seemed limited; an exit led left, which would take us away from our route and possibly back towards the warehouse we were trying hard to forget. The road ahead appeared to lead off into deep countryside and not in any direction we wanted to go. I flicked around the sat nav's map, looking for a viable route that wouldn't take us days to navigate. And then fate made the decision for us.

We heard the strange, pulsing, throaty 'chug-chug' sound first. I instinctively gripped the wheel, and both Josh and I looked left toward the sound at precisely the same moment to see the familiar shape of a tractor with a bucket attachment heading our way. We could see several men lounging in the empty bucket, and it felt as though we noticed each other at the same moment. Shock and realisation must've made a funny picture of our faces. But I wasn't laughing. Instead I saw red. I opened the car door and found myself moving without thinking. As I exited the car I walked towards the, now blocked, exit and picked up the first decent-sized rock I could put my hands on. I turned back towards the oncoming tractor and hurled the rock.

It arced upwards and towards my intended target.

The rock landed and skittered just short of the oncoming group.

Josh was shouting about getting in the car. There was a chorus of shouts and jeers. Josh banged on the roof of the car, shouting that it was time to go. I picked up another, smaller, rock and hurled it again. The lighter stone seemed to have a flatter trajectory. It sped through the air and smacked against one of the men sitting in the tractor's bucket. Hands left immediately to his left eye as the small rock ricocheted into the bucket of the tractor.

Jeers and shouts rose from the small horde. Several men pushed forward and ran from the tractor, incensed and screaming. It was definitely time to go.

I quickly jumped into the driver's seat. With the engine still running, I jammed my foot on the throttle, and the car lurched forward. Josh just about managed to pull his door closed as we took off around the roundabout, the tyres on my poor little car screeching on the road surface. Everything in the rear of the car slides chaotically to the left. I saw bags and tins and boxes roll around in the back. We quickly came around and exited onto the road we had just come off. The tractor was fast approaching the roundabout, and a few of the angry men were already there. A few had picked up rocks and were throwing them at us in retaliation. Several bounced off the side of the car with clangs and thuds. One well-placed rock clattered against the window. I didn't hear the window break, but it made almost like a snapping sound. Josh flinched and looked back at the window.

"Shit."

I glanced in the side mirror and saw a looming figure brandishing a large pole. I saw him swing and then heard a loud 'bang' towards the rear of the car. The sound made my foot bury the throttle, and the car sped away as fast as a small, underpowered hatchback can.

The sat nav said something about turning back, but I ignored the droning electronic voice and pressed on back down the road.

"Fucking hell!!"

I checked the rearview mirror, and our pursuers were nowhere to be seen. We continued to race down the road, maybe a little bit too close to one or two cars, evident when I heard the passenger wing mirror slap against a parked car's mirror. A few minutes or so later and we were heading into the countryside again. I figured the band of lunatics would either take too long to get to us or just loose interest. I drove for another handful of minutes before I pulled over and killed the engine.

"Why are we stopping?"

"I have no idea what the fuck we're doing. We need a plan

and fast; we can't just drive around hoping not to run into those fuckers again!"

Josh rubbed his head; I couldn't tell if he was thinking of frustrated.

I tapped at the sat nav, trying to find a viable route back. Our only options were to either go back the way we came or take a larger detour through what looked to be country roads. I was aware that the sun was low in the sky; we'd squandered the day, mostly being angry at each other and feeling sorry for ourselves. I suddenly felt angry at myself for not being more proactive.

Josh was rummaging through a bag, a small black case, not much bigger than a pad of A4 notepaper. He appeared to be flicking through the contents and then pulled out a map. He looked at it, seemingly taking in every detail, and then flipped it over.

"What are yo..." I began to say, but he shushed me before I could continue.

He unfolded the map and refolded it again, almost turning it inside out.

"I've got it," he finally said. He tapped at a point on the map.

"Got what?"

He pulled a small pen from the pouch and marked an area on the map and then handed it to me.

My eyes adjusted to the strangeness of the map; it felt heavy and laminated. There were a bunch of marks and symbols I didn't recognise.

I could see he had, haphazardly, circled a small region.

"Bagby. It's a small airfield and not that far away. I know it reasonably well. It's likely to be deserted, and we can hole up there until the morning."

I looked at the map and saw that it was, indeed, right next to Ripon, and I knew we weren't too far, at least in the car, from it. I tapped in the nearest village name into the sat nav and then zoomed out; I easily found the place on the electronic map. I pressed “Go” on the small panel, and within a few seconds it gave us a route.

“In half a mile, turn right” said the voice

“I think this will work,” I said, handing the map back to Josh

"Of course it’ll work."

I fired my little car back up and pulled onto the main road, following our new route ahead. Normally there would be banter or some kind of conversation, but we both just sat and stared ahead. I think we were both still too raw to really go beyond the basic niceties.

Even so, I felt a small surge of confidence in knowing we had a new goal. And a way forward.

ELEVEN

"Well, this doesn't look good," said Josh, craning his head forward, assessing the scene beyond the windscreen.

I sighed and turned the engine off. I checked the rearview mirror, and as confident as we could be that we were alone, we both gingerly stepped out to survey the road ahead. I say 'road ahead', but it was impossible to see the road because blocking the entire width of the road was a stack of cars, three vehicles high.

"This", I said, "is a problem!"

"Uh-huh. Who the hell did this? And why?"

"I have no idea, but I think it's safe to assume they're not wanting strangers passing through."

"Just how did things get so fucked up so quick?" said Josh, raising his voice.

"I don't know, fear is a strange thing."

I looked at the strange structure up and down. Cars of all ages and types had been stacked to make the wall. From old cars which looked like they'd not run in years to a brand new Audi. I kicked the nearest car at the bottom, a midrange Ford POS, almost expecting the makeshift wall to topple. All that happened was a dull, metallic thud. We peered through the gaps in the cars where they'd been stacked and saw nothing but the road beyond. In the distance, a small group of houses, but nothing more. No signs of activity or any life, save for a bird or two.

"Fucking weird," said Josh

"Pretty much. I think we need a new route."

I turned and headed back to the driver's seat and found the option on the sat nav to find an alternative route. I blinked and sighed at the four or five different options. They all would take us on a ten or so mile diversion, at best.

"Why does everything have to be difficult?" I asked to no one.

Josh was leaning down and looking through the driver-side door.

"It's bad, huh?" He said, more than asked

"The shortest route is going to take an hour, at best. And that's assuming we don't hit any other snags along the way."

"It's worth a chance," added Josh

"If we go now, we can get there just about sundown. I don't want to be driving about at night."

Josh half jogged around the car and wrestled himself back into the passenger seat while I confirmed the route on the sat nav. As soon as he got in and closed the door, I turned the car to the right in a circle to bring us level to a small road that led off to the left. I took the exit, following instructions issued from the small electronic box mounted on the windscreen. I hoped that this would be the last of our problems, at least for today.

Not long later, and I noticed that the car felt funny; it felt stodgy when steering. A tiny voice at the back of my head started to worry, but I pushed it away and continued on. We came to a small bend to the right, and as I turned, the car seemed to slide suddenly, and there was a grating sound, followed by a repetitive banging. Josh and I looked at each other, and I brought the car to a stop and got out. I looked around the car and saw the problem; the rear tyre had suffered a puncture and ripped most of the rubber around the edge of the wheel. There was a sizeable gash in the tyre which didn't look like it could be repaired. Luckily I had a spare In the rear.

"You got a flat tyre," said Josh from the other side.

"I know. I can see it right in front of me."

"No. You have a flat here!"

I trudged to where Josh was and saw what he was pointing at; the front tyre had suffered a similar fate.

"Well, that's just great; two busted tyres and one spare."

"And it's getting dark," Josh added

I groaned and rubbed my head

"We aren't getting to Bagby tonight. I don't much fancy stumbling around in the dark trying to find it."

"Agreed. What do you want to do?"

I looked up and down the road; it was quiet, but I didn't want to leave the car here, and we certainly couldn't stay with it out in the open.

"Fuck it! Let's push on as far as we can and maybe we'll find somewhere to pull in, out of the way, further down the road."

We jumped back and slowly pulled away. The car didn't sound good, and I kept our speed to something just above a crawl. The car was difficult to steer, but I got a little more confident and felt like I could pick up the pace. The noise the wheels made grew steadily worse, and within a mile or so were making a hideous scraping, grinding noise. I desperately searched for somewhere to pull off the road into. It was a race between finding a safe spot and the approaching full dark of the night. I didn't feel confident that we'd win. But as the blue of the day faded from the sky, a small clearing opened up to the right. I steered the car to the right and gave the little vehicle a final burst of gas to get us clear off the road. The car rolled over the firm ground and eventually came to a stop with a dull grinding sound. The veil of night was dropping fast; the light blue of the day had been replaced by a dark blue that appeared to be fading into black at an alarming rate. In the last gasps of the day I could already see a star or two emerging.

"Bloody Sod's law," said Josh, with a deep sigh, "and we're only five miles away as the crow flies."

I opened the door and sat in the car while looking at the small expanse of bushes and trees. The smell of burnt rubber and something else, almost like burning electrics, filled the air.

"We could always hoof it on foot," said Josh. "It wouldn't take too long."

"What?" I responded, "Now?"

"Why not? We could just cut over a few fields. It's not that far."

"At night." I added, "We could trip or fall over anything, and let's not forget we have friends somewhere out there, and there might be someone else wanting to make friends, too."

Josh blew out air, obviously frustrated

"I guess. It's frustratingly close to hot and cold drinks, a working toilet and facilities."

"We have drinks and snacks here. And as for facilities, there's the finest trees and bushes England has to offer!"

Josh smiled and laughed.

"Let's get some rest and start again in the morning. In the meantime we can have supper."

Rummaging around in the devastation and disorganisation of the rear of the car, we pulled out several packs of biscuits and assorted treats and a few cans of soda, which Josh insisted on calling 'fizzy pop'. I'd lost a few of my speech traits since coming to the UK, but soda was something that had stuck, and I felt almost silly saying fizzy pop. Although, come to think of it, soda is originally soda pop back home.

We ate biscuits and Jaffa Cakes. taking sips of Dr Pepper and Coke every so often. We didn't talk much; I felt a sort of pressure between us. Instead, Josh fished out an iPad from his bag, and we watched several episodes of a cartoon he'd found. After eating I felt suddenly tired. I reclined the seat and used my jacket as a blanket. Josh did the same, and soon he was breathing heavily. I stared out the window for a while, trying to pierce the darkness. I was both tired and scared to sleep. Memories of the events of the morning played out in my head. At some point sleep must've come for me. Because my next memory was waking up with a stiff neck.

I blinked, and instinctively my hand went to my poor, aching neck. The windows were steamed up, and the light of the morning crept in. Beyond the shade of the trees I could see that the skies were blue and clear of clouds. I looked to the passenger seat and saw Josh, still very much asleep. I felt like a hot bag of dicks. Almost everything ached, and it was a good deal colder than last the evening. The night had stolen the warmth from everything. I took a deep breath and carefully opened my door so as not to wake Josh. I had the door open and was easing myself out when Josh let out a long, wet, rasping fart which seemed to last too long. I involuntarily froze and was both amazed and disgusted at the same time. I quickly pushed myself out of the car and slammed the door as hard as I could. It wasn't going anywhere, but it was still my car. Dammit.

I yawned and stretched, taking in the fresh morning air. I quickly took in my surroundings, and I was happy to see that it was quiet and nicely secluded. We couldn't hide from anyone passing by on the road, but we were out of the way from prying eyes at a distance. Hopefully we'd have enough time to figure out the way to Bagby.

The passenger door opened, and Josh shambled out. From the look of him, he appeared to have just as bad a night as I had. He yawned loudly and made a terrible throaty retching noise. It sounded like like a terrible demon was trying to escape from his body.

He turned and saw me staring.

"Morning," he said with a sheepish grin.

"Morning," I answered.

"I feel like shit."

"You are not alone."

"The car smells like something crapped out a dead rat."

"That's all you, buddy."

"I could do with some breakfast, but I have some more pressing issues."

He looked a tad concerned. You might say nervous.

"What's wrong?" he didn't seem himself

"I need to pee."

"So", I said with a shrug, "go pee."

"I can't," he said, looking a little more embarrassed. "You're here."

"What?"

"I can't go with other people around."

"How on Earth do you survive in the real world?"

"I use cubicles."

He saw the way I looked at him.

"Do judge me. I'm cock-shy."

"Just go fifty feet over there, find a bush or a tree. I'll go over here."

I walked away and turned to see Josh looking around and scratching his head before shuffling towards a bank of trees. I found myself a small, dense copse of bushes. I saw a large bushel of dock leaves and grabbed a few before navigating behind the bushes. I looked back and saw Josh disappearing behind a tree and smirked to myself as I unbuttoned my jeans and pulled them down with my underwear. I crouched down and once I'd finished, used the dock leaves. Although somewhat awkward, it was oddly freeing. I buttoned myself back up and jumped out of the bushes without looking back. I arrived back at the car and was rummaging around looking for baby wipes, which I'd half seen the day before last when I threw a bunch of stuff into the car.

I managed to find the pack just as Josh appeared.

He didn't look happy.

"You good?"

"No," he said. "I couldn't go."

"Why?"

"I dunno, I just feel weird about peeing in the open."

"I never figured you for stage fright."

"It's a thing."

"I'm sure it is." handed him a wipe

"But I didn't go."

"Just clean your filthy dick, spankers."

He sighed and took a wipe and rubbed his hands.

I rummaged around in the chaos of the back seat of the car and found an energy drink. I pulled the tab and took a glug of the peculiar-tasting fizzy beverage.

Josh opted to grab a can of Coke from the pile.

"I guess we better get going sooner rather than later; I don't much fancy getting caught by anyone unsavoury."

Josh squinted, focusing on something in the distance, or at least that's what it looked like.

"If we head for that high peak in the distance, it should get us there."

"Let's get organised; I'll feel better once we're under way."

I gestured towards the small, dirty white cable that trailed from my dash and towards the passenger footwell.

"Charge your phone before we head off."

Josh nodded and connected his phone as I stretched once again. Feeling a little more alive, although I would've killed for a cup of hot coffee.

I went to the rear of the car and found my trusty backpack. It wasn't massively large; it could hold a laptop and a few other bits and pieces, but I took it everywhere. I began filling it with some of the food and drink we'd brought with us. There was a small first aid kit I stuffed into one of the pockets, and I made sure I had packed all the cables that I kept in the car for charging various electronics. After a few minutes the bag was stuffed full. I grabbed my jacket and laid it over the backpack which I had dumped on the ground. Josh was standing, looking off into the distance at something or nothing.

"You might want to take some stuff with you," I said

"What for?" He asked, "We're heading home, non? And besides, there will be something to eat and drink at the airfield, I'm sure."

"Fair enough. Grab your phone, and let's go."

I picked up my bag and slid my arms in and through the loops. I holstered it onto my back and adjusted the straps until they were comfortable. I picked up my coat and stuffed it through the one of the straps and let it dangle.

"Ready?" I asked

"No," replied Josh

"Excellent," I said, striding off in the general direction of the airfield.

An hour or so later and we were labouring over a roughly ploughed field. We'd already crossed several fields, although they were pretty easy going. We had some difficulty in navigating through a few hedges, and there was an incident in getting over a small fence where I was stuck on some barbed wire for longer than comfortable. But, we had made decent time. We were hot and starting to tire; this dull brown field was fighting us every step of the way. The ground was uneven, and more than a few times each of us tripped over a rock or stumbled because we lost our footing in a small hole. The only good thing was that it wasn't uphill. Beads of sweat had formed on my face, and I could feel the clammy, sticky heat of sweat around my armpits and down my back. The backs of my knees felt strangely damp, too. Josh was confident he could dead reckon the way, and I was sceptical at first, but to his credit he managed to steer us in the right direction.

"Using visual points of reference is my ting." he said with a smile

We continued on for a while; it felt like hours, but a sneak peek at my mobile phone told me we had only been walking for 90 minutes. Josh complained about the heat and his feet. We were already halfway over another field, and so to push us on, I suggested we take a break at a small group of trees which lined the edge of the current field. We soon arrived at the trees, and we both slumped down in the shade and looked out past where we'd walked from.

I handed Josh a can of coke. He grabbed the can, had it open and was downing its contents as quickly as possible.

I found myself a small carton of orange juice and settled back onto a tree and tried to relax for a few moments. It was seemingly all too easy to try and forget the events of the previous day, but every now and then the memories would intrude into my thoughts, flashing visions of fire, smoke and violence. I felt sad but mostly guilty for leaving Charlie. Part of me knew that there was almost no hope of saving him, but there was that stubborn part of my mind that refused to acknowledge that fact. Josh had been prudent and had, most likely, saved our asses. My own temper had nearly got us into trouble. But still. Maybe there would've been a chance.

Our fifteen-minute break turned into a forty-minute break. We eventually wrestled ourselves into a standing position. My limbs ached, and there was a stinging sensation on the ball of one of my feet. I stretched and pulled on my backpack. Josh pointed us in the direction we needed to travel, and we set off, clambering through the small bank of trees before emerging onto a small dirt track which appeared to frame another field, although this time it was green and lush. An entire field of tall grass; walking over it was definitely preferable and easier to manage than the last field.

We continued to put one foot in front of the other until we came to our next hazard to navigate. A smallish drainage ditch that we had to get over. There was a gentle dribble of water at the bottom, although it seemed rather stagnant. Neither of us fancied trying to jump over, for fear of falling in the water, and we both didn't want to take shoes and socks off to cross either. We elected to take a detour, operating on the assumption that there would be a place to cross sooner or later.

As we traced the route of the ditch, I could feel the heat of the day increase. We'd been at this for a while, and I felt largely uncomfortable. Josh didn't look any better than I felt; even with no additional bags, we had begun to sweat profusely. I watched several droplets of sweat cascade off his nose and fall towards the bone-dry dirt ground.

After ten or so minutes of walking, we found a suitable place to cross; a small bridge had been made to span the ditch that would allow a tractor or other farm machinery to cross.

We trudged on through another field, this time bone dry and pretty much flat. A few weeds were poking out here and there. For whatever reason this field didn't look to have seen any work for a while. We crossed the field with ease and found a small public path to follow where the grass was knee-high. A path had naturally emerged from the many people who had walked it. Although you could see where nature was intending to reclaim it. Grasses had started to grow up and out and were attempting to fill in the spaces where humans had trampled them down.

At Josh's direction we followed the path and then veered off into another field. We had to trample through the long grass and through several large bushes before we emerged onto yet another field. Plants, or, I can only assume, vegetables of some description, had been planted in almost perfect rows of raised soil. Small bursts of green appeared at regular intervals. We walked down a row each.

Half over, Josh pointed in front of him

"I think I see it. I think that's it."

He seemed more animated than I had seen him in the last few hours, and I strained to see what he meant.

"Over there," he said, pointing towards something that, to him, seemed obvious but somehow eluded me. "The airfield."

Even when he told me what I was looking for, I failed to see it. I just followed and let him lead. His pace quickened, obviously excited.

Between Josh's excited strides and the uneven ground, it was difficult to keep up. A large hedge blocked our path, and we managed to eventually struggle through where it had thinned out a little.

We had to stoop to get through; small branches scratched at my face. I had an irrational image of a small branch entering my eye and blinding me for life.

I stood up and stretched, surveying the airfield, if you could call it that. There was no paved runway; it was just grass. A few buildings dotted the periphery. I could see about five or six small aircraft, tied to the ground from their wings. Josh was already making his way over to one of the small buildings.

"C'mon," he shouted

I took a breath and followed him at a much slower pace. A large flagpole with a windsock fluttered around, although the lack of wind made the thing flaccid and sad.

I cautiously looked around, waiting for someone, anyone, to burst from a dark corner, a bush or one of the small buildings. Josh had disappeared inside one, and I stood waiting, watching to see what happened next. Nothing. It would appear as though we were alone.

I heard Josh shouting something from within. I took a few steps towards the building and was met by an excited Josh who was holding several chocolate bars and cans of Orange Fanta.

"Breakfast is served," he announced, obviously pleased with himself.

We sat on the grass and looked out over the pristine greenness of it all. It was quiet, and Josh seemed to be happier than before. We both sat and drank a can of orange soda, sorry, fizzy orange or orange pop if you prefer. The hours had drifted by, and the sun was high in the sky. The heat felt like it was pushing down on us. Yet we managed to enjoy a moment with a cool-ish beverage in the shade.

"I take it you have an idea?" I finally asked

"I do," replied Josh. "We take one of the planes and fly it back to an airfield near your house. It won't take long to walk back. We can do it in about twenty minutes, I'm sure.

"Wait a minute. Are you serious?"

"I am," he replied. "I am licensed, and I'm pretty much only a few hours away from being able to take my commercial and multi exams. We can borrow one of the 172's or maybe a 150 and fly it back. Once things calm down, I can sort everything out afterwards."

I obviously didn't look comfortable.

"Have a little faith."

"I've never been in a small plane."

"Don't worry about it. They're pretty safe and well maintained."

"Pretty safe" I started to say

"We can either spend the next few days or nights or however long it'll take to walk back or maybe hitchhike, and hopefully we won't get fucked over along the way home. Or..."

He paused for dramatic effect before continuing

"Or we could borrow a plane and be landing back near home in under twenty minutes."

"Twenty minutes?"

"More or less"

I took a deep breath; for some reason getting into a small plane made me nervous

"Alright."

Josh obviously saw how nervous I looked.

"Don't worry," he said in his best cheesy American accent. "Captain Josh will look after you."

"Oh fuck!"

We ate a hearty lunch of biscuits and cold drinks. We sat for a while just staring into space until Josh clapped his hands and briskly stood up, which seemed to snap me out of my sugar trance.

"Right," he said. "Let's get cracking."

I suddenly felt a pang of weirdness in my stomach

"I'll find us a bird; you get your bag and pack up what you need and go to the toilet and stuff."

He marched off with purpose. Leaving me alone in what he had called the clubhouse.

I wasn't normally a nervous Nelly, but I felt an element of apprehension about flying or being flown. Maybe it was also the fact that it was Josh. I'd never flown with him, and he never offered to take me flying. I think Charlie went up with him once, although not much was said.

I decided to take a pee and then pack up whatever we had.

Washing my hands, I found it strangely eerie that we hadn't seen anyone in almost a day. It was also something I was glad about.

As I was adjusting the contents of my bag, Josh stomped back into the room.

"Good news, I found the perfect one, and she's already outside."

"Great," I said through half-gritted teeth

"Don't worry. It'll be fine."

He rubbed his hands and began to rifle through a nearby cupboard. Within a few seconds he pulled out two large headphones with long wires. He battled with separating the cables from one another before handing me one.

"This is your headset," he said. "Keep hold of it for now, and we'll get you plugged in when we're ready to go."

"Okay," I said with some trepidation.

The headset looked new but old. It was a strange green colour with a flexible microphone protruding from one of the earphones. A cable extended from one of the sides of the headset and ended in two plugs which looked like something from my dad's vintage music system. I carefully wound the wire up and saw that the plugs appeared to be slightly different in size.

Josh seemed to regard me with humorous eyes.

"Come out when you're ready; I'm going to check the plane out."

"Cool"

I finished packing up my bag, zipped it up and then carried it out using the shoulder straps as handles. I emerged from the building into the bright and oppressive midday sun. I saw Josh a little way off at a small plane. He was busy winding a rope up, which he seemed to tie into some kind of knot before dropping it onto the ground. He saw me and waved me over. As I got nearer, the smaller plane seemed to gain a little size, but not much.

"Your chariot awaits."

The plane was white with a blue stripe that ran down the side and up onto the rear tail. Wings were mounted into the roof, which extended out and slowly rocked in the breeze every now and then. The plane had a single propeller mounted on its nose.

"What do you think?" asked Josh. "Nice, eh?"

The white paint had seen better days and there was some dirt on the underside of the wing

Before I could point this out, he ushered me to the right-hand door

"This is the passenger side; you should be comfortable

with this, since you're a Yank," he said. "We fly from the left seat, generally."

I said nothing and pulled open the door. I was greeted with a fairly high seat and a somewhat roomy cabin. I could see another set of seats in the rear.

"Shove your bag in the back and then jump in. The seatbelts are easy to figure out. I just need to finish my walk-around."

I pushed my bag onto the rear seat and then climbed inside. There was a strange smell of oil, electrics and age that I couldn't quite put my finger on. I found two halves of a belt and managed to clip them together. I saw that Josh was intently examining each part of the plane. He walked around the aircraft, touching various points, at times kneeling down or reaching into things. He didn't seem to notice me; he seemed utterly focused. It was a strange thing to see and a different side to him that I'd never seen before. It gave me confidence that this was maybe a better idea than I first suspected. After ten or so minutes of Josh doing his thing, he opened the door and climbed in.

"I've already checked the fuel and oil, and we're good for about two hours of flight, which is more than enough."

He wriggled in the seat, getting himself comfortable. He quickly did up his lap belt and then reached back and hooked in a shoulder strap. He took his headset and plugged each end somewhere under the instrument panel, which was filled with buttons, dials and readouts.

He pointed towards the far end of the panel near my window.

"You can plug your headset into those points at the very end."

I looked around and saw two connectors for the headset. I fumbled with the cable and managed to eventually got them in.

"Once the engine is running, you won't be able to hear me until I turn on the radio."

Josh pulled on the large headset, and I followed suit.

Another wave of anxiousness washed over me. But I took a deep breath and told myself that Josh knew what he was doing. That this was his thing. It certainly seemed like he knew what he was doing as he tapped on certain dials, twisted various controls and ran through some kind of checklist. After a few minutes he opened his window and shouted through the small hole.

"Clear prop!"

I have no idea who he was shouting at or why, since we were alone. I can only assume it was habit.

His hand was already on a key that I, strangely, didn't see him insert. He turned it, and I heard a dull, muffled click from within the confines of the headset, and then he twisted it again. The engine spluttered, and the propeller turned a few times before there was a coughing sound and then silence.

"She's a bit on the cold side," shouted Josh

He pushed and pulled some kind of lever near his window a few times and then tried again.

The engine turned over; the propeller turned a few times as I heard the engine struggle to come alive. He pushed another lever, near the key, gently in and out. Suddenly, several coughs from the engine turned into a rapid succession of spluttering, and a second later, the engine burst into life. It was loud, even with the headset on, which seemed to provide a fair bit of buffer to the sound. Josh was busy pointing at various instruments and setting more dials. He pushed a button, and suddenly there was an electric buzzing sound in my ear.

"Can you hear me?"

The sound came through into my headset and was coloured with a tinge of static and electronic distortion.

"Yup! It sounds a little weird!"

It was strange when I talked, because I could hear myself when I spoke. It was very strange.

Josh reached forward and adjusted my microphone so that it pretty much touched my lips.

"Try that," he said. "I couldn't hear you very well."

"Umm. Is it better?" My own voice sounded louder, although no less confident.

"Much better," he said

The plane throbbed and vibrated as the engine ticked over. The propeller was a blur of motion out the front window. It suddenly occurred to me that I couldn't see very much in front of us. The front of the plane seemed to sit very high.

"Alright," he said. "I need to do some power-on checks before we take off, and then I'll take you through a few things before we head off."

I nodded and simply observed. I heard a slight click in the headset and heard Josh's voice again.

"Golf bravo victor, taxiing for power on checks"

Josh looked around and then pushed a lever to the middle of the console. Next to two levers, one blue, one red. He eased it in, and the engine pitch changed and rose. The plane seemed to bounce, and we were suddenly moving forward. Josh seemed to be super focused and was looking left and right as he moved forward. I felt my nerves rise, but there was also an element of excitement. The plane slowly bounced over the grass. Josh swung the plane around almost 180 degrees, and we came to an abrupt stop.

"This should be into the wind, although there's not much wind today," he said, pointing towards the windsock, still looking very sad.

Power-on checks seemed to involve running the plane at high RPMs for a small period of time. The plane made some worrying sounds as I noticed the sudden drop in RPMs every now and then. Josh assured me that this was normal and part of the standard series of checks that needed to be done prior to flight. I took a deep breath and resorted to looking out the window.

I spotted a pheasant gambolling around near the clubhouse when Josh's voice came through my headset again.

“Okay, are you ready?”

“I'm going to go with yes?"

He laughed.

“We'll head down to two-four, and then it's game time.”

He paused, and I got the sense he was assessing me or rather, my competency in keeping it together.

“Golf bravo victor, taxing to hold at two-four”

Josh drove, if that's the right term, the plane forwards and then spun back around. The little plane trundled and bounced over the grass. I couldn't see anything to indicate what was the runway and what wasn't. We appeared to just be running on grass.

“Right,” announced Josh. “We're taking off from runway two-four. Being in a small plane is not really different in terms of physics from being in a larger plane; we just need less speed to take off, and there are less complicated systems that control flight. Basically don't touch anything, but if you feel like you're getting nervous, then try and hold your knees rather than touching the yoke.”

I nodded

“And make sure you keep your feet away from the pedals, please.”

I immediately pulled my knees back and away from the footwell.

We came to what looked like the end of the nicer groomed grass, and Josh brought the plane to a gentle stop.

“Just a few more things to do and then we're good to go.”

There sure seemed like a lot of things to do before you could take off. Which I guess was a good thing. This certainly wasn't like jumping in a car and driving. I felt a little bit more at ease.

Josh pressed and manipulated other controls. I heard a dull whirring somewhere. I looked out the window and saw the end of the wing sort of drop down a little.

"Those are flaps," said Josh, reading my mind. "They'll give us a little extra lift for takeoff." "Interestingly enough," he added, "they can also be used to slow us down for landing."

"Oh."

"Right, all good?"

"As good as I'll ever be."

"Excellent. Let's do this."

I noticed that he pressed a button on the control column, or yoke, as he called it.

"Golf bravo victor taking off from two-four and departing to the south"

Without pause, Josh pushed the throttle in, the plane immediately responding with additional revs which caused the plane to lurch and bounce forward. Josh swung the plane around, and as soon as he did, I could see the perfect groom of the grass extend in front of us. The pitch of the engine surged. The plane gathered speed quickly, and suddenly the long runway looked a fair bit shorter. The plane bounced over the ground, and I anxiously grabbed my knees. I looked out of the window, and the grass passed by the window in a blur.

"She wants to fly," said Josh

"Not helping."

I saw that he pulled back on the control column, and suddenly the bumpiness of the ground disappeared. Holy shit. We were flying.

"I'll keep us near the ground to gather speed," he explained

The plane seemed to quickly pick up speed now that it was freed from the confines of the Earth.

Josh pulled back a little on the controls; the plane made a little lurch, and we rose higher into the sky. The ground dropped away quickly.

"How high are we?" I asked

"Passing six hundred feet now."

"Is that all? It seems higher."

A few minutes later and we appeared to level off. The

horizon rose up into view. Josh quickly pushed a small wheel-like device several times.

"Let's trim this bitch out," he said to himself, at least I assume so; I had no idea what was going on.

I stared out the window. I could see for miles and miles; the land stretched out like a crazy patchwork joined by the ever-threading and intertwining roads.

"This is pretty sick."

"It's not something that gets old. Even now I still can't quite believe I can do this."

He looked and tapped on several instruments; his fingers found a small dial on the panel and started twisting. The small digital numbers on the tiny panel changed. Josh looked at the panel and looked at the map he had cradled on his lap.

Josh spoke into the microphone, and I assumed this wasn't aimed my way.

"Leeming zone, this is Golf Mike Delta Bravo Victor, requesting MATZ penetration and basic service."

There was a slight click, or maybe pop, when Josh released the small button on his control. And then there was nothing. Just the thrum of the little plane's engine. I idly looked out the window and saw the landscape passing below.

Josh tried again, repeating himself. Again, nothing.

"Strange," he said. "Maybe Humberside is up and running."

Again he twisted the small knob on the panel; the numbers changed. I understood now. This was some kind of radio frequency.

"Humberside radar, good morning, this is Golf Mike Delta Bravo Victor, requesting basic service."

Again, the radio call was met with silence. Josh, looking both puzzled and frustrated, frowned and repeated the same phrase several times. There wasn't a peep from anyone.

"This is borderline impossible," he said finally. As he looked down at his map; his finger searched for something, and he found it, tapping at the surface. He twisted the radio frequency to the new number that he'd found on the map.

"London Information, golf mike delta bravo victor, requesting basic service"

Nothing.

"Maybe the radio is out?" He said

He looked at his map again and quickly found something of interest. He held his finger on the point on the map while he adjusted the radio frequency with the other. I was a little nervous that he didn't have his hands on the controls, but, amazingly, the plane seemed to just keep flying straight.

As soon as he dialled in the new frequency, a series of rapid beeps filled my headset and invaded my ears.

"Well, we can receive," he said

He put his hands back on the controls and adjusted the small wheel again. The plane lurched a little, which gave me a start.

"I have one more thing to try," as he turned around and rummaged around in the back of the plane. He pulled from a small plastic box a small black walkie-talkie.

He held it up, showing me, almost victorious.

"Emergency radio," he said with a smile

I gave a thumbs up, not really knowing what to say or make of it all. I was just happy we weren't falling out of the sky.

Josh pulled his headset out of the panel. The radio popped, and I was severed, in terms of communication, with him. I watched as he plugged his headset into some kind of adaptor that was on the radio. He clicked a few buttons and appeared to set the frequency. I couldn't really tell; it was too small to really make out from my seat. I could see his mouth moving as he spoke, but I couldn't hear a word. The sound of the engine and the sound-dampening effect of my headphones were isolating me from him. After a minute or so, he unplugged from the small radio and plugged back into the plane's radio. He reached back and placed the small black device back in the box. I imagined it would've made a small, plastic clatter as it did.

"We seem to be alone up here."

"Is that strange?"

"There's no precedent for it," he explained. "It just doesn't happen."

"Except it's happening."

"All we can do is carry on and keep an eye out for any other air traffic."

He checked his watch and looked out the window and referred back to the map on his knee and then turned the control a little to the left. The plane started an easy turn.

"This should bring us onto a course that will take us straight home." He explained, "It's a fairly straight shot, and we should see some recognisable features."

I could already see, in the distance, York Minster and several notable power stations. I looked out and down from the window and saw that we were already passing by a large service station on the A1.

"Wetherby"

"Already?"

"She moves quick. We're doing," he peeked at another dial, "about one hundred knots, which is just over one hundred miles an hour."

"Fast. Pity we couldn't make that time on the ground.

"Plus it's a straight line, no roads to navigate."

"This is pretty impressive, Josh."

"And by general aviation standards, this is slow. There's a DA42, which is only marginally bigger than this plane, and that'll do about 220 miles per hour."

Josh squinted at the horizon and then at the instruments. He then looked at a small device on the top of the window which looked to be some kind of compass. Although I hadn't noticed it before.

"Weird"

“What’s weird? What's wrong?” I asked, suddenly feeling nervousness creep back into my psyche.

“Nothing’s wrong. Not exactly. I plotted our course here.” He tapped on the map attached to his knee. When I plan routes and headings, you adjust for magnetic drift. It’s a known thing when plotting courses using compass headings.”

“Okay,” I said, not really knowing what he was talking about.

“Magnetic drift is a fairly static thing; you can adjust for it and then have the correct heading, allowing for winds. It seems the course I’ve plotted, already adjusting for the magnetic drift, isn’t correct. It’s almost as if there’s more magnetic drift than there should be. Which isn’t possible.”

“I’m going to say okay, like I completely understand.”

I swore I heard Josh tut.

“It’s not a problem anyway; I know where we are and where we’re going since I’ve flown this area a tonne, especially when I was first getting my licence.”

As if in response, he moved the controls a little to the left again, and the plane tilted and moved slowly. After a few seconds he moved it back, and the plane levelled out.

“That should be it.”

To be honest, it didn't seem like it was a big deal; we were sort of still following the same direction, or so it seemed. But this was Josh's show, so I didn't say anything.

In the distance I could see black smoke rising from the ground, and squinting, I could just about make out the city center of Leeds to the right.

“That’s Leeds, right?”

“Yup,” he said. “Looks like more fires.”

I suddenly felt a nagging ache in the pit of my stomach.

A few minutes later and we could see more smoke, this time in front of us.

“That’s home.” he said

The plane buzzed on, and the closer we got, the more we could see. Large plumes of smoke were now winding into the sky. Our view from the plane had masked the true extent of the chaos, but as we drew closer, we could see that whole groups of houses appeared to be on fire.

"I'll take us down to have a look."

"What? Land?" I said with some urgency

"No," said Josh. "We'll drop down to about five hundred feet and get a proper look."

Josh pulled a small lever; the engine seemed to change pitch a little. He then pulled the throttle, and the plane's RPMs dipped, and we suddenly started losing altitude. Not worryingly, but enough to know we were heading towards the ground.

As we dropped down, the world below grew larger, and more and more details revealed themselves.

He pushed the throttle back in, and the plane seemed to pick up speed. But it wasn't all that was happening inside that was piquing my interest. It was what was happening outside.

Being so close to the ground, I could see cars that had been burnt out, now blackened hulks sitting on the side of the road. Several houses had been burnt to the ground, and several more were engulfed in flames. I was wondering where the emergency services were when I saw a burnt-out fire engine. I saw a few people on the ground; I couldn't make out what they were doing, but they just appeared to be walking around aimlessly. A few ran by others, going from car to car. I recognised one of the main roads which led into Selby, which we were now following. Josh turned to the right to take us towards the town center. More thick, black smoke erupted from the train station. There appeared to be more activity on the ground below. Several groups of people were running around, throwing objects at one another. There appeared to be some kind of brawl, a small mass of people throwing things, stomping, hitting and pushing other people. I certainly wouldn't want to be down there. More abandoned cars littered the roads, and there seemed to be all kinds of debris everywhere. Like someone had emptied the contents of cars and trucks everywhere. It was hard to take in singular details; the whole picture looked like chaos.

"What the fuck is going on?" Asked Josh

"I have no idea."

"How has it got this bad in only a few days?"

I said nothing. The scene below spoke for itself.

"Let's check out my house," he said, turning the plane to the left.

We flew over the canal and out past the local shopping precinct. A small estate of houses, which were fairly new, sprawled out to the left. This is where Josh and Charlie had been sharing a house.

"Holy shit!" He said, "It's like a fucking bombsite."

I leaned towards him and saw more smoke and destruction. More people were dotted around, not really doing anything, or so it seemed.

Josh turned the plane to the left again, and we headed away from the estate and towards more familiar ground, at least for me.

"Are we checking out my house?"

"Yup! Yup!"

Everywhere seemed to be covered in trash and debris. Surreal; my last memories of this place were of quiet, almost strangely so, and now it was chaos, mayhem and destruction.

As we approached the familiar rows of streets which formed my mental image of home. I was too shocked to really be in awe of how things looked from the sky. Instead I saw the rows of fire-gutted houses. Several small wisps of smoke reached for the sky in a surreal tangle. Neatly parked cars appeared to be burnt out; some had survived better than others.

"I think your street has looked better."

He dipped the plane right so that I could see out of the window; I suddenly could see more of the ground than before. I was acutely aware that the plane was now at an angle and that I could look out the window and only see the ground. I couldn't really focus at first; I couldn't understand what I was seeing, but then I realised that it was my street and my row of neighbours. I saw the telltale black marks on the front of what was my nicely pristine whitewashed house, which appeared to have been gutted by fire, which had taken most of my row of houses.

"Shiiiit!"

"You have insurance, right?" Asked Josh

"I think insurance is the least of our worries right now."

The whole street seemed like it had been plucked from a post-apocalyptic war zone. This wasn't how I imagined it would be. I didn't realise how bad things were going to get, and now I could hear Charlie's words in my head. I suddenly realised I'd failed to take what he said seriously. I regret not planning, not listening. I felt the pangs of guilt and shame, followed by a wave of sadness sweeping over me.

"What do we do now?" I asked

"I have no idea," said Josh quietly

For a few minutes we circled the area, seemingly entranced by the chaos below.

"Maybe we should head back to the airfield," I eventually said

There was a long pause. The dull drone of the aircraft engine filling the nothingness.

I hear Josh sigh through the headset.

"I think you're right."

He looked at his map and then began another turn. We quickly levelled out before increasing power, and we began a slow rise into the sky. I kept looking behind at what we were intending to come back to and what we were now leaving.

Would we ever see this place again? Would it ever be the same? I did want to believe so. But something inside me, at the back of my head, said the opposite.

Somewhere I thought I heard Charlie laughing.

TWELVE

We sat in what, Josh had reminded me, was the clubhouse and not the office. I'm not entirely sure what the difference is, but it seemed to matter to him. Sometimes a little bit of trivial shit is easier to deal with than the bigger issues. Even so, we sat and drank a can of whatever we could fish back out of the fridge.

"What are your thoughts?" I finally asked Josh, mid-slurp.

He looked at me and then put his can of Dr Pepper down on the table next to him.

"I honestly have no idea. I can barely process what we saw."

I nodded. There was a certain surrealness to everything. I would've even said that it had a dreamlike feel to it, if you dream of fire and destruction.

"At least it all makes sense," he added

"What do you mean?"

"The lack of internet, mobile phone signals, the destruction, everything. It seems to be pushing from the South to the North."

"You think we're safe here?"

"I don't know." Josh looked sombre. "I know that I have nowhere to go and no other options or even a glimmer of a plan."

I took a sip of my drink, leaning back in the chair I had selected, and considered our options.

"Do you think we could make it to Charlie's sister's place?" he ventured

My eyes snapped to Josh's in an instant.

"That's not a great idea. I can imagine how that would play out: 'Oh, hi, Jessica, how's it going? Charlie? Oh! No, he's dead, and here's the blinker: we're responsible.'"

"We're not responsible," said Josh in a matter-of-fact tone

I wondered if he was convincing me or himself.

"Anyway, I don't know where she lives; I only know she's in Northumberland and she's moved several times."

"No." I said, "I have a marginally better option."

"And?" Said Josh

"I have relatives in the North."

"You? How? And where?"

"On my father's side, Uncle Joe. I'm not entirely sure where exactly. I have the address saved in an e-mail, which I can't get to right now."

"Well, I guess that's pretty useless."

"Dacer...no, Dacre!"

"What?"

"That's the name of the village they live in," I said with more than a hint of defiance.

"Where in God's name is that?"

"Cumbria?"

"Oh goody," said Josh. "I'm glad it's only just down the road."

I gave him my best withering look

"What other options do we have?"

"I concede," he said after a few moments. "I just hope your family doesn't turn out to be cannibals or part of some weird cult."

The next few hours were a sort of blur of activity. Josh rolled out a few maps of the country, and we eventually found Dacre near Penrith; it was actually just west of Penrith, which was good and bad. We'd found our destination without much trouble, but now we were faced with having to get there. Josh knew there was another, larger, airport at Carlisle, but then we'd be faced with a large journey of about twenty-six miles. Not ideal.

Josh actually managed to find another small airfield not too far from the village.

While we were talking, Josh had scribbled a few notes and circled various points on the maps we had spread out.

"What's with the hieroglyphics?"

"Possible routes and what I think might be good visual reference points. Makes it easier to navigate from the air."

"Oh," I said, not totally understanding.

He smiled and sort of shrugged. It was the same sort of gesture you'd do when Grandma asked about those fancy 'smartie phones' she'd heard about and what about that Facebook thing that could tweet people or something?

While Josh sat down and did what he called 'pilot shit' on the desk with equipment I hadn't seen since high school, I set about repacking my backpack with whatever I could find. Josh said we had a weight limit that we most likely wouldn't hit, considering that all we had were basic snacks and foodstuffs. I was now regretting my eagerness to bring just snack foods, and I was starting to crave something real and moderately healthy. Josh hadn't raised any such thoughts, but then I wondered if Josh just normally lived on snacks and junk food. I ended up poking around the clubhouse and offices and the rudimentary kitchen to find anything I could to take with us. I found some old, but still edible, chocolate digestives, and there were one or two chocolate mini rolls in a kitchen cupboard. Other than that, nothing else.

I looked at my hard work: several small boxes of various

tools and equipment, some plane supplies at the request of Josh, a small bottle of oil and screen wash, as well as sundry cleaning items. I packed all but a few items of food. The Good Samaritan in me was compelled to leave a can of coke and the last lemon curd bun in the fridge. Maybe someone else would need them more than us, but looking at the goodies, I felt like we had enough to last a little more than a few days, and hopefully it wouldn't be that long until I could locate Uncle Joe.

I was inspecting our haul when I became aware of Josh behind me.

"That's a decent amount of booty."

"I think we're all set. I guess we just need to load up and get out of here?"

"Pretty much, although you'll have to dial back the eager!"

I looked confused and to be honest I was until Josh explained

"We can't set out now." He said, "It's late in the afternoon, and we'll be flying around in the dead of night when we get up there. It's not safe and I don't have night privileges."

"Oh."

"It'll be safer if we hunker down tonight and then head out first thing."

"Great," I said with more than a little sarcasm.

The prospect of spending another, semi-uncomfortable night at the airfield didn't fill me with joy. Although it had been safe and away from whatever chaos we'd seen earlier. I did have a nagging fear at the back of my mind about what we'd do if the chaos moved further north while we were asleep. But then I guess we'd deal with that too. No matter how unlikely an event that felt like it might be.

"At least we're warm and dry." Josh added, "It looks like it might rain."

I nodded, and suddenly I felt very tired. It's almost as if some kind of switch was flipped when I realised we'd be spending the night and not flying away somewhere. It was another exhausting day, and tomorrow would be another one. I wondered just how many days would be like this. My thoughts inevitably turned to the coming week. I hoped we could find Uncle Joe. Although it might be a bit weird since I had no real contact with him after he and Dad fell out. I guess family drama is weird. But Dad seemed to think that I could go to him in a bind, and that was good enough for me.

My hopes of repeating a night of solid, if somewhat frigid, sleep were dashed when I jolted awake, having seen the face of Charlie burning in anguish. Although I didn't see it happen for real, it didn't seem to stop my brain from conjuring up the image, probably thanks to many hours of watching horror movies over the years. The guilt felt like it was weighing me down, both physically and mentally. I didn't really know how to cope, other than power on through. I rolled over, having found a fairly comfortable leather couch in the clubhouse. I stared into the darkness of the clubhouse and heard Josh snoring away somewhere. I closed my eyes and felt the tug of sleep once more, until I heard it. Faintly, at first, but then seemingly louder. Calls, shouts. Almost a scream. Familiar voices, patterns of talking or communicating or just sheer emotional shouting. The same caterwauling as we'd heard from the group at the warehouse. Could it be the same group? Had they somehow tracked us, or maybe they'd roamed here? Ever marching north. It seemed to be more plausible that it was someone else or another, isolated group. But what was with the screaming and shouting? I got up and stalked to the window and peered into the inky night, looking past the recognisable shapes of the planes and out towards the fields. My eyes could see nothing past the airfield. Just a jumble of shapes. I don't know what I was expecting to see. I couldn't see or hear anything. I opened the small panel in the top of the window in an effort to hear more. Nothing. Did I just imagine it? Maybe it was my dreams again. I got as close as I could to the window. I felt like I was holding my breath, trying to hear something, anything. I sighed; my imagination was doing an absolute number on me. I shuffled back to the couch and tried to sleep. I closed my eyes and was vaguely aware of my surroundings and could hear the faint, high-pitched sound of a wire being blown against metal in the gentle wind outside. I heard the first few drops of rain on the sheet roofing, the odd little ping- or pang-like sound. The sound grew with consistency. More drops were falling, and then with what sounded like more force. Within a few minutes there appeared to be a steady rate of rain, each drop seemingly echoing on metal and tin work. The sound drowned out anything else I might hear. I concentrated on it, and it was this sound that I eventually fell asleep to.

Any idea that either Josh or I had for an early start was immediately dashed when I awoke. Josh was still snoring a little, and my eyes were focusing on the brightness of the day. There was no sound of rain, and the sun had come out. The day seemed a little too bright for the time of day I was expecting, and a quick check of the large, antique-looking clock on the wall confirmed that we'd slept in. Ten past ten. We should be well on our way by now. But here we were. I started to move around a little, and my movement must've triggered something in Josh. The snoring ceased, there was a rustling of fabric, and he plodded out from one of the offices into the main clubhouse, bleary-eyed, his hair pointing in almost every direction in little tufts and wisps.

"What time is it?" He croaked

"Ten ten."

"Shit."

"I know."

He moved with semi-purpose, and I followed suit. I got up and stretched and then made for the toilet.

"I'll put the kettle on," he shouted

Within half an hour we'd managed to brush teeth, have a quick wash and down some coffee, all the while looking over maps and making sure we had everything we needed. There was an excitement in the air as we worked. I think we both could feel it, it was the same sort of excitement that you feel the day before a big vacation or Christmas Day. By eleven we were outside in the bright but slightly overcast day. Josh tasked me with loading everything into the plane. He quickly showed me where little lockers were on the plane where I could stash smaller items and other bits and pieces we'd might not need in a hurry. He made it clear that everything should be as secure as possible and to distribute the weight of everything as evenly as I could. While I was pushing boxes and bags into small spaces, Josh busied himself with checking over the plane again. It didn't take him as long as it did the day before, and he was already in the pilot's seat just as I was shoving a small plastic bag full of loose confectionery into a small corner of a box. We'd stumbled upon someone's secret stash of pick and mix in a dark corner of a cupboard while looking for note paper.

I checked over my packing, and it looked good. I scooted out and pushed the seat back into place so that I could fit in the plane and hopped back in. I scooped up the headset just as Josh shouted, "Clear prop!" and turned the key.

Unlike yesterday, the old plane fired up the first time. I felt a sense of déjà vu. The radio clicked on, and I could hear Josh through the headset.

"Okay, just like yesterday, we're even using the same runway."

"Cool." I said and nodded.

Josh seemed to speed through his checklist, and soon we were bouncing over the grass of the airfield.

I stared out over the fields past the green strip of land that was the runway, from where we'd come. I felt a pang of regret leaving my car back there. Josh was busy going through what I now know is called power-on checks. Another minute and we were coming to a stop by the side of the runway.

"Okay, ready?"

"As I'll ever be."

I felt a rush of excitement as Josh pressed the radio button on the back of the yoke.

"Golf bravo victor taking off from runway two-four, departing to the northwest"

Josh quickly pivoted the plane around, and we were suddenly faced with the familiar expanse of grass, slowly picking up speed. The plane bounced and jolted a few times, and suddenly we lifted into the air. I looked outside towards the ground and saw the green grass rushing by and dropping away. It was a strange experience, but not an unpleasant one. As the plane lifted off, my gaze drifted over the buildings and out towards the fields where we'd come from. I thought I saw movement. I blinked a few times, making sure it wasn't just the brightness of the day. Sure enough, at the edge of the field next to the airstrip was movement. A shape moving in an awkward manner. I blinked and focused and saw it hobble forwards. Did it look up? Could it see us? It waved its arms threateningly in much the same manner I'd seen from our not-friends in the previous days. I felt a slight chill. I nudged Josh and pointed towards the figure.

He nodded.

"Looks like we left just in time," he said. "If we'd slept in another hour, we might have had to deal with them."

"Them?" I asked

Josh nodded again, and I followed his gesture and saw a little way behind the lead figure were several more of the shambling shapes. Some moved easier than the rest. But they moved with purpose. At this height we couldn't make out any details, but we didn't need to. What had happened to these people? Could the same happen to us? Just what the hell was going on?

No answer came. No blinding light, no chorus of angelic music played, delivering explanations for our queries. We just had to deal with everything in front of us, ourselves.

"I'll circle around, and then we'll head out."

The plane banked a little to the right, and we turned in a wide circle. The whole landscape rotated, and I thought that a few of the figures below were maybe looking at us. I felt a sense of relief and satisfaction that we were in a position where they couldn't reach us. I gave them the finger, not that they could see, and turned my attention away from them and towards our journey ahead. All being well, we wouldn't have to deal with them again.

We came around, and I saw the airfield buildings down below us, and we slowly turned to the right and levelled out, heading towards what I assumed would be Thirsk.

"Heading 330," said Josh. "It won't take too long; we'll be at our first checkpoint in 3 minutes."

I stared out at the window of the little plane, watching the ground slowly pass us by. It was a surreal feeling. I looked out as we flew over the town. I wondered how busy it would've looked before today? There didn't look to be any signs of life, no movement at all, at least not that I could see. I looked out the front of the plane and saw clouds.

"I'm taking us up above four thousand feet," he explained. "We're going to be going over military airspace. Even though no one is still answering, we don't want to get on the wrong side of an intercept. Especially if they're on high alert."

I hadn't thought about other planes or even helicopters at all. It occurred to me that I'd forgotten about just how crowded the sky was just a few days ago, and now there wasn't a single plane in sight.

"Should we even be flying?"

"There's nothing to say we can't. Besides, this is the best

way to travel. It's quick, and there's virtually no chance of having someone getting in our way."

I nodded and returned to gazing out the windows and watching the patchwork of varying greens pass below us. Various roads zigzagged their way through the landscape

Small villages passed by; I peered at the ground below, struggling to see any semblance of life or activity. I did think I saw some movement, but it was difficult to pick anything definite out. There were certainly no cars or trucks driving around. It was almost like life had paused. It felt very alone in the sky except for the constant drone of the engine and the light buzz of static in my headphones. I sighed and sat back; a blue sky peppered with light fluffy clouds opened out in front of us. I could see peaks of mountains in the distance and a large motorway winding its way up the country.

"That's the A1," said Josh, pointing at the large, empty stretch of blacktop. "But I'm more interested in that," he added, pointing to the right.

I looked forward to trying to see what he was looking at in the distance.

"Look down and to the right of the A1," he said

I looked down and focused on the motorway, and then all of a sudden it popped out at me.

How had I not seen it sooner?

A massive stretch of tarmac led off towards the right. I could see smaller sections intersected at the very ends. Large buildings congregated to the right-hand side. It was some kind of airport.

"RAF Leeming," explained Josh

Our plane got nearer, and the tarmac loomed larger than ever. As the buildings inched their way closer, I could start to pick out details, and I could see, even from our present height, that they were drab and functional. Painted in a sort of dull green. Other buildings were painted in a boring grey.

"It doesn't look like anyone is there," I said

"I know. They didn't respond on the radio, and there are no calls from any aircraft."

As we passed over, we could see a few of the large hangar doors had been left open. A few 4x4-looking vehicles had been left outside. Looking like someone had just walked away from them.

"This is weird," said Josh

We both peered down from the plane as we slowly cruised over. Josh elected to circle over the airfield and make a few radio requests, or calls as he put it, into the field. Trying to ask for some kind of help. Something called basic service. I would later learn that this was part of helping pilots steer clear of each other and avoid accidents. But at the time it seemed like some kind of alien language.

We continued to circle a few times, Josh having abandoned trying to make radio contact. After another wide circle, he levelled the plane out and headed back over the motorway, heading northward. I looked back at the large airfield and considered asking Josh if we should land there. But what would we do? We'd be in a similar position as before. With no one to turn to and no idea of what to do next. Better to keep to our plan and try and find my uncle and take it from there.

As we neared the motorway, I could see what appeared to be a large industrial estate.

Josh looked at his map.

"Leeming Bar".

As we passed over the grey, featureless warehouses with their off-white roofs, I could see several roundabouts marking the end of the construction. A large service station with a huge truck parking area resided at the top of the estate. The concrete almost gleamed in the daylight. But I could pick out a few trucks that had parked there and quite a few cars dotted around, too. A small wisp of dark smoke wound its way into the air at the far end of the truck stop. It looked like someone was burning something. My eyes refocused, and I could pick out small figures walking around, and at the very edge of the truck stop, I could make out several bright triangles of fabric. Were those tents?

"There looks to be people down there," I said to Josh

Josh looked out of his window

"Oh yeah. Looks like some kind of camp."

He peered down at the ground for a moment before looking back at the plane's console.

"It looks all very Walking Dead down there."

"Please," I said, "Zombies are so played out."

I looked down again.

"If anything, it looks almost like Revolution."

"What!?" Scoffed Josh "That abortion of a TV show?"

"Hey, it was great until it wasn't."

"You said the same thing about Lost."

I sat back in my seat, leaving the truck stop below to pass by. The view ahead was green; the hills and mountains ahead were growing and becoming more detailed.

We followed the A1 for a while until we got to Scotch Corner. I have no idea why it's called that; we were miles from Scotland. I didn't ask, and Josh didn't say, so I assumed he had no idea either.

As we approached the junction, which appeared to be a huge roundabout with a small set of services to one side, we slowly turned left and headed towards the ridges which loomed up ahead of us. We followed the road, the A66, closely. We gained height, slowly, with the road. We passed a multitude of small farm holdings and other random buildings on the way. The landscape was a mad patchwork of greens in all shades, peppered with lighter and darker oranges and browns. Small villages popped up and disappeared. I had no idea where we were or how far we'd come. Distance seemed almost irrelevant in the sky. There was no real way to judge the distance we'd travelled. I felt kind of panicked but tried to settle in and enjoy the ride.

Mountainous peaks rose up from the ground, and I saw a large quarry below as Josh announced we'd need to go higher. The little plane humming and vibrating its way through the sky. We followed the road, and I could see why Josh had elected to take this course. Rocky peaks emerged out of the ground everywhere we looked. There wasn't really a safe place to land, or so it seemed, if we needed to. The only real place would be the roadway below us.

We passed over the top of the rocky outcroppings, and the landscape seemed to drop away from us and open out into a sprawling green landscape. It seemed brighter and warmer, and I noticed that there were suddenly very few clouds in the sky.

As we passed the edge of the mountains, new roadways wriggled their way through the landscape.

"We can take a more direct route now," said Josh. "Our next major reference point is in fifteen minutes."

I looked at the road below and followed its snaking shape into the distance. The cockpit had suddenly got a lot warmer, and I fidgeted and tried to stretch my legs.

A river flowed below, and I distracted myself with mapping its course with my eyes as it headed off to the right. My attention was suddenly brought to the front of the plane by a glistening body of water in the distance, surrounded by a deep green of trees. I wondered if that could be it. I'd heard so much about the English holiday camps but had never been. Charlie had told me about the great time he had had with his sister there, and the three of us had planned to go next year. The irony being that we should've been there this year, in fact probably right now, if I'd gotten my act together. I wondered just how differently things would've played out by now if I'd just got a part-time job sooner and not frittered away my savings. I tried to push the thought out of my mind.

As we got closer I could see a smooth, domed shape glistening brightly in the daylight sun.

"I think I see it," I said

"Let's not jump to any conclusions."

He busied himself looking at the map secured to his knee. He placed a finger on the map and looked outside, then proceeded to do it several times before he announced that we had arrived at our last major checkpoint, or visual reference point, to give it its proper name.

I'd never been to Center Parcs, but both Charlie and Josh spoke in hushed, revered tones whenever it was mentioned. It was one of the things they both agreed on without any thought or discussion or disagreement. At the end of the day, Center Parcs was the shit.

That's as it may be; I never went, and it was never really an option. Apparently in the last few years the prices had gone through the roof. Josh wanted to focus on his flying, and Charlie, well, it seemed like Charlie lacked the proper motivation. Which was a shame, because they made it sound like some kind of magical place. And here we were, several thousand feet in the air, and Center Parcs looked every bit as magical as they had made out. A strange oasis hidden in a forest. A bright, shining, mirage-like jewel. Josh explained that it was the main dome that was bouncing the light from the sun. As we got closer, the glare seemed to reduce, and I started to notice other details.

As we passed overhead, I looked down over the central lake. I could make out small houses and several larger buildings.

"That dome is the tropical swimming pool," explained Josh. "It's pretty sweet. has a few slides and a hot pool. Even a wave machine."

"I can see slides outside," I said

And then I saw it.

"Holy shit!"

"What?" said Josh

"There are people down there."

"What do you mean?"

"People. As in normal, frolicking people. They look like they're on vacation."

"Holiday."

"Whatever."

"Let me see."

Just pushed the throttle level in and put the plane into a tight turn.

I instantly grabbed my knees and helped my heart almost leap out of my chest.

"Fuck."

Josh seemed to ignore me. All I could now see out of the side window was the ground. The world in front didn't look that much better; the horizon was at a peculiar angle.

Josh stared out of my window, glancing at the instruments every now and then.

"Fucking hell," he said. "There are people on the water slide."

I quickly glanced out the window in time to see several human-like shapes move down light blue-coloured slides, which appeared to snake and turn outside.

"Looks fun," I said

"Super fun"

He sort of sighed, and then he levelled out the plane into a more sedate turn and then levelled off. I saw the large dome of Center Parc withdrawn and fall behind.

"I guess we're not stopping off?"

"Alas, no. We have a plan and a schedule; we should keep to it. Besides, there's nowhere to land. At least not properly. I don't fancy landing anywhere that isn't an airfield."

I shrugged and continued to watch the landscape slowly move by. The mountains where we'd threaded through had now turned into a backdrop for the rolling fields and winding roads below. Various farms dotted the countryside, and cows and sheep seemed to carry on as normal. It occurred to me that maybe things were different in this part of the country; maybe life would be normal here.

In front of us the landscape was just as impressive, and in the distance there was the telltale glint and sprawl of houses and other buildings that marked a denser population. I started to get a little excited and a little nervous. Who knows what we'd find, but it was more the prospect of seeing Uncle Joe after all these years, more than anything else.

For whatever reason I was sure I could find him, even lacking the address I needed. The place was small, super small, even by UK standards. Someone must know who they were. I clenched and unclenched my fists.

"How far are we?"

"A different way for asking the 'Are we there yet?' Question"

"Yurp." I left a suitable pause. "Are we there yet?"

"Almost," said Josh. "Penrith should be that way, where that bank of buildings are."

Josh pointed out to the right of the plane.

"Your uncle should beeeeee"

He looked at that map and looked at the compass at the top of the windscreen, consulted the map again and then pointed just a little to the left of center.

"That way," he said with confidence, "we'll land at Berier."

I nodded, happy with the plan. We'd travelled a fair amount of distance in short order. I dreaded to think how long it would take using a car, even on a direct route. Given what we'd seen on the way. We continued to follow the road below. As we'd gotten nearer to Penrith, more buildings peppered the roadside, and I could see a large motorway which cut through the landscape from left to right.

"Thats the M6," said Josh

We flew over a roundabout and turned a little to the right. Another one was a little way down the road, but it looked like we were cutting a corner. We'd take a path that would have us flying over the edge of Penrith and then the motorway. As we neared the motorway, I could see a large industrial complex below. Lots of small and large units that had done goodness knows what now appeared to be standing still, empty. There was activity below. The plane turned a little to point north, and I saw a large truck stop below, or what looked to be a truck stop. A large line of green and white trucks were parked around the edges of what looked like a large dirt area with strips of concrete or tarmac making several strange roadways through the middle. Clustered in the middle were cars, motorhomes and assorted vehicles. Dotted around were humans moving around. I wondered what they were doing. Were they friendly? There was no question that life had changed in similar ways to what we'd seen. The evidence was down there in front of our eyes and through the view of Penrith. How different an image it was from the one we'd seen only moments ago. Something had touched the lives of everyone down below. That something didn't look to have made its way to the holiday village, where people, even now, seemed to be having fun. How long would it be until it lasted? How messy would it get?

I looked away from the scene below and looked out on the lush green terrain ahead of us. In the distance a large mountain appeared to erupt from the Earth.

I was about to ask Josh about Scotland when the plane was filled with a strange sound, or rather a vibration which appeared to run through my very being.

I could see Josh had furrowed his brow. I wasn't going to ask, at least not right away. My own heart was beating a little faster. Even though I didn't know the intricacies of planes, the sound made it abundantly clear that the plane wasn't happy.

Josh's had darted to a small control next to the throttle. He pulled it all the way out, and the sound of the engine lowered.

"Uhhhhh," I said involuntarily

"Hold on," said Josh through what sounded like clenched teeth

The plane shuddered, and my worst nightmare came true. The blurred whirring of the propeller had disappeared. Along with the familiar, if a little jarring, noise of the engine. All I heard was the wind outside and a multitude of swearing from Josh. Our plane had suddenly turned into a glider.

"Pitch for sixty," I heard Josh say through the radio. Although it was obvious it was for his benefit and not mine. He looked left and right as if searching for something.

"Okay, wind is coming from the south; we'll swing around and see what we can see."

The plane made a slow turn to the right. We levelled off with the motorway to our left-hand side. Josh looked forwards, and I could almost hear the gears in his head spinning and whirring.

He flicked a small paddle below the throttle, and the plane made a whirring noise.

"Flaps out," he said. "Okay, we're going for the motorway."

Josh lined up the plane with the motorway, which stretched out in front of us. The plane bumped a little, and I let out an 'Urk'.

"Just a little wind. We're all set up for a landing. Let's see if we can't fix our issue."

Josh reached between his legs and below the seat.

"Fuel on," he said. His attention turned to the panel. He placed his fingers on certain controls, checking everything.

"Master on, we've got power."

He pumped a small lever by his window a few times and then turned the ignition key.

Nothing happened.

"Fuck," he said, which didn't provide much encouragement

"Fifteen hundred feet. We're doing this."

His attention turned to the outside world. He glanced inside and out. The aircraft glided through the air, losing height. The long strip of blacktop came looming into view.

"Seven hundred feet. Just think of this as landing on the largest runway ever."

"Okay," I said, but I really wanted to tell him how fucked up this was and how I knew it was a mistake to fly. But here we were.

The ground seemed impossibly close.

Josh pressed the flappy-looking lever again, and the plane whirred.

"Flaps full. Five hundred feet."

The road was fairly straight but bent to the right and seemed to drop off. I tensed up. Didn't we need a straight bit of road? My throat went dry. I found it hard to swallow.

"Two hundred."

Josh exhaled; I could see his hand flexing on the controls. He was calm and focused.

"One hundred. Fifty."

The plane shimmied to the side and then bounced a little. The jolt surprised me. Another few bounces confirmed we'd touched down on solid ground. Another bump and the front wheels touched down. Josh wrestled with the controls. He coaxed the plane around a smooth bend which turned into a gentle slope. We followed the road around and down. A sign for an exit appeared, saying it was half a mile. We already appeared to have good speed and so kept our momentum. As the plane turned a little left, we saw the exit. We veered a little too much to the left, and Josh swore. He corrected just as we passed the exit. The exit turned into a small hill; a sign next to the road informed us that it was a large roundabout. The plane slowed quickly, and we finally came to a stop at the base of the hill.

Josh Rick Flared and clapped his hands in a single, almost deafening blow. He turned off the radio and removed his headset. He pressed various switched and fumbled with whatever the control was at the base of his chair.

He sat back and stared out the window, appearing to be looking up the road.

"First off-field landing, nailed!"

"Well done, Captain."

"Oh my god. I think I need a stiff drink."

"Maybe," I said, looking up the hill. "They might have something?"

Josh followed my gaze, and we both looked up the road to the crest. Several people had gathered and appeared to be watching us. They look like they were holding something. We didn't know what.

"I sure hope they're friendly," said Josh

THIRTEEN

"I don't think they're friendly." whispered Josh

"Ya think?" I said back

"What the fuck did yez say?" barked the gruff voice.

The owner of which was a tall, lanky and grizzled man. I have no idea how old. Maybe he was fifty or sixty. Hell, maybe even forty. He had the strange look of age with no age mixed with a sort of sickly green pallor. He didn't look sick, but then he didn't exactly look healthy either. There were a few others around him; four, maybe five men and a woman. They all had this weird, almost desperate look about them. Everyone was a little dishevelled, a little dirty. But they all had this green, pallid look about them and deep sunken eyes, like they hadn't slept in months. Their overall demeanour made me super nervous. Not to mention they were fairly aggressive, not physical. But when they came down from the top of the road, they came at us quickly. And the leader guy, if that's what he was, seemed to want to shout at us about what we were doing on his road.

"I said," he yelled, "What did yez say?"

"I don't mean to be rude," I said, "but this isn't your road; it's a public highway."

"And we had an emergency," added Josh

“Shut up, you,” yelled the man, pointing a somewhat bony finger towards Josh’s face, which startled him a tad.

The lanky man turned to me.

“I don’t like the look of yez. I see the way yeh look at me and mine.”

“Look,” I said in my best, even-tempered way, “Maybe we got off onto the wrong start.”

I held out my hand to shake his

“My name is...”

He cut me off with a wave of his hand

“Don’t care.” He shouted “yer trespassing and yeh comin’ wi us”

I had defiantly had enough, and there was no way we were going anywhere with this guy.

“Fuck that.”

“P!” said Josh with some urgency

“You can fuck right off!”

The tall man looked like I’d told him I would drink his children’s blood and burn them alive.

“Yer come wi’ us if yeh like it or not.”

I started to take a step back, but there was nowhere to go. We had our backs to the plane, and we were pretty much surrounded. At the very least we were outnumbered.

“Bri,” said the man. “Take the little un.”

One of the men from behind the lanky old man stepped around him and came towards me.

“Get ready,” I whispered out the corner of my mouth

“What?"

As the man approached, I had already moved my right leg backwards. I steeled myself and let him come closer. He came within six feet. I tried to focus on speed and accuracy rather than raw power, just like Uncle Joe had shown me years earlier. I shifted my weight onto my left leg, lifted my right and pushed forward into the man's left knee. I had always remembered what Uncle Joe had said about striking. Don't hit **at** the target. Hit **through** the target.

The man yelled as his knee buckled. The dice had been rolled; there was no going back. It was now a pitch battle for survival, at least that's how I perceived it. I moved to the left and shoved the lanky old man to his right, hoping that in his advancing years he might not be as quick or stable as he once was. He staggered a little bit and recovered far quicker than I expected. I turned my attention back to the man on the ground who was now trying to get up using his good knee. He shouted mostly in rage, it seemed. I whipped my left leg around in a sweeping roundhouse kick and delivered it to the back of his head. There was a dull thwack, and the blow caused him to stagger forward and splay out onto the ground. There was some commotion behind me; I assumed Josh was in a similar situation. I spun round and came face to face with a woman whose eyes were wild with hate and violence. Rage and instinct had taken me, and I delivered a simple one-two combination of punches to the woman's face. She fell back with a squeal and began screaming on the floor.

I turned to face the larger mass of individuals that seemed to be falling on Josh; they had somewhat ignored me, and I felt compelled to rectify that situation. I kicked at the nearest leg and struck a blow on the side of his face from the rear. I followed up with another low kick to the legs and a few punches to the liver. The man called out with that strange shout, which was more anger, or rage, than pain. Even so, he stumbled and fell, and I went for the next person. Josh seemed to be faring okay. He was moving backwards, keeping people at arm's length. It suddenly occurred to me that maybe he'd never been in a fight before.

He threw a couple of punches. The first missed his target by a few inches. The second one landed nice and square on the face of a rando. His head snapped back, and Josh seemed as surprised as the receiver of the punch.

I heard a sound from behind me and turned just in time to see a huge fist coming at me.

I didn't so much feel the blow as hear it, or maybe that was how I experienced it. I found myself staggering backwards and toppling on the ground. This wasn't good; I needed to get up and quick. I had a hand on the ground and pushed up. A large figure loomed above me. I found it hard to focus on any details and just saw the ragged outline of a man. I didn't see the second incoming punch, but I felt it as it snapped my head to the side, and I fell back to the floor again. I pushed myself up, eyes wide, breathing hard. I felt compelled to get up. I saw a set of boots next to me and looked up.

"Fuck you," I said and spat the bloody contents of my mouth on the boot.

Another punch snapped my head forward and sent it bouncing on the hard ground. Darkness started to fade in around the edge of my consciousness. I tried to speak, but the only noise I could make was a strange gurgling that tasted warm and metallic. I coughed and felt warmth splash on my chin. I spat, almost involuntarily. Strange as it may seem, I felt nothing, at least not pain. Maybe it was the adrenaline. I realised that I couldn't see out of my right eye.

I heard Josh shout something, but couldn't make out what it was.

"...okay! Okay!" was the only thing I made out.

I felt rough hands pull at me, lifting me up. I couldn't see much; the edges of reality seemed grey and black. I tried to focus, but the world seems louder than before. My head lolled, and voices seemed to be muffled. I don't quite know what happened next. I was aware, at first, of shouts from elsewhere.

I heard running and shouting. From elsewhere I could hear whimpering and crying. The hands that held me up suddenly vanished, and I fell to the floor. I didn't even know what was happening until I realised I was crumpled in a heap. How could I have let myself get so vulnerable? So weak. I thought I was stronger than this. I cursed myself for not being better. Was this train wreck inevitable, or was this solely the product of my rashness? I felt a little sick, queasy. I took in a few deep breaths, and then everything swam a little at the edges, so what little I did see of the world seemed to bend and blur. It felt like I was drunk, seeing the world through some kind of haze. I could make out shapes, but no detail. Everything appeared to be soaked in a reddish blackness. I felt a hand on my shoulder. It wasn't the same violent grip as before, but gentler. I heard a whisper in my ear.

"Let's go; this is our chance." It was Josh's voice.

I put my legs under me and pushed. I felt Josh throw my arm over his shoulder, and he helped me stumble to wherever we were going. The screaming and shouting seemed louder, more urgent. There was pain and anger in those voices. I didn't know what was going on, but it sounded hectic.

"What's going on?" I asked. At least that's what I intended to say, but the words came out wet and slurred.

"I don't know, but we're getting out of here!"

Josh helped me along, my feet slipping and dragging as I tried to plant them on the ground. We stumbled a few times, and I was aware I was more of a hindrance than a help.

I coughed and spat more blood on the ground.

"Fucking gross," said Josh

I grumbled, and we kept moving. The sound of shouting was behind us now, and we kept moving, trying, I guessed, to put some distance between us and them.

I felt a little more steady and was managing to put more weight on my feet, but I felt tired.

"Okay," said Josh. "Let's stop here."

Part of me wanted to keep moving; another part of me desperately wanted to stop, maybe grab a nap. I felt Josh turn us around; I think we were looking at what was going on. I saw vague shapes in the distance moving, although I couldn't tell you how far we were. I might've even seen the outline of the plane. Why couldn't I focus or see anything?

I heard movement from behind us, and I think Josh heard it too, as he seemed to turn to face the sound. I felt it more than I saw it. Was I turning into Daredevil?

"Hey there," I heard a female voice say. "Are you guys okay?"

"I'm good," said Josh

"I need a nap," I heard myself say

"Looks like your friend got on the wrong side of someone."

"Terrible life choices and a shocking temper!" replied Josh

"Where are you guys from? We saw you fly in."

"Not the landing we wanted. But we're from a bit farther south?"

"How much farther?"

"Leeds way."

I heard motion from behind, but no one moved. Hurried footsteps. And then voices. Whispers.

"What do we do with them?" asked a baritone voice

By 'them' I assumed he meant us.

I felt Josh tense, and it must've shown in his body language because the woman seemed like she tried to sound calm

"Don't worry." She said, "We're not here to harm you. We can help, if you want it."

There was a pause before Josh replied.

"My friend needs help."

"We have a small camp just up the road," she said

"Camp?" I said, "Is it band camp?"

"I say we ditch them," said the deep voice

"I say you can go fuck yourself." I gurgled.

The woman laughed

"I can see why your friend gets into trouble."

There was a pause; I think maybe I heard movement or something. I couldn't quite put my finger on it, and then a grunt followed by several steps running away from us.

"You'll have to forgive Duncan; he's not the most trusting. But you're welcome to come with us. We can offer shelter and something to eat. Your friend looks like they need more than a few plasters."

“That would be nice,” said Josh

I felt kinder hands grab me from behind and let them take me. Each of my arms was wrapped around an unknown person's shoulder.

“Don’t take this the wrong way,” she said. “You’ll need to go into quarantine first.”

“Quarantine?” Asked Josh

“It’s only for two days, but we need to make sure you’re not infected.”

“Infested?” I said with just the hint of a slur

“Everything, or at least as much as we know, can be explained later. Right now we need to keep moving, because Amos will be back with more people. Either you're in or not. If you’re in, come with us now, and we’ll talk once we get you patched up and have made sure you’ll not go ballistic.”

I could feel my face aching; the adrenaline was starting to wear off, and I was aware I probably didn’t look the best, either.

“Okay,” said Josh. “We’re in.”

The camp, as it turned out, wasn’t a camp at all but a roadside service station that led to some weird tourist information place that a bunch of people had barricaded themselves into. At least that’s what I got from Josh. By the time we reached this, so-called, camp, I couldn’t see anything but blurred movement. I could pick out rough details, like a bunch of trees, but I had problems focusing. I’d be lying if I said I wasn’t more than a tad concerned. In fact, I was super worried. The whole place was protected by a barricade of heavy goods vehicles. One of which pulled away to let us in. I heard the rumbling of the large engine. I suddenly had a flashback to the warehouse. The visuals in my head were surprisingly sharp. I’d prefer them to be blurred, too.

We were escorted into the compound in the back of a

pickup truck. People, apparently, eyed us suspiciously. Josh whispered into an ear, giving me details I just really didn't need to hear. Something inside my chest clenched. The irrational part of me wondered if we were walking into somewhere that we wouldn't be walking out from.

By the time we arrived and it was time to get out, I felt a little steadier on my feet. I still needed a little help, but I could largely stand and move around on my own, but I wasn't ready to break my 100-metre sprint record just yet. We walked for longer than I cared to before coming to a small set of steps. I stepped up and a few steps in, and suddenly it was dark and cool. We were inside some kind of building. I felt like I could see details a little easier in the dark. Inside was a set of three beds, each with its own small cabinet. Josh helped me onto the nearest bed. My muscles ached, and I felt relieved to lie down. It occurred to me it had been days since I'd slept in a real bed. Even though it wasn't my own, it was good enough.

Annoyingly, Josh kept me awake, following orders not to let me fall asleep. Concussions and stuff. Whatever. Eventually someone came to look us over; she had a kind voice and a gentle yet firm touch. She looked me over once I had washed my face, which was quite painful, I might add. Apparently there was nothing too broken about me, aside from the beating my pride had taken along with my face. Amazingly, I didn't need anything more than a temporary stitch and some cleaning up. There was a nasty-looking cut on my cheek, but that would heal, and maybe I'd have a scar. I didn't want to see. I just wanted to sleep. And the lady doctor, I assume she was a doctor, eventually said I could get some sleep. She wanted to look over Josh, too, but I didn't even make it to seeing her start an exam. I just seemed to flake out.

I woke up, and it was dark. A small light glowed next to my bed, casting a soft orange hue on the walls of the makeshift room. The soft orange light was soothing. I blinked a few times, details coming into focus. I realised I was looking at the light, and looking back at me with piercing, intentional eyes and a wild, unkempt hairstyle was a small purple troll figure. We glared at each other for a few moments before I relented and turned over onto my back and blew a small huff of air into the room. I looked to the right and could make out that the doors to the container had been closed, although they had been modified. They had windows cut into them, and the glass, or plastic, had holes in them to let in air. A slight, cooling breeze drift in and over me. The room was warm, but not unbearably so. My face hurt. I tried moving my jaw, and everything ached. I looked out to the left and saw Josh, seemingly asleep on the bed next to me. It was confusing. It looked like night, so it must be. I wondered how long I'd been asleep and what time it was. I yawned and wondered what would happen next, and maybe I should get up and look around and maybe go for a pee. I closed my eyes and felt a dull throb in my right cheek.

When I opened my eyes again, sunlight lit up the room, and from the bed I could see clouds in the sky. It appeared to be a nice day.

"Is it awake?" Came the familiar voice from the left.

I turned my head to see Josh sitting on a chair by his bed. He looked to be reading a book.

"Am I dreaming?" I asked, "You can't be reading."

"Mi-mi-mi!" He replied in a high-pitched voice, "There's not much to do but wait it out."

"Wait for what?" I said as I propped myself up. I was aware of a dull, pulsing headache and a stabbing pain on the right side of my face.

"We're being quarantined, remember?"

"How come?"

"Some bullshit or whatever."

"They haven't told you anything?"

"I think they're waiting to see how you'd do?"

It occurred to me I was missing something

"Wait. How long have I slept?"

"Over a day."

"I feel like I've had five minutes."

"I don't want to say you look it," said Josh with a smile, "Buuuuuut..."

I held up a hand.

"What's been said?"

"About what?"

I tried to express my frustration with an expression that would say 'really?'. Instead my face seemed to scrunch up, and I felt a stab of pain.

I slowly eased my legs around and sat on the edge of the bed.

"Quarantine. Talk to me."

"Well, Terry," said Josh, "they've said nothing; they wanted to wait until you woke up. At least that's what I was told."

"Anything else?"

Josh faked thinking for a bit with a sort of wistful look.

"No." He finally said, "But the food is good."

My stomach rumbled at the mention of food, and suddenly I felt hunger pangs.

As if on cue, there was a click and the squeak of hinges. I turned to see an older lady, maybe fifty or so, with long, greying hair tied back. She wore a protective mask and glasses and was dressed in white overalls with blue gloves, completing the outfit.

"Why hello," she said in a friendly voice. "It's good to see you finally awake."

"I'm not sure how good I feel to be awake, to be honest."

"Well, my dear, don't take this personally, but I feel like you've seen better days."

"Is it that bad?" I asked

She looked at me for a few seconds before giving me her opinion

"It probably looks worse than it is."

"So, when are we getting out of here?"

"That's precisely the reason I'm here. Check-up time."

The lady approached me and held up a small portable device which looked a little too gunny for my tastes. I frowned and flinched as a small shaft of paint arced through my face. The lady chuckled a little.

"Don't worry, it's just a temperature check."

She held out the device, and it beeped. Once, then again. He nodded and looked happy.

"Temperatures are good. Let's take a closer look at you."

She gently took me by the face; she moved my head from side to side. She seemed to be looking for something, although I didn't know exactly what.

She gently pressed her hands on my throat.

"Sore?" She asked

"No"

"Good"

She gently turned my head and looked at or in each ear.

"How are your eyes? Your good one. Is it clear or blurry?"

"My left one is fine. Seems normal. The right one..."

"Not so good," she smiled. "I guessed."

She gave me a little wink.

She held my wrist and looked at her watch. Checking my pulse. Which made me nervous. I have no idea why.

"How are you feeling? Frustrated? Angry? Tense?"

"Always," said Josh

"Hmmm. Doesn't surprise me."

"Hey!"

The lady smiled.

"You're fine, duck. Your pulse is a little high, but maybe it's stress and all the excitement. It's not surprising considering the little adventure you've been on."

"Excellent. Thanks, doctor...?"

"It's Vivian. Just Vivian."

"I'm..."

"I've already introduced you," interrupted Josh. "While you were sleeping."

"Rude," I said

"In any case," said Vivian, "it's nice to meet you."

We shook hands, and then she stood up and turned to Josh.

"Right then, young man. Your turn."

Josh got the same treatment as I did, although Vivian took twice as long with him. She checked his pulse twice and asked a few more questions. Asked more about family medical history. After a final temperature check, she seemed happy.

"Okay, let's get you two some supper?"

"Supper?"

"Yes, supper."

I had heard what Josh had told me, but it didn't really sink in. My stomach growled, and even Vivian heard it.

"Let's go; you sound hungry," she smiled

I slowly got up. Pretty much everything was stiff and ached. My first few steps were more like awkward hobbling. By the time I got to the door, my legs felt like they had loosened up, and I was starting to move more like a human and less like a stunned fly.

We emerged from what I now could see was a converted cargo container into a dying light of the day. A sort of mini outdoor kitchen had been set up, consisting of several tables that looked like they were used for food prep and a makeshift cooking area, which looked to be a thrown-together setup which involved some kind of large metal barrel and several smaller grills over a hot bed of wood which was already alight. The orange flickering light illuminated the area, and there was someone stirring several large pots of something that smelt good.

Vivian escorted us over to one of the tables and prompted us to take a bowl each.

"This is Dan," she said, nodding towards the man labouring over his steaming pots

“Dan!” She said again

He seemed startled and turned around. Dan was a portly man, about fifty and sporting a red, jolly face. He wore a bandana and an apron and was currently brandishing a large metal spoon.

“Vivian,” he said with a broad smile. “New recruits? All clear I take it?”

“They are, and they haven’t decided to stay; we haven’t got that far yet. Can we get a head start on supper?”

Dan sniffled and considered the request for a moment. In hindsight I do wonder if it was just for dramatic effect.

“Of course, but only because it's you."

He moved back to the stove and grabbed a pot, and heaved it onto the table in front of us. He stirred the mixture a few times before withdrawing a ladleful. He motioned for us to present our bowls, which we did, and he filled them up with hot, steaming, fragrant food. I peered in, trying to assess which it was we’d just received. It looked like a kind of Bolognese, minus the spaghetti.

“Chill. Not my best work, but not bad considering we’re on limited supplies.”

I smiled and thanked him. Josh received a bowl full, and he stared at the contents like he was wondering if it would reach out and throttle him. I picked up a fork, and Josh fumbled for a spoon as we were escorted by Vivian through the car park.

"Normally we eat together.”

She pointed towards an area which was set up with improvised tables and chairs.

"Pat wanted to chat first. But I don't think she'll mind if you eat and talk."

Vivian led us into the main building, which seemed quite busy. It was weird; whoever these people were, they obviously hadn’t been here very long, as the main foyer displayed various welcome signs and information on the center itself. They looked to be in the process of stripping out the place. Several people were packing things from shelves into random bags and boxes. A small stack of stuff had started to build up at the entrance. I ignored the majority of them and concerned myself with not spilling any chilli on the floor. We followed Vivian into the center. The whole situation was all too weird and seemed like some kind of fever dream. I mean, here I was, far from home, carrying a bowl of hot chilli through a tourist information center being escorted by a benevolent carer after crash landing in a small plane. Like I said, weird.

As we reached the back of the store, Vivian called out to someone, a tall lady wearing jeans and a tank top. She turned to face us as we approached.

“Ahh,” she said, smiling. “I take it you’ve both got a clean bill of health.”

"They're as clean as far as I can see. Although the scrapper here will be in a bit of pain for a while.”

“Thanks, Viv, I’ll take it from here.”

Vivian turned and walked away; she winked at me as she left.

“So”, she said, “how are you feeling?”

“Okay,” said Josh from behind. I shrugged a little.

“Good,” I added. “Just a little confused.”

“Well,” she said, “we can’t have you standing there with your food getting cold. C’mon, let’s sit down and talk outside.”

Strangely enough, we walked back out the way we came. It seemed weird that we were escorted inside and now we were being escorted out. But life is strange. Or maybe I focus on the wrong things. As we exited the main building, we turned left towards an old motor home. Back home we’d call these RVs, but I think the English name is more accurate. Several collapsable camp chairs were dotted here and there. The lady took one and invited us to choose our own.

We sat, and instinctively I dipped my fork into the bowl and spooned a small portion of the chilli into my mouth. It had a strange texture, and it appeared to be made mostly from canned vegetables, but it was super tasty and very hot. I made a large 'O' with my mouth and fanned my free hand in front of my mouth in an effort to cool it down. My face ached as I did, and I instinctively grimaced.

"I don't think I've introduced myself." said the lady, "My name is Patricia, and this is our little safe haven, for now."

"That's funny," I said. "My name is..."

"Safe haven," said Josh, butting in. "Safe from what?"

"To be honest. We have no idea. Josh, right?"

There was a pause, and I assume Josh nodded. She continued.

"All we know right now is that there is some kind of infection. We don't know what it is, where it's come from, or how it's transmitted. We only know how to spot it. I can tell you that it takes about two days for the infection to take hold. After that you'd start to have an elevated heart rate and temperature. For the first six or so hours you'd be sweating like you'd run a marathon, slowly getting hotter. You'd get frustrated and agitated for no reason. After twelve hours you'd be shouting, screaming. Taking your anger out on anyone or anything near you. After a day, you'd almost be in a blind rage, either that or completely lethargic."

"So the guys that attacked us?" I asked

"Infected."

"They did seem a little sweaty and green around the gills."

"What do you think it is?" Asked Josh

"No idea. But odds are it has something to do with what's been going on in London."

"You mean the attack?" I asked

Patricia nodded

"What happens after two days?" Asked Josh

"Obviously there's no long-term observations. Whoever is infected is asked to leave to protect the group."

"Seems a little harsh." I offered and consumed another fork of chilli.

"But you've experienced the consequences of the infection.

Those people you had a run-in with are from Amos' group. They're all infected. In fact, a few of our group who were infected went over to him."

"Over?" I asked

"Amos has taken over the truck stop on the other side of the motorway."

"I remember seeing something like a camp when we passed over it. Didn't look to be in a great state either."

"We're not in the best of shape here, either, but at least we're not beating each other to a pulp."

There was a long pause as we took it all in. I heard Josh slurping on a spoonful of chilli.

"So how come you're here? Do you have a plan?"

"A plan?" Said Patricia, "There is no plan; we all just sort of came together, purely by chance. The only plan we have is to stick together and wait this out. Survive as best we can. And hope that some kind of help will arrive at some point."

She paused and seemed to reflect for a moment.

"But I have to say. I don't think this is going to be a quick fix. I think we're going to have to figure some things out on our own for a while."

"Which is what this is?" Asked josh with what sounded like half a mouthful of food in his mouth

"To a degree, yes. We're largely just a bunch of strangers that were forced together, but it works. And it works because everyone pitches in."

"Is this part of the pitch?" I added

"Pitch? I'm not pitching anything; you're free to stay or go. But. If you stay, you work. You do what you can. You help out. That's the only way we can survive together."

"Has it really come to this, after only a few days?" I said

"Society has always been a thin veneer on human evolution." Said Patricia, "But this whole thing has shown just how thin that veneer was. I think the big surprise is just how quickly things went south, as you Americans would say."

We sort of looked around for a second, taking in how life

was. I was suddenly aware of several dark figures standing and slowly moving at the edges of the car park.

"So", said Patricia, "what about you two? Where are you headed?"

"My uncle has a place near here."

"Uncle?" Patrician seemed surprised. "With that accent, I wouldn't have thought you had family here."

"Strange as it may seem. My uncle moved here years ago, when I was a little younger."

"So how did you two end up here, exactly? How bad is it that you ended up here?"

"It's bad," I replied

I didn't skip on the details of our adventure but purposely didn't mention Charlie and managed to gloss over that entire portion of our so-called adventure. Josh didn't say anything either. I felt a heavy sadness and wondered if we'd eventually lie to ourselves so much that he would be forgotten. But deep down I knew I couldn't forget. I wouldn't forget.

"Where does your uncle live?"

"Dacre"

"Dacre? Really? That's just down the road."

"You know it?"

"I know of it. Not a very big place."

"That's perfect." I smiled and again, felt pain

"Look, why don't you and Josh stay the night? It's not safe to venture out after dark, and you could obviously do with the rest. See how you feel in the morning. If you want to go to Dacre, off you go. We'll point you in the right direction. But we'll be here if you need to come back."

Patricia's offer was warm and, I'm loath to admit it, sensible.

"Sure," I said

"I don't suppose," interjected Josh, "that there is any more chilli?"

FOURTEEN

Even though I had been asleep for over a day, I slept through pretty soundly and was awakened only by the movement of people in the main foyer, which is where we had bedded down for the night. The rest of the people here camped out in a few tents, their own cars, and a few, like Patricia, had their own motor homes. They were busy emptying or making better use of the center for a central community point. Somewhere to eat and meet as well as have some emergency beds for strange weirdos that arrived out of nowhere. I was surprised to see that Josh was already up and moving around. He was even helping out, it seemed. Sweeping out an area of the building which had already been cleared and emptied of whatever displays were there.

I looked around trying to see if there was a pretty girl around. Imagine my surprise when it was just burly dudes. I stood up from the makeshift nest of my coats and a few travel blankets liberated from the store. Mine looked like they'd been thrown around in a storm. Joshes were perfectly folded and stacked.

I wondered why no one had suggested sleeping in the quarantine area. I included myself in that statement, but then I figured it was probably more about making a statement, or what was the term? Bad optics? I guess it would be super weird if we were in quarantine and walked out only to go back.

I took myself off to the bathroom, purposefully avoiding the mirror. I splashed water on my face. I felt cooling water and then the dull sting from my wounds. When it came to brushing my teeth and other toiletries, I swore a little. Pretty much everything we brought with us was still at the plane. I wondered how safe, or unsafe, it would be to try and get back there and get our stuff.

I wandered out of the bathroom and found Josh, bottle of cola in hand, sitting on the floor, back against the wall.

"Hey," I said

"Morning. Sleep well?"

"Yes, thanks. Well. As well as you can on the floor. What time is it?"

"I have no idea; it's just morning. So what's the plan? Are we going uncle hunting?"

"If that's good with you? Sure." I paused for a second. "If you wanted to stay here, I'd understand."

"What?" Said Josh, who almost looked hurt at the suggestion, "and leave you alone to have all the fun. Plus, who's going to bail you out of your next set of fisticuffs?"

We laughed; it was maybe a little tense.

We tidied up the area we'd used and then went to find Patricia, who we found sitting outside her motor home, cradling either a tea or coffee. I'd suddenly remembered that it'd been a while since I'd had coffee.

She smiled and waved as we approached.

"Morning. Sleep okay?"

We didn't immediately answer. She laughed.

"Another few days and it'll be a little more comfortable. I assume you're going looking for your uncle?"

I nodded.

"Thank you for your help." I said, "It was much appreciated."

"You're welcome. But I'm not quite done yet."

I looked puzzled, and so did Josh as we turned to look at each other.

She nodded towards the front of the motor home, where two backpacks were resting against the front wheel.

"Take those. You've got some basic supplies in them, plus a few extras."

"We can't," I started to say

"Yes, you can," asserted Patricia, "and you will."

"We have a whole heap of stuff in the plane."

"Forget about it. It's too near Amos' little empire, and it's more than likely that he and his crew have already stripped out whatever you were carrying."

"Are you sure?" I asked, looking at the bags

"Of course I'm sure. Don't be silly. Take them."

Her tone reminded me of Mom, and I felt a sort of familiar reassurance.

"Remember. If things don't work out with your uncle, you're welcome here anytime. Josh can have his broom back."

Josh laughed. Was that nerves I was picking up on?

I pushed the thought aside and picked up the first backpack. Although it was well packed, it wasn't overly heavy. Not wanting to appear rude, I decided against rummaging through the bag to see what had been packed for me. I shouldered the backpack and felt its weight and adjusted the straps so that it was snug. I heard a faint zipping noise behind me and turned to see Josh peering into his pack. He'd already pulled a bottle of water out and was looking, with great concentration, at what else was lurking in its depths.

I looked to Patricia and mouthed 'sorry'. She said nothing but kept smiling.

"Dacre is about four miles from here. I've put a map in each of your packs that will help. But if you follow the A592 you'll get to it just fine."

I smiled; my face ached, and it felt a little lopsided and rather larger than I was used to.

"Thank you."

"You're welcome. C'mon. I'll see you off."

Patricia walked us through the car park and towards a group of three men. One of whom, according to Josh, was the dude who wanted to leave us behind at the plane. Douche.

As we approached, they seemed to straighten up, and one man hurried off and climbed into the cab of the truck they were standing in front of.

"Be careful out there," said Patricia to both of us

She raised her hand, and the truck started up with a growl. The engine rumbled and then appeared to strain. There was a dull hiss, and then the truck inched forward, revealing the exit to the service station.

"Thanks again." I said, "Maybe we'll see you again?"

"Maybe."

"Thank you," added Josh a little sheepishly.

We walked out and turned left and started to follow the main road. We'd got no further than a few feet from the station when the truck rolled back into place, turning the service station back into a makeshift camp.

From the outside the whole place seemed smaller, and as we walked by we could see a few people moving around, doing various jobs, carrying boxes and bags of stuff to and from the vehicles parked outside.

"Strange place," I said to no one in particular

"Maybe, I guess it's a backup if we can't find your uncle."

"I sure hope we can. But you're right. I never really considered what we might do if I can't find Uncle Joe."

We walked in silence for the first hour or so. The going was pretty easy; we just had to follow the road, which was well paved. No trudging over fields or navigating difficult terrain. We didn't see anyone, at least not human. A few birds flitted around, and every now and then there was a slight rustle of leaves deep within a small bush or through undergrowth.

We had made decent progress when I suggested we stop for a break. Josh didn't argue. We sat down on the grass next to the road. My limbs ached a little, almost as much as my face did.

"Is it bad?" I asked Josh.

"Not really. It probably looks worse than it is."

"I'm not sure I'm comforted by that statement."

I wrestled my backpack off and opened it up. I carefully removed the contents. We'd each been given an almost identical backpack with an almost identical load out of basic items that would get us to where we're going and beyond.

We each had three small bottles of water. Two nut-based chocolate bars. I had an apple, and Josh had a banana. There was a small box which contained a few plasters, some dressing, a super small bottle of sanitiser and some safety pins. The bag also contained a poncho, folded up in a plastic bag. The final item in each bag was a small multitool. I looked at the metal device and flipped out each tool in succession.

"I'm not sure how capable that is," said Josh busy unwrapping one of his chocolate bars

"Better than nothing. It's a nice gesture. She didn't have to help us."

"True, true," he said, chomping away on a chunk of chocolate bar as busied myself exploring the rest of the backpack.

I went through each of the pockets which were empty, apart from one; on the inside of the backpack was a small zipped compartment. I patted it down and felt something hard inside. The shape, through the fabric, was hard and difficult to make out. I unzipped the pocket, removed the object and came face to face with the googly eyed plastic purple-haired troll. I sighed and stuffed the annoying little thing back into the main backpack.

I opened one of the water bottles and took a deep swig of water. It was still nice and cold.

I considered opening one of the nut bars, but I didn't really feel that hungry, so I packed everything back into the bag, minus the bottle of water.

We sat and watched the world pass by for a good half an hour before I suggested we get underway again. Josh had gone through his banana and the entirety chocolate bar.

"Eat now, starve later!" he said with glib enthusiasm.

"Cheery."

I looked up and down the road. Nothing. Just the sound of the breeze blowing through the trees. Birds were singing somewhere.

"This is weird," I said

"How so?"

"Just everything. One moment it's silence. Some semblance of normality. Then utter chaos. Then back to something that looks like normal."

"Sounds like you've just described life in general."

'Whatever."

I turned towards our destination and started walking.

"Are you okay?" Asked Josh, catching up

"Yeah. I just hope I can find my Uncle Joe. He'll know what to do or at least have a plan."

"What? Is he some kind of badass?"

"You could say that. To me, he's the best kind of uncle to have. He always knows what to do or where to go or what to say. You'll see."

"Groovy. As long as he has food."

I tutted at Josh, and we walked on with only a few miles to go.

I stood in front of the sign which read 'Dacre'.

"I guess this is it," said Josh

"Yeah."

"I don't suppose you have any idea where to go?"

"None. wish I could remember the address."

We both had our reproduced maps out, which clearly showed the village and its roads.

"If I were your uncle," said Josh, "where would I live?"

I sighed.

"We're going to have to search every street."

"Eh. Are we going door to door?"

"Not quite."

"Sooooo?"

"We're looking for something that seems. Uncle Joe-ish"

"At least I know we're looking for something specific," said Josh, not even trying to hide the sarcasm

"Trust me. You'll know it when you see it."

I strode forwards with confidence. But quietly, inside, I was doubtful. There were a million possibilities and a million reasons why he wouldn't be here. Why, he could be and most likely was somewhere else. But my gut told me to do this. To keep looking.

I heard the quickening footsteps of Josh from behind, hastening to catch up.

The road to Dacre had narrowed somewhat, but I was grateful that it was very well maintained and pretty easy going. We passed several large farmhouses on the way, still and quiet. The elevation of the road slowly grew, slowing our process a little. The walk took longer than expected, but after passing a turnoff to somewhere called, I kid you not, 'Sparket' we arrived at a small village.

"Is this it?" asked Josh

"Maybe."

Small cottages, some clad in stone, others painted white, lined the road which snaked out of view.

There were no obvious signs that said we were in the right place, but as we walked into the village, the first cottage to our right had a small name tag indicating that we had arrived at Dacre.

We stood for a few moments, taking everything in. Listening for any signs of life or activity, but there was nothing. Everything was perfectly still. We turned right down a small road which had a large metal gate that was propped open. I could see several houses with white exteriors bunched together.

I went up to the first door and knocked.

"What are you doing?" asked Josh

I knocked again and waited, but no one came.

The second and third houses were the same. Empty and devoid of life, or so it seemed.

The fourth house had a fairly modern Ford Focus parked outside. This looked promising. I knocked on the door, a little harder than maybe I should have, and the door gently crept open.

"Creepy!" sung Josh from behind

"Hello?" I said, gently pushing the door further open, "My friend and I are lost and need help."

There was nothing in reply. I gingerly stepped forward and put a foot on the step.

"You're not serious, are you?"

I took a step up and peered inside and then instantly took a step back outside.

"Jesus Christ"

"What?"

"Inside," I said through several coughs.

Josh took a step, and the smell hit him too. A potent, acrid smell which assaulted the senses. It seemed to linger in the air, which felt strangely warm in my throat. The smell was strange, wet and almost mossy. I have no other way to describe it. Josh screwed up his face in disgust. He quickly closed the door.

"Fuck this place!" he said

My throat felt rough, like the smell had got inside and was

living there. Slowly eating away at the flesh inside. I felt sick. I stopped and removed my backpack and pulled a bottle of water out and one of the chocolate bars. I took another swig of water, which eased the scratchy feeling. Josh had followed suit, and I assumed we both had the same relieved expression on our faces. I broke off a small piece of the nutty chocolate bar and devoured the slice. The strange taste in my mouth was replaced by chocolate caramel sweetness. Josh looked longingly at the bar.

"I bet you wish you saved some, non?"

Josh said nothing. He almost looked like a scolded child. I laughed and pulled off another piece and handed it to him.

"Thanks," he said, and the chunk disappeared in an instant.

I packed the chocolate bar back into the backpack and kept the water in my hand. We marched back to the main road and continued into the village. The next street was a turnoff to the right, lined by more quaint white cottages. A long line of stone houses lined the road on the right-hand side, and I could see a larger building in the distance.

Lush green foliage blocked our view into some of the houses. The only sound was of our footsteps. We approached a larger house, and I could see inside from the small window. I couldn't make out any movement or activity. The house sported a small yard with a double garage and a hefty-looking wooden gate for both aesthetics and security. And that's when I saw it.

"Look."

"A 4x4?" he said, unimpressed. "So what?"

"It's not just a 4x4." I said, "It's a 1970s Ford Bronco."

"Is that a good thing?"

"It's an Uncle Joe thing."

I pushed the gate, and it slowly opened; the metal hinges made a deep whining sound.

I approached the vehicle, and it seemed largely original, retaining its boxy features and larger, knobbly wheels. I peered inside and saw that the interior had been refitted. This had to be Uncle Joe's. It would be too much of a coincidence. One of my earliest memories was helping Uncle Joe work on cars. He once had this old Mustang that spent most of its life in bits. But piece by piece, Uncle Joe had put it back together. By the time I was entering my teens, he and my father had fallen out. Over what, I had no idea. But for some reason Uncle Joe had come to England and settled for a while. The family lost touch, and it was only after I told my parents that I was going to spend some time in England that my dad gave me Uncle Joe's address.

And here we were. I peered through the back window trying to see what I could see when I suddenly heard a strange sound behind me.

"Irk" followed by a sort of wheezing, high-pitched sound.

"That's enough."

The voice was deep, firm, sort of raspy and noticeably American. I slowly turned around and recognised the stern face. I immediately smiled.

"Uncle Joe. It's me."

He stood behind Josh, his arm tightly wrapped around Josh's neck and also the underside of his arm, leaving his right arm in a strange position.

"Cabbage?" He said, obviously surprised, "Is that you?"

I nodded

"Holy shit! You look terrible."

"Thanks. "That's my friend, Josh."

Uncle Joe released Josh who gasped

Joe slapped Josh on the back.

"Nice to meet you, Josh," he smiled and extended his hand. "No hard feelings, buddy."

Josh's hand was grasped and pumped firmly. Josh seemed to be in a state of shock.

Uncle Joe was almost the polar opposite of my dad. While they looked uncannily alike, although they were not twins (my dad is the eldest by two years), Uncle Joe looked like my dad if my dad was locked in a gym for a few years. He was broad and muscular without being oversized. He'd spent a good deal of his life in the military doing, well, military things. When I was younger I used to try and get him to tell me stories of what he'd seen and done, but this aspect of his life had remained a permanently closed book. He and my dad had argued over the military. Exactly what, I have no idea. They both had remained frustratingly closed-lipped.

Uncle Joe ushered us into what was, in fact, his house.

It was a modest abode, well furnished, nothing too fancy. Several bookcases were stacked with everything from finance to politics to mechanical engineering. There was a healthy amount of sci-fi and horror, too. Uncle Joe seemed to have broad reading tastes. We followed him through the house, down a hall which turned into the kitchen.

"You want a drink? I have coffee, juice, and soda."

"Water will be fine."

Uncle Joe looked at Josh

"Do you have Coke?"

"Sure do," he said, opening the refrigerator. He pulled a can from the door and handed it to Josh.

He poured me a glass of water and handed it to me.

"It's good to see you, but what the hell are you doing here? And why do you look like you've gone one round with Mike Tyson?"

"I came looking for you, and we got, sort of, jumped."

"Sorta? By whom and how many?"

"Must've been six or seven."

"You're missing the part where you spazzed out and started the whole thing."

Uncle Joe nodded; his eyes seemed to narrow.

"I see you've still got that temper. It's a pity you never continued training."

"I learnt enough."

"Not enough to stop that." He pointed to my face. To which I had no reply.

"Oh snap," whispered Josh, leaning over. "You got served. By your uncle."

I scowled at him but was rewarded with a bolt of pain.

“No use in dwelling on it. What’s done is done.” He leant against the kitchen countertop. "Just what are you doing in England?"

"Finding myself, I guess. Although it's not going so well."

"I don't think it's going well for anyone right now."

"What do you make of all this?" I asked

Joe shook his head.

"It's too much to process."

"What do you think it is?"

"Define 'it'. I don't know if there is an ‘it', but whatever is going on seems to be happening and happening quickly."

"What do you think?" I pressed

“I have absolutely no idea. All I know is we heard something bad happened in London, Glasgow and Edinburgh. Communication outages, yadda yadda yadda."

"We didn't hear anything about Scotland,” said Josh, placing the now empty can onto the counter.

"I figured it would be just another part of the news cycles, and we'd be done within a day or so. I'm glad I'm not a betting man."

"So what do we do now?"

"There's nothing to do, cabbage. We just have to wait and see how things play out."

"What about military contacts? You know people."

"Sure. But that’s back home, and even if I could communicate with them, I don't think they'd be any more informed than we are. Heck, we don't even know if what's happening here is an isolated incident or if it's happening back home, too.”

"Don't you have some kind of secure line? or a sat phone or something?"

“No.” he said flatly, "And those days are far behind me. Your dad made sure of that."

I sighed, and, to be honest, the statement got my hackles up.

"So what was your plan?"

"To be honest, we didn't have one. The only plan was to come and find you. We needed to get away from Selby and anything further south. It's pretty much chaos."

"And if I wasn't here?"

"We stumbled upon a small group of people that have set up a camp at some kind of tourist center a few miles down the road. They helped us. I did think about going back there and seeing about making myself useful."

"And by 'stumbled upon'," added Josh, "we mean totally rescued."

Uncle Joe nodded.

"You're a lucky so-and-so," he said, "but you always have been. I worry about that luck of yours running out. Especially in times like these."

I said nothing. My painful face was enough of a reminder to know he was right. But I didn't want to admit it, dammit!

"We were hoping to get ahead of whatever was coming this way."

Uncle Joe thought for a few seconds.

"If Scotland is just as bad as the south of England, it looks like we could be caught between two fronts."

"What do you think?" I asked

"What do I think? I don't know what to think."

"What are you going to do?"

"Nothing"

"Nothing? What do you mean, "nothing"?

"That's exactly what I said, Cabbage. Nothing. There's nothing TO do."

"But there are people just down the road. They could use your help. We could use your help."

"My help?" He said, somewhat astonished, "What can I do to help? I'm just an old warhorse."

"You're more than that, and you know it," I said, not able

to hide the frustration in my voice. “Besides, you can’t just sit here on your own.”

“Sure I can. I have a small generator, supplies, and water filtration. I can ride this out, whatever this is.”

“And what about me? Do I factor into this plan of nothing?"

My tone was harsh, almost accusatory.

“You are, of course, welcome to stay. And your friend, too.”

“You don’t sound enthralled,” I said. I turned to Josh. “Maybe this was a mistake.”

“C’mon, Cab, I didn’t mean it like that.”

I turned around and started to walk back towards the hallway and the front door. I pushed past Josh, who looked alarmed, eyes wide and startled, not knowing what to do or where to look. I figured he’d catch on and follow me.

I heard my Uncle calling me from the kitchen as I opened the door and stepped outside into the fading daylight

“Hey! Cab. “C'mon, you can't just walk away like this."

"It worked for you, didn't it?" I spat back.

"Now that's enough."

And I stopped. Uncle Joe had that sort of weird power. My dad had something similar, a look, a tone that would make you stop and take note. Uncle Joe’s tone had a hint of concern or caring. A softness that made people like him, even when he was being a dick. It was part of his charm; it was almost his superpower. I didn’t want to admit it, but Dad’s tone was meaner. I wondered if it was, in part, down to the very big physical differences between the two brothers. Uncle Joe had a physical presence which said, straight off the bat, 'You don’t want to fuck with me.’ My dad didn’t have that. He even used to say that Uncle Joe's love of physical conditioning was a vain and foolish affair.

I turned back to face my uncle. I felt frustrated and angry and more than a little disappointed.

My arms hung at my side.

"What's going on?"

I said nothing. Dark thoughts and my internal rage boiled inside.

"I don't understand," he continued. "I haven't seen you in years, and I say one thing, and it's like I'm talking to your father again."

"Does everything have to be about Dad? Why can't you accept that it might be you that's the issue?"

"Me?" He looked taken aback. "I've done nothing."

"Exactly," I shouted. "Nothing for anyone but yourself."

I felt a wave of heat over my face, and my breathing was heavy.

"You seem to be good at looking out for number one, but if there was ever a time that we needed people like you, it's now. But you're too busy hiding out here: a dead person in a town of dead people. All that experience and knowledge. You're someone who can do something, help people. If maybe you weren't so stubborn, like Dad said, you'd be around."

I noticed that Uncle Joe's features hardened a little; there was almost the barest of twitches, and then the warmth drained out of his face.

He took a stride forward towards me and then stopped, almost as if he willed himself to stop.

"Let me tell you something." he said, his voice low "I know he's your Dad and all, but you have no idea what you're talking about. Your father made his choices, and I made mine. And here we are. It changes nothing."

"Exactly," I screamed. "Why couldn't you have just been there, and then he'd be alive?"

I coughed the words out, almost instinctively.

"Fuck you." I shouted, "I'm going back. You can stay here."

I turned and started to walk up the street. I heard footsteps behind me and the struggling breath of Josh trying to keep up. My uncle didn't say anything. He didn't call out or shout or try and get us back. I didn't even know if he was watching or not. I stormed out of the yard and turned left to head back to the main road. I stole a quick glance and saw only Josh standing, looking a little dumbfounded. The man had gone inside. Hurried footsteps told me Josh was catching up.

"Fuck him," I whispered under my breath and strode back down the road and towards where we had come from.

The journey back to the camp took longer than I expected. I shared the rest of my food and water with Josh. I was physically and mentally exhausted, replaying the events of the day over and over in my mind. Again and again. They merged with imagery of the Charlies truck exploding. I realised I'd lose composure again, lashing out at those nearest to me. This time verbally instead of physically. First Josh and now Uncle Joe. It felt like some kind of perverse carousel that I couldn't get off. For the longest time it was a joke, something funny to comment on. A few months ago it was nothing but a mere annoyance and maybe something of an embarrassment at times. Especially when I found myself alone after time had passed. Shame and embarrassment stung like a hot poker. I pulled the hood of my hoodie over my head and kept moving. To Josh's credit, he said nothing and just followed along. We ate and drank in silence as the night settled in. The sun had long gone, replaced by the night. A multitude of stars dotted the canvas of night. In the distance we could see small pinpricks of light here and there. House lights, maybe. The large swaths of lights from roads and towns were invisible. My mind turned to how long the power would stay on, maybe this was it and the power was disappearing. A hot wave of fear swept over me, followed by panic. All the worst bits of every bad post-apocalyptic movie played out in my head. I didn't want this to happen. I didn't want this life.

'Can't we go back to normal?' I asked myself silently

There was no answer. I looked up into the night sky and saw the moon, surrounded by a blanket of stars. The universe had spoken, it seemed. Maybe our time was up, finally. Or maybe not. This could be nothing but a blip, a road bump in our evolutionary path. Maybe in a few months things will bounce back, and this will all seem like a bad dream. Maybe we'll get season six of 'Z Nation' finally?

I tried to keep a positive outlook. But there was something nagging, pulling at the very edge of my waking mind. The thought was there. Sitting, waiting, demanding to be heard; that this was it. This was the new life and life would be hard, harder than before. And that this was now truly survival of the fittest. I took a deep breath, and we pressed on, putting one foot in front of another. In the distance I could see a small ring of lights and a dull orange glow which lit up the side of a building. The camp. I hoped that Patricia had meant what she said about welcoming us back.

FIFTEEN

I didn't realise just how late it was when we arrived at the truck-based barricade of the service station. At first we were met with wariness with a tinge of hostility. When we identified ourselves, there was a visible relaxation. Patricia had come to meet us, but nothing was really said. When we met at the gate, her eyes flicked between me and Josh, and she had given a sort of sympathetic, motherly expression. My mood had turned dark and inwards. I felt crestfallen, and the miles of walking had exhausted me to the point where I didn't feel motivated to talk. Josh, on the other hand, seemed to perk right up. He was all 'hellos' and 'heys'. He did most of the talking and, to his credit, left out all the nergly details of our heated discussion with my uncle, but I could tell that she could read between the lines. All I wanted to do was sleep; we were shown the same "bed".

I slumped back onto a pillow after rolling out the duvet and stared at the ceiling of the visitors center. Now a ramshackle mess in the midst of transformation into something else. A modern-day castle, maybe.

"The strangest outpost." I said out loud.

My eyes felt heavy, and I took a deep breath. I didn't know where Josh was; maybe getting food. I wasn't hungry; all I wanted was to sleep. I expended the rest of my reserves with washing and brushing my teeth. I finally settled back onto the makeshift and started to think about how we would fit in here.

I never completed any coherent thought as I quickly descended into a deep sleep.

I only realised I'd fallen asleep when I woke up the next morning. The light of day shining in through the main entrance of the visitors center. I could already see the sun slowly rising in the early morning sky. I pushed off the duvet and sat up, rubbing my eyes. I stretched and yawned. I felt a dull pain in my stomach. I needed to pee.

I emerged from the toilet, a little more relieved and refreshed after emptying my bladder and splashing some water on my face, and I did it in that order, thank you very much.

There was movement outside, and I decided to investigate. Dan was up and about busying themselves at their cooking station. They turned as I emerged from the building and waved.

"Morning," I said, somewhat dazed and very much aching from the day before.

I looked around at the ragtag mixture of vehicles parked in the small car park. I guess this would be home for a while. How long? Who could say? I wanted to be excited, or at the very least enthusiastic about it. But I still noticed the black cloud which hung over me from yesterday. I felt my mood darken as I thought more about the altercation with my uncle. I felt stupid. Was this another bridge burnt? I suddenly realised that I didn't have many left to burn.

I sighed and looked around. Some people milled around, but everyone was largely asleep, or so it seemed. I felt a little lost. I wandered past the outside makeshift kitchen, Dan busy at work cobbling together a meal for everyone. Maybe it was breakfast, or maybe lunch. I didn't bother to ask. Instead I walked past and weaved my way around the small cars parked next to the preparation area. At the far end of the car park was Patricia's motorhome. Was this the modern equivalent of the king's castle, or in this case, the queen's? Although she didn't present herself as a leader or queen or whatever, it seemed as though she had some sort of authority, or at the very least everyone seemed to look to her for guidance and make the decisions on what move to make next. Even the surly, somewhat burly, Duncan deferred to her. I mulled over the hows and whys as I made my way to the previously non-stationary home. To my surprise I saw Josh sitting in a camping chair, a cup in his hands, talking to Patricia, who was sat opposite him in her own chair. She looked up as I approached, my sneaker making a sort of scuffing noise on the tarmac.

"Good morning," she smiled

"Hey," said Josh. "How ya doing?"

"Good." I said, "I needed the sleep."

"Busy day, I assume."

"Eventful is more like it."

"Josh mentioned that things didn't go well."

"Not overly," I said. I felt my face getting warm

"Well," she said, putting her cup down on the ground, "now that you're both here, what are you planning to do next?"

I looked at Josh, who shrugged.

"I can't speak for Josh, but I hoped that your offer to stay and help was still on the table."

"Of course it is, luv. Josh and I have already spoken this morning, and we've agreed on ways that he can be of service."

Josh smiled, and the phraseology struck me as strange.

"So, is there some kind of master plan?"

Patricia relaxed into her chair.

"To be frank, we don't have much of one. Our key aim is to tread water and hopefully figure out what the hell is going on."

"Sounds like a solid plan."

"It's the only one we have."

"So what can we do?"

"At the moment we're clearing out the main center, storing everything we can and turning it into a central hub where people can sleep and eat and come together, where we can discuss things in the open and resolve any conflicts. I'm wanting it to be our town hall, as it were."

"You're planning for the long haul." I stated

Patricia nodded and she seemed lost in thought for a few seconds

"I have no idea how long this," she waved an absent hand in the air "is going on for, but I intend to ride it out. For now, grab yourself a tea, coffee, water or whatever you want, and then go see Steven inside. Lend a hand where he needs it. It's not glamorous work, but it's necessary. See how you feel about the place; give yourselves a day or two, both of you. If you like what you see and wants more responsibility, we can talk."

"More responsibility?"

Patricia nodded and took a sip from her mug.

"More responsibility means making a bigger impact on everyone's lives, which means more perks and rewards and privileges."

"Care to elaborate?" I asked, intrigued

"Everyone here works, does something. They contribute. But there are those that do more for the whole, risk more, and in return they're rewarded with a few little extras. That might be food or alcohol or something else. The long and the short of it is simple: you get out what you put in."

"Sounds reasonable."

"We can talk more, but, like I said before, give yourself a day to settle in. Meet and say hello to new people. If it turns out this isn't your thing or you want to move on, fair enough. No one's forcing you to do anything you don't want to do. But while you're here, I ask you to contribute something, to help us out."

"I'm happy to help."

"Good," smiled Patricia. "Right, get that drink and I'll check in with you later."

Patricia pushed herself up from her chair.

"I have some work to do, so I'll catch up with both of you later."

"Cool," said Josh

"Okay, see you later."

Patricia turned and almost skipped up the steps of her motorhome.

"What are you doing now?" I asked Josh

"I have a few things to do for Pat."

"Cool, I'll see you later?"

"Sure thing. We could catch up later at either lunch or supper?"

"Yeah," I replied. "That would be good."

I spent the large majority of the day by myself. Josh was doing whatever job he'd found for himself or whatever Patricia had found for him. Meanwhile I busied myself stripping the rest of the store in the service station. It wasn't too taxing; it required very little thought. It was simply packing things into bags and boxes and moving them into a makeshift storage area, which turned out to be the back of an old van parked outside. I worked all day, and I didn't have too much interaction with anyone. I introduced myself to Steven, who seemed nice enough and turned out to be a sort of foreman for the whole outfitting project. A few people arrived and helped for a while and then disappeared, no doubt finding a different, more engaging job. But I liked this; the stone-cold monotony of it was what I needed in that moment. I worked through what would be lunch and grabbed the odd bottle of water when I needed to. The shop and its shelves were arranged closely; I could imagine them being tightly packed with all manner of goods, or at least it would've been. A few remnants languished on shelves, but for the most part it had been stripped bare. As the day drew to a close and the sun started to head towards the horizon, I had managed to finish stripping everything off shelves and had disassembled most of the shelving, which was now stacked neatly in the back of the old van.

I looked back, slightly sweaty, and surveyed my work. A few more shelves on the wall needed to be removed as well as the serving counters and a few storage cabinets, but it was a decent amount of work for a day.

My limbs ached, and I rubbed my neck to ease a dull throb which had developed through the course of the day. It was while I was surveying my handy work when someone approached. I couldn't remember her name, Helen? Hannah? She had startling red hair, and I couldn't help but wonder how she would maintain it when everything was looking like it was crumbling. She approached with a neutral smile and made eye contact.

"Hi," she said

"Hi," I replied

"I've been asked to come and get you. You're wanted at the gate." a seriousness in her tone and expression.

"Sure, lead on."

This didn't look good. She turned around, and I followed.

What the hell had happened now?. Had Josh done something? Shot his mouth off? Said something? Wasn't that my party trick? My superpower? I tried to think as to why I might be summoned. As I approached the gate, or rather the dirty old lorry trailer, I could see Josh wearing a passive look on his face. As I approached, he faced me and raised his eyebrows. What kind of trouble was this? Were we being kicked out after just one day?

Patricia stepped forward with a somewhat serious look on her face.

I started to open my mouth to say something, but she got in first.

"You have a visitor."

She nodded towards a makeshift set of stairs next to the end of the trailer, made out of shipping pallets.

'Visitor?' I thought, 'What the hell is going on?'

I headed to the stairs and climbed up onto the top of the trailer, half expecting someone behind me to push me off and banish me forever. Instead, as I looked down at the other side, I saw the familiar shape of an orange Ford Bronco, with Uncle Joe leaning casually against the hood. He held his hand up in a half wave as our eyes met.

"Hi, Cabbage."

I heard a snigger somewhere.

He smiled. "Can we talk?"

The trailer was edged forward, and I went out, but only after my uncle and his Bronco reversed thirty or so feet from the gate. As soon as I was clear, there was a squeak, and then the slow rolling sound of tyres on tarmac followed by the hiss of brakes. Even though I could vouch for my uncle, the people of this little outpost were careful about strangers, especially ones that looked kind of imposing, as he did. I kind of forgot about that or managed to see past it, probably because he was my uncle. But people only saw the guy who looked like he could strangle a tree.

I walked towards the orange 4x4, and he got out as I got nearer. I leaned against the hood of the car, and it felt very warm. There was a strange familiarity to it. Of heat and the smell of oil and fuel, with a faint hint of burnt electrics. Old cars ruled.

"I'm sorry about yesterday. I didn't mean to make you or your friend feel marginalised. It was a poor choice of words on my part, or maybe I didn't explain myself fully."

I nodded and considered what he said for a second.

"I'm sorry for flying off the handle. I'm probably more angry at myself than you."

"Do you want to talk about it?"

"It's been a rough few days, and I'm not really ready to, to be honest."

Uncle Joe nodded. There was an awkward pause for a few seconds before he broke the silence.

"I've been thinking too, about what you said. In part, maybe you're right. Maybe I'm so used to being here alone. I think maybe I just wanted to hole up and forget about everything."

He took a deep breath before continuing.

"Which is why I'm here. I wanted to find you, clear the air between us and maybe change our trajectory."

"How so?" I asked, a little confused

"I packed up the mule with as much as I could get in her, and I figured maybe I could lend a hand. Here. With you."

I smiled and nodded.

"That would be cool," I said

"So, ahhhh! What are these guys like? They seem a little, edgy"

I laughed.

"That's just how you make people feel. I'll talk to Patricia; she's the top dog around here."

Uncle Joe stayed next to his Bronco as I waved to the lone sentry on the trailer to let me back in. Once inside I gave Patricia a quick rundown on what my uncle had to offer, effectively vouching for him. I neglected to share the details of our little spat. She seemed eager to have someone with his skills and experience joining their, our, little crew, and so the trailer was drawn back, and he was allowed to drive his Bronco in and park it in a vacant spot next to the station. The only proviso was that he would spend two days in quarantine, as Josh and I did. He didn't seem too put out when I mentioned this, more interested. I had expected more resistance, but he seemed to take everything he was told in his stride. His only real demand, if you can call it that, was that no one touch his truck or its contents. Myself included. The moment this was mentioned, I had the desire to run over and see what he had inside. Most likely it was supplies and survival equipment, maybe a weapon or two. But my interest was piqued. And I discovered I wasn't alone, either. As the days passed, more than a few people walked, somewhat too casually, by the Bronco and looked in through the slightly tinted windows, trying to discern what was locked within.

Towards the end of the second day, Uncle Joe was given the all clear. He emerged from the makeshift quarantine area with little to no fanfare. I was waiting for him as he emerged and took a long stretch in the afternoon sun.

He noticed me, waved and strode over.

"Hey," I said

"Hey yourself." He scratched his head. "Did you have to do that? "

I nodded

"What do you make of it?"

I shrugged

"There's some kind of infection. Makes people go weird and angry."

He nodded and thought.

"Something similar happened back in Dacre. Some sort of mass hysteria, or so I thought. Not a good time. Everyone eventually left."

"There's a whole camp of people, similar to this one, a mile or so down the road. All infected."

Uncle Joe nodded.

"It's not a particularly comforting thought. Having that so close by."

"So far I haven't heard or seen anything from them. Maybe they'll keep to themselves."

"Maybe. But I would bet that changes at some point."

I took a deep breath. I was in no mood or even shape to consider going for round two with the rival camp, at least not like last time.

"First things first," he said. "Apparently I need to have a sit-down with a Patricia. Is that right?"

"Yeah," I answered. "She appears to be in charge around here."

I pointed towards her motorhome, indicating the queen was in.

"Well," he said, rubbing his arms, "I guess I better see what gives and then"

I watched him stride off around the front of the building, heading towards the parked vehicle and, it seemed, impromptu throne room.

"All hail the queen," I said out aloud, quietly.

I smiled to myself and headed for someplace where I could find a cup of coffee.

The next week was, how shall we say, interesting. If Patricia was looking for change in her little empire, she got it, thanks to Uncle Joe. Within a day of being at the station, Uncle Joe took charge of bolstering the perimeter of the area. He talked to a whole bunch of people and had almost every vehicle moved to a more central area, pulling any stragglers away from the edge of the existing perimeter. The existing haphazard perimeter was added to with scavenged vehicles pulled in from the road where they were abandoned. Some smaller cars within the service station were cannibalised for parts to bolster the growing makeshift walls. A bank of earth was slowly erected with a lot of help from everyone, myself included. Over a period of that week, not only did the look of the place change, but the feeling too. The visitors center had gone from a random array of vehicles together to something that resembled an actual compound. The progress was such that Uncle Joe took charge of security and the organising of teams that would go out and collect much-needed resources and equipment. At first this didn't go down well with Duncan at all. I had heard that something had gone down, that there was some kind of argument or disagreement between Uncle Joe, Patricia and Duncan. Alas, I was not there to see exactly what happened; in fact, no one else really saw what happened. I had spent the majority of my time inside working on redecorating and making several large tables that would be a meeting and planning area for when we would venture beyond the confines of the service station.

Like I said, the exact details of what happened would only be known to the three involved. But Duncan was sporting several dark circles under his eyes. He was quiet and sullen, very withdrawn for a day or so before eventually coming round after Uncle Joe sat down with him with a bottle of some kind of booze. Something which he had brought with him from home apparently. The entire contents of Uncle Joe Bronco continued to be a mystery, even to me. And to be honest, my interest in its contents disappeared in the activity of daily chores and new projects to tackle.

I only saw Josh once or twice in that week. Mostly at meals. We talked a bit, but I felt like we were starting to drift, almost like we were starting to live separate lives. By the midpoint of the second week I was starting to train with my uncle. We'd do basic physical fitness drills for an hour, then lunch, then another hour of martial arts, which consisted of basic striking drills. A final hour was dedicated to grappling, which was new to me. I had always been fairly good at the striking but never bothered to really look at grappling. I was a bit apprehensive, but after a few sessions I'd started to get into it.

When we started our workout sessions, it was just me and my uncle, but as the days marched on, we seemed to pick up more and more people. Some people would come and join in just for the fitness stuff; others would come in for the martial arts. A few would do everything a few days a week, maybe. But it was me and my uncle who ground it out each day. Day after day. As the days turned into weeks, my confidence and competence grew. I had begun pestering Uncle Joe to take me on one of his recon missions. Over the weeks he had led several volunteers beyond the confines of the newly rebuilt walls to scout and scavenge basic materials and supplies. I had wanted to volunteer, but he had urged me to wait, to train more. I had pushed back and hard. I wanted to go out. I wanted to do my part. At least that's what I said. But more than anything I wanted to confront my demons, my failure. In reality I wanted to strike back at those who struck at me. The simmering rage burnt in my stomach like a hot poker. I had replayed the moment when Amos and his crew had got the better of me again and again in my own head. The thought, the memory, wove its way into my dreams. And it was in those dreams where my true pain hid. Images of flames seared my dream state; a faint image of a face formed into a fiery visage and mouthed words that were unintelligible. I often fell on my bed, exhausted from the day's work, hoping not to dream. Sometimes I was rewarded with a dreamless sleep; other times not.

It was after one such vivid dream that I had cornered Uncle Joe and demanded that he take me out.

"Slow down," he said. "What's the rush?"

"I need to get out there and prove myself."

"You don't have to prove anything to anyone, least of all me."

I paused and looked into his eyes

"I need to prove it for myself."

My uncle looked at me. He nodded and thought for a moment or two.

We looked at each other, and I felt his eyes look at me in a new way.

"Okay," he finally said, "tonight. But you do as I say and keep that anger in check, you hear?"

"Yes, sir!"

"Okay," he nodded again; he seemed deep in thought. "Be ready by nineteen hundred. Come meet me at the Bronco."

I nodded, and he walked off towards the service station building with purpose. A smile crept over my face. I felt excitement and then, almost immediately, a sense of...it's difficult to say, apprehension maybe, even dread. Nerves. This is what I wanted. I needed to embrace it. I took a deep breath and started counting the hours until 7pm.

SIXTEEN

Six forty-five found me walking out of the service station and towards the middle of the car park, where a small huddle of cars were now somewhat permanently parked. Amongst them, my uncle's Bronco. I threaded my way past a Ford Focus, a Fiat 500, a Volvo V50 and a battered Vauxhall Corsa, which looked like it had seen far too much abuse in its lifetime. My uncle's ride stood out like a sore thumb. It was tall, wide, and far too boxy and brutish for British streets and small villages. As I approached, I could see my uncle leaning inside from the rear of the vehicle.

"Hey." I said aloud

His head popped round from the back of the 4x4, and he smiled.

"Hey yourself."

He closed the back with a satisfying, metallic thud.

"Ready?"

"As I'll ever be," I said

"Good. What are you packing?"

I motioned to the small backpack.

"Water, energy drink, snack bar, headlamp, first aid kit."

"Any gloves?"

"No"

"Fail," he said and reached into the front passenger-side door of the Bronco, which technically should be the driver's side on English roads. But, American car.

He rummaged in the stairwell for a few seconds before withdrawing and handing me a pristine set of gloves. They were black, with brown trim. They had some kind of flexible rubberised plastic along the tops of the fingers and on the top of the hand area, which would offer some protection.

"Neat," I said, pushing a hand into the first glove.

"How do they fit?"

"Tight," I said, flexing my fingers

"Good, the leather will give a little with some use. Look after them."

"Leather. Snazzy."

I pulled on the second glove and did up the small Velcro strap on each wrist. I continued to flex my hands as my uncle led us away from the cars and towards the main entrance of the service area.

"Who else is coming?" I asked. I was keen to see who he had paired us with

"No one," he said. "It's just us tonight."

I was kind of taken aback and a little confused.

We approached what was now a holding area. A twenty-foot square marked out with wooden pallets stood on end. It served as a temporary barrier for anyone going in or out. The pallets were a temporary measure until something more permanent could be sourced. The large trailer which was once a barricade had now been moved to the side of the main service station and was acting as a storage area for anything we could scavenge. As we entered the area, a sentry waved at us, or rather, my uncle. He responded by nodding back. A sort of frosty air descended over him. Where previously he was all smiles, now, he was all business. The sentry crouched down and pulled something out of the top of the wall where he was standing. My uncle pushed on part of the makeshift gate, and a door-sized aperture swung open, revealing the green of the outside world and the grey of the road which stretched ahead.

I stepped through, and Uncle Joe closed the gate behind us with a slight whine of hinges and a clang of metal on metal. A few steps and there was another metallic bang; the gate had been re-secured. We were now locked out.

I followed my uncle as we took a direct route over the roundabout and headed up the A66. To our left was a small expanse of grass lined by a dense wall of trees. You could see the shapes of fields and houses beyond. I wondered if anyone was still in the farmhouses out there. I turned my mind back to the present. I began my interrogation in earnest.

"Where are we going?"

Without missing a beat, my uncle replied.

"Recon, and there's an old farmhouse I want to check out."

"Not very specific," I said

"It's as specific as it needs to be," he said flatly

I paused for a second.

"Is this a test?"

"Do you think it's a test?"

Confused, I decided to stay quiet and see where our outing would take us. A tight knot started forming in the pit of my stomach, followed by a wave of anxiety.

I felt sure that we would follow the road all the way to the large roundabout over the M6. I had thought that we'd return to the plane that Josh and I left behind or maybe explore down the A66. Instead, after a few hundred meters, my uncle turned left and started heading up the verge of the motorway and towards a section of the trees which was much thinner.

"There's a small road just beyond the trees," he explained. "We'll keep to the back roads for now."

I said nothing and followed. Another few hundred meters of walking and we were at a junction; to the right was an exit onto the A66, the road we'd left. We turned left and started walking up the lane. Every so often I would turn around, walking backwards, making sure there was no one behind us.

We walked in silence for a while, putting one foot in front of the other. I followed Uncle Joe over a closed farmer's gate and into a field. The ground was fairly soft and noticeably harder to navigate than the easy tarmac of the roads. We gained a little altitude, and I could already see the motorway slightly below us. Somewhere, just out of sight, would be the little plane that brought us here. It seemed like both such a long time ago and only yesterday.

Uncle Joe turned and continued to walk backwards for a few steps before turning back.

My legs burned as we continued on; Uncle Joe showed no signs of slowing down or letting up. From the road the small hill didn't look like much, but actually walking up the thing was a whole different kettle of fish. I forced my legs to push on; each step felt like a dull burning pain in my thighs. My heart rate was rising, and I was starting to get a little breathless. I couldn't even tell if my uncle was breathing heavily, let alone panting. The guy was a mountain goat. I realised that it would be futile to try and keep up with him.

"I need a moment," I said, huffing. Trying to claw more oxygen into my system.

My uncle come to a sudden halt and turned around

"Okay, let's take a moment."

He turned around and surveyed the area, his eyes sweeping over the landscape.

I sat on the ground and looked out towards the motorway and the small town of Penrith beyond.

Despite power still being available, it was strange to see a town bathed mostly in darkness. In fact, the majority of buildings seemed to be dark. Whether this was out of choice or simply that no one was there, I didn't know. But as night started to close in, the whole landscape slowly descended into darkness, with only a few pinpricks of light marking any form of civilisation. I watched for a while; Joe was looking through a pair of binoculars. "Glassin'" he called it. I don't know exactly what he was looking at, but for a fair few moments he paused and watched intently. I looked around, wary of anyone that might try to sneak up on us. There was nothing out there but rocks and hills and maybe the occasional sheep or cow. Even in the new darkness you could easily pick out the shape of someone, once your eyes adjusted. Uncle Joe sat down next to me.

"So", he said, continuing to look towards the hills in the distance. They were nothing but black shapes, but they still stood out against the slightly lighter sky.

"How are you holding up?"

"Is this the start of a pep talk?" I asked with a grin

"No. This is the start of me asking if you're okay. We haven't spoken so much lately, and you've been through a lot in a short time."

I sighed.

"I'm good," I said

"Are you, though? You've thrown yourself into training; in fact, it's almost all you ever do, aside from chores."

"Is that a crime?" I snapped

"Certainly not," he said, ignoring my shortness. "But you've isolated yourself from anyone; even Josh hasn't seen much of you. He's worried. I'm worried."

"You shouldn't worry about me. I can take care of myself."

"I do worry about you, though. You can't do this alone, and you seem to be pushing people away."

That hit hard; I felt the tickling of anger bubbling from deep within me. But I knew he was right.

"And something's bothering you. In fact, it's eating you alive."

I didn't want to talk about any of this. I just wanted to carry on. I said nothing. Hoping, maybe, that Uncle Joe would drop the line of questioning I thought he was taking.

"You mentioned something," he said, "when you were at the house. It was in the heat of the moment."

'Shit' I thought

"You said something about 'saving him'. Who were you talking about?"

I gritted my teeth, my jaw set and I felt the muscles within flex and pulse

"What did Josh say?" I asked

"Nothing. I haven't spoken to him. I want to speak to you."

I sighed and took a few breaths. The silence was deafening.

I rubbed my eyes and ran the same hand through my hair.

"I know I haven't been around for a while, but we're family. And regardless of what has happened between me and your dad, I still care about you."

There was another long pause. I thought I heard an owl somewhere.

Uncle Joe wasn't going anywhere, and I knew he wouldn't quit. I felt tired all of a sudden. Not physically tired, but mentally. I could feel the mental pressure. The burden almost pushing me into the ground. Or at least it felt like it.

I looked at a few lights in the distance. I took a deep breath and looked my demon in its eyes.

"When Josh and I set out." I said, "There were three of us. Our friend, Charlie, was with us."

And so I sat there, in the darkness, and told Uncle Joe everything. Of how we came to leave, how I'd voted to go. And how I failed my friend. I don't know how long I was telling the tale, but Uncle Joe sat and listened. He never stopped me for questions or interrupted; he just let me talk. And to be honest, I think that's what I needed. Once I started, I didn't stop. In my head it was a quick story, but when I stopped at arriving at the service station after our altercation with Amos and his gang of weirdos, my voice was hoarse, and I felt more tired than before. But strangely, I felt lighter.

We sat in the darkness for a while. Embraced by the night. He broke the silence first.

"That's a whole lot to be keeping to yourself, Cabbage. I don't pretend to have all the answers, but I do know you need to find some way of forgiving yourself, if nothing else for your own sanity."

"Do you think I'm responsible for Charlie's death?" I asked

"No," he said. "Nor do I think there was anything you could do to change the outcome based on what you said. But in the end it doesn't matter what I think or say. What matters is how you move forward. And I need you to move forward. To find a way to survive in whatever world this ends up being."

"You sound worried."

"I am," he said, flatly. "You're family. My brother's kid. My responsibility. I can imagine your parents are worried sick right about now. And I need to find a way to get you back to them, even if I'm not around."

"What are you talking about?"

"I'm talking about all eventualities. I'm talking about giving you as much knowledge and information as possible to get you home, even if I'm not there to do it. And part of that is learning how to deal with loss. The loss of people closest to you."

"You're like the toughest dude around here."

"And yet fate has a strange way of working."

I looked at my uncle, still gazing into the night.

"You're worried." I said

"I'm concerned," he corrected, "about the future."

He handed me the binoculars and pointed towards the motorway.

"Take a look at the truck stop next to the freeway."

I held the binoculars to my eyes; they were deceptively heavy

"They call it a motorway over here." I said

I turned the focus knob until the blurry image solidified. I managed to pick out the edge of the motorway in the darkness and the road just next to it. I followed it until I saw the road twist upwards. I knew that the truck stop was just there, beyond the tall building that seemed to have been an office of some kind. I expected darkness at the truck stop. But there was light. The light of many fires burning, contained within what looked to be oil drums. There had to be at least thirty of them, dotted around the site. Illuminating the immediate area. I could see figures walking and stumbling in the dark, large shadows cast by the fires. There were makeshift tents and shelters everywhere. It's like some kind of shanty town I'd seen on the news in some third-world country, but instead of somewhere far away, it was right here. It didn't seem real.

"Jesus", I said, "you're worried about them?"

"The encampment is getting larger by the week. There are more and more people cramming themselves in there. I can only assume they're carrying the same infection that Patricia quarantined us for. Supplies are limited and getting more and more scarce. I've been taking small groups out on scavenging missions, and getting hold of food and supplies is getting harder. So far we've kept to our own territories. But at some point both sides are going to meet. And as it stands, they outnumber us by a fair amount."

"You're worried about escalation and our ability to defend ourselves?"

"For starters. But I'm more worried about if this isn't an isolated case but more of a trend. And based on what you've said about everything that went on where you lived. I'm betting something similar is playing out not only down there, but all over the country."

I took a deep breath and blew air heavily from my lungs. It was easy to view what was happening here as something isolated. To view it as something temporary that we'd eventually overcome. It was something else to realise that this could be all of our futures.

"You're going to have to be strong," said Uncle Joe. "Not just physically, but mentally. And sometimes that means knowing when to ask for help, knowing when to put your hand up and say something is wrong, and knowing when you can and can't deal with what's in front of you."

I sighed and looked at the ground.

"It's okay to feel sad about people we've lost. It's okay to feel a sense of responsibility. But you can't punish yourself, or others, for decisions that you never made or. And he paused for a second or two, as if considering his next choice of words. "couldn't have made. It'll drive you mad."

"In my head, I know it makes sense," I said, "but in my heart, it's like a whirlwind of confusion and hatred and several other emotions I can't put a finger on."

"Take that twisting knot that seems to wrap itself around your heart and squeeze, and try and refocus it. Use it to point towards something else. Either something more productive or an enemy."

I considered what he was saying.

"By enemy you mean them?"

"I mean anyone or anything that stands in front of you."

"And how do I do that?"

"As strange as it sounds, you need to start by forgiving yourself."

"That does sound strange."

"We're in strange times, Cabbage, and we're all going to have to find ways to survive this, one way or the other."

"That sounds even stranger."

"I know, but it'll become less strange, one way or the other."

"That sounds super ominous." I said

Uncle Joe laughed.

"Ominous is my middle name," he said

"I thought it was Francis!"

"And we shall never speak of that again.

He pushed himself up and stretched.

"Let's push on."

My legs complained as I got to my feet. I wiggled my toes in my boots and rolled my shoulders, shook my legs out and took a few deep breaths. For some reason I felt physically lighter.

"Okay," I said, "let's go."

We continued our way towards the edge of the field, continuing north and turning a little to what I thought was west. We eventually came upon a hedge-lined road, turned, and followed it. The road eventually led to a smaller, poorly paved track. We walked in silence for the majority of our journey. The walk gave me time to think and reflect on what Uncle Joe had said. I felt mentally exhausted and wanted nothing more than to crawl into a small, warm hole and sleep. The realisation hit me that carrying around this guilt, this burden, had tired me out, had drained me to the point where I had pushed people away by distancing myself from others.

I had lost myself in these thoughts when my uncle brought me to the present when he stopped and held out his hand. We both crouched down, and I followed his hand signal forward. I saw the outline of several buildings in the darkness. No lights were lit, but we crouched and remained there, carefully watching for any sign of movement or habitation.

Seconds seemed to stretch into minutes into an unknown amount of time. We waited in the darkness. I felt tingling in my feet when Uncle Joe whispered to me.

"Okay, let's check it out. Quietly."

We got up and advanced slowly towards the looming shape of the buildings. As we approached, I looked around, watching for any telltale signs of movement. It was amazing just how much you could actually see at night when your eyes adjusted.

As we approached the building, Joe took a peek inside the nearest window.

"Looks good. But let's take it easy."

I followed him, and we stopped at the door. He peered in through the small window. He put his hand on the door, and, amazingly, it slowly opened with a slight squeak. He stepped forward a little and peered inside. I thought I heard him stifle a cough as he stepped through the door. He beckoned me forward, and then it hit me: the smell. It was like I was ported back to Dacre again. The memory of that strange, foetid smell evoked an almost immediate sense of panic inside me. I felt my heart race, and I desperately wanted to turn and run. I swallowed and took a breath in through my mouth. The air tasted as weird as it smelled. I stifled a cough, but I kept it together and followed my uncle as he stalked down a narrow hallway and into what appeared to be an ample kitchen. He quietly looked around, opening cupboards. He pulled out several cans and placed them on the countertop along with several packets of something else. I looked through other cupboards and found a few jars of something, maybe jam or peanut butter; it was difficult to really pick out too many details in the dark. I removed my pack from my back, unzipped it and began loading up our haul. Uncle Joe looked around and out the rear window. He helped pack up the rest of the items, and we both donned our packs before quietly stalking down the hallway and back towards the door. A set of stairs led up to the next floor. He motioned upwards, and we started to climb the stairs slowly. Every so often a floorboard would creak and moan. Each time my heart would skip a beat. As we went to the top of the stairs, the air seemed thicker and warmer. It was getting more difficult to breathe. My nose and throat stung. I put the back of my gloved hand against my mouth. It didn't help much.

The first floor was more cramped. As we got to the top of

the narrow stairs, a door stood ajar in front of us. Looking back along the hallway were two other doors, a bedroom and bathroom, I presumed. Joe stepped forward and glimpsed through the narrow opening in the door.

"Oh shit," he breathed, carefully pushing open the door fully.

He stepped into the door and coughed. I felt a wave of heat escape past him, and with it a wave of strange-smelling air. My eye watered. Taking a deep breath was a mistake, and I gagged and coughed a little as I stepped into the large room. I saw a double bed, maybe a king-size bed, in the middle of the room. One had some kind of dresser or a chest of drawers. But what drew my eyes wasn't the dresser or the bed. It wasn't even the weird stains that adorned the sheets. It was the huge throbbing mass which was attached to the wall and seemed to be growing into the edge of the bed.

I couldn't quite make out precise details, but I could see it move and pulsate in the darkness. I could hear strange, slick sounds come from it. I was aware that what looked to be tendrils of...something...were stretched out above us on the ceiling. I tapped Uncle Joe on the shoulder and pointed up. He nodded, seemingly calm.

"What the fuck is this?" I whispered, trying not to lose my calm.

I was ready to leave; I was ready the moment I stepped through the door. I could feel my heart beating heavily in my chest. It was getting difficult to breathe fully, and I felt a wave of panic wash over me, almost like I felt like I was drowning. I edged towards the door, trying to find some cleaner air. My body screamed at me to run, run and hide. It took all of my willpower to keep me rooted to the spot. I was lost in thought, trying to focus through the smell, when there was a quick flash of white light which startled me. My vision cleared, and for an instant I saw color and details that I didn't want to see. Greens, reds and greys all merging and swirling into one. Slick and wet, like a leathery gelatinous mass. After a few more flashes and I could make out its movement as it heaved and pulsed, somehow rooted to the wall and threatening to engulf the bed. We were suddenly back in the dark. My night vision was temporarily ruined. I blinked a few times and closed my eyes for a moment. The imagery of what I had seen burned into my mind. I shuddered and heard the sound. Something between tearing and squishing.

"Let's go," said Uncle Joe.

I didn't need to be told again. I made my way straight down the stairs. For a second my senses were clear of the smell, until I briefly turned around to see my uncle reaching the bottom of the stairs. A waft of hot air, along with that smell, assaulted my senses, and I instinctively moved towards the open door and fresh air. My uncle grabbed my arm and held up his hand. Careful.

I peeked outside to see if anyone unsavoury was around. I waited a few moments, almost panic-stricken, my heart racing harder and faster again. I felt the need to rush out into the night and run down the road far away. My uncle was next to me, peering into the darkness. He slunk past me and stepped outside. I followed without waiting and took in a deep breath of clean, fresh air. My uncle turned and held his finger to his mouth, and we walked back down the road.

We walked at a steady clip for several minutes, putting distance between us and the buildings behind. I felt more at ease as we walked down the small country road. Where normally I'd be mostly creeped out, I felt a sense of relief now that we were away from those houses. Or rather that thing.

"What did you make of it back there?" Asked uncle Joe

"Not pleasant. What do you think?"

"I think this is trouble; we haven't seen the start of."

"What's that meant to mean?"

"I need to think. This is not something I was expecting to see."

"Do you..."

"I don't have any definite answers," he said, expertly

cutting me off. “Right now, we need to get back to the center and figure out a plan before external forces force our hands.”

“Amos?” I asked

“Between him and his camp, the thing in the house and whatever else is going on. We’re sandwiched into a situation that's going to get rough and quick.”

We'd reached the end of the road and had come to a small junction which opened up onto the main road which would lead back to our makeshift camp, which was now home. I could see dim, flickering lights around the station and a few pinpricks of light in the distance in whatever little farmhouses or towns still had people hiding out or just getting on with life. We walked towards the station, and I wondered if and when life would return to normal. Or would this be the new normal? Skulking around at night, raiding houses for supplies and keeping out of harm's way? This wasn’t the future I thought I’d live in. I don’t suppose anyone thought of this kind of future. For a few seconds I wished I could go back to playing video games and eating pizza. My stomach growled at the thought. Pizza would be great about now. Maybe a meat feast with pineapple and jalapeños. I sighed and kept walking, following Uncle Joe, who was unaware of my pizza desires.

That thing was weird, and the smell was nasty, but he was acting decidedly different after we left the house. More aloof than usual. I couldn't put my finger on it, but now my gut was telling me something wasn’t right.

“C’mon,” he said. “Let’s pick up the pace. We don’t want to be last for supper.”

SEVENTEEN

“So what are we looking at?” asked Duncan in a tone that didn't lend itself to being immediately patient.

There were six of us around the table that had been set up in the main building, specifically for meetings like this. The meeting had been convened two days after we got back from our trip. Uncle Joe had volunteered us for immediate quarantine. And so we sat in the familiar containers waiting for Vivian to give us the "all clear". By which time the rumour mill was in full effect, and as soon as we emerged from our self-confinement, we were rushed into a meeting.

Around the table were Vivian, Patricia, myself, Uncle Joe, Duncan and Callen, an annoying jerk that had stumbled upon us by chance a few weeks ago and was all smiles and answers. I smelt an absolute tonne of bullshit whenever he talked, but everyone seemed to take a liking to the guy. I didn’t 100% trust him. He’d said nothing most of the time and not only managed to find his way into everyone’s good books but also into a position of trust. Which is why he was sitting across from me wearing that shit-eating grin of his. I’m not sure what Uncle Joe thought. Every time I brought it up, he managed to evade the question or change the subject. The most I got was a "Just keep your cool. Give him some room."

I realised that I'd missed a good chunk of what had been said, lost in my inner thoughts.

"I have no idea," said Uncle Joe. "not sure about the exterior, but it looked wet, almost like some kind of organ. Plus it was very warm in that room, like it was radiating heat along with the smell."

"I've seen them before," interjected Callen. "Down south, lots of them?"

"Where?" I asked; my tone was somewhat accusatory, but I genuinely wanted to know. And maybe find out for sure if he was full of shit or not.

"Canada Water", he answered

"Where the fuck is that?" I asked, quite genuinely I might add

"South London. Sort of near the Tower of London. You should go. You'd love it!"

"Wait." I said, "You were in south London after London was closed down."

"I sure was. It was a hell of a time. Managed to head west, towards Heathrow. Caught a few good pieces of luck, and here I am."

"Sounds like quite the story."

He smiled and said nothing.

"If we can get back on track," said Patricia, gesturing to the image. "What can you tell us, Callen?"

"Nothing, really. They smelt like hot ass. Didn't hang around. I mean, I wanted to have a closer look, maybe find something important out, but the crew I was with had other ideas. I tried to make them stay, but they just weren't up to it. At the end of the day, majority rules. But, to this day, I sure wish they'd listened to me. We might soon have good intel on whatever those things were."

"We?" I asked, "I thought it was just you?"

"It was. After we got out of London, we all went our separate ways. Families, loved ones. You know the deal," he explained with a smile that I couldn't quite read

My bullshit meter was pegged, and alarm bells were ringing. I met eyes with my uncle, and he, ever so slightly, shook his head. I took this to mean that he could smell bovine excrement too, but now wasn't the time. I didn't acknowledge his small gesture; I merely kept my mouth closed and took everything in.

"I was hoping for something other than what Joe came to us with, but thank you for your input, Callen."

"Always a pleasure," he said with a smile that was too wide.

"What's your assessment, Joe?"

"I've never seen anything quite like it; they're obviously not a device or not obviously man-made. I think it's safe to assume they're not indigenous. We need more information. But if what Callen says is right, then these things could be everywhere. We need to assess how many there could be and try to understand what they are."

Patricia rubbed her head

"This goes way beyond what I was prepared for. We're hardly equipped to understand what's going on with Amos' people at the truck stop, let alone a potential biohazard, which is what you're both implying."

There wasn't any answer from anyone at the table. There was a long pause as everyone seemed to look at everyone else, until my uncle spoke up.

"I do have a suggestion."

Patricia nodded. "I'm all ears."

"With each passing week there's something new to deal with. We're starting to feel the pressure because we move from task to task or event to event. Our manpower isn't increasing. We're starting to be stretched thinly. Which gives us little option but to deal with the priorities. My suggestion is we split our labour into three operations. One group works on fortifying our position, making sure the encampment is secure. Another group will focus on recon and acquisition. They go out, find supplies and provide a watchful eye on what's going on over at the truck stop as well as anywhere else there could be activity. The third group will be tasked with finding out as much information about those things as possible as well as a rough estimate of how many there could potentially be."

"That's pretty thin," said Duncan

"It is," said my uncle. "But if we concentrate on just two things, the third is going to bite our ass; I can almost guarantee it."

"I'm in agreement with Joe," said Patricia. "It might be a stretch, but maybe we can devise some overlap."

Uncle Joe nodded in agreement.

"If I may," asked Vivian, "we're hardly in any position to do any real research. It's all we can do to treat basic wounds and ailments. We're not equipped for serious examinations or research."

"That's a given," replied Uncle Joe. "As part of our acquisition push, we need to think about casting a net further afield to secure more equipment and supplies."

"We're already pushed for space as is," said Patricia. "Can we afford to take up more? Are you thinking about bringing one of those things in here?"

"If we are, then we need to talk about infection risk," offered Vivian. "I don't like the sound of this as it is, let alone talk of bringing something like that inside."

"No. We do any examinations in the field," said my uncle. "We minimise the disruption to the specimen and minimise the possibility of infection to anyone else. At least for now."

"So what's the division of labour between these groups?" asked Duncan, "Who does what?"

Quiet descended on the small group; I shifted around in my chair.

"Realistically, I guess there's only me to do the examination of whatever it is Joe found," said Vivian

"That wouldn't be an option," said Patricia. "Joe?"

"I'd have to figure out the details, but the broad stroke

would be myself taking the lead on recon and acquisitions, and Duncan would take point on base security."

"Which just leaves me with no one."

"Callen," said my uncle. "Callen can take point on this; he has combat experience."

Callen shifted in his seat and for a split second I thought I could see nerves flick over his face, but somehow he managed to reset with a broad smile

"Happy to help wherever I can."

"This will be a good opportunity to prove yourself in the field and to get back in the leadership saddle."

"I guess it'll be a good way to get rid of the ring rust."

Callen stretched and flexed his arms.

My uncle nodded, and I noticed that Duncan didn't look 100 per cent impressed, but he said nothing. I guess I wasn't the only one who didn't buy whatever Callen was selling.

"Okay," announced Patricia. "Sounds like the beginnings of a strategy. Anything else? "

She patted the tabletop softly, waiting for anyone to chime in.

"No? Good. Joe, figure out the staffing and time frames for all this chaos. Time is one resource we definitely don't have enough of."

There were several nods and a hint of a murmur around the table. I stifled a yawn as everyone started to get up and go their separate ways. Duncan, however, hung around for a brief second or so and quietly said something I couldn't make out to my uncle. He walked Duncan to one side, and they had a quiet chat that lasted a few minutes or so. I couldn't make out what was being said. I imagine that Duncan wasn't happy with them. Or maybe someone. Maybe I would have an ally in Duncan against Callen.

Duncan and my uncle parted with friendly smiles and nods. Whatever was said, they both liked the outcome. Duncan went one way, and my uncle strode back over to the table.

"Trouble in paradise?" I asked

"Seems like Callen isn't making friends in the right places."

"I don't like that dude." I said

"I never would've guessed," laughed my uncle

"So how come he's around all the time, and all of a sudden he's going to be heading up the specimen examination portion of this master plan?"

Uncle Joe stopped abruptly in the middle of the corridor.

"Firstly," he said, "Callen isn't heading up anything; Vivian will be in charge of the examination of the specimen, if that's what we're calling it. Secondly, you need to keep your disdain for Callen on the DL. I don't care if you don't like him or if you think he's the best guy in the universe; we need to keep it business-like when it comes to dealing with everyone else. Thirdly," and he paused a little before he continued, "you sound a little jealous."

I looked, awkwardly, for a second. Busted.

"I was hoping you'd give me a shot at heading up the expedition, what with all the extra training and whatnot."

My uncle nodded and took a minute.

"Cabbage", he said, "you'd play a lousy game of cards. I want you here. Eyes and ears to the ground. I also need you as part of the acquisition team. I want you to shadow me for the first few runs, and eventually I want you to build a small team. IF".

He paused as if to emphasise the last word.

"If you can follow orders, take direction and put the team and our collective mission first.

"I can do that."

"I know you can," he said, "but you still need to show it to not only me but everyone else. You need to earn their respect."

I nodded, and he turned to walk away.

"Hold up," I said. I tried to make it non-threatening, argumentative or abrupt. I'm not sure if I succeeded. Even so,

Uncle Joe turned back around and faced me. A passive look on his face. Super difficult to read.

"In the meeting you said you'd never seen one of those things before."

He nodded, not saying anything.

"But out there, when we found it, you said that you'd seen something similar. What gives? Which one is the truth?"

"Both," he said in a tone that was decidedly matter-of-fact.

"What did you mean, then?"

For a split second my uncle looked genuinely pained. In a rare break of character, he took a breath and paused, almost awkwardly.

He took a few steps forward and looked around before speaking quietly.

"I didn't lie," he said. "I haven't seen specifically one of those things before."

"But", I said

"BUT", he said, cutting me short, "I have seen something similar, many years ago."

"What was it? And where?"

"I still don't know that what," he said

"And the where?"

He looked at me and blinked a few times; seconds ticked by before he spoke again. I felt a sort of brooding tension.

"Your father's lab."

EIGHTEEN

Confusion was the order of the day. I had no idea what I should think or how I should react. I could barely process the existence of whatever weird, hot and disgustingly foul-stenched thing was sat in the house a few miles back. Let alone the existence of many more of them. Let alone the possibility that my father might somehow be involved. And in the military, no less. Or at least for the military. My uncle was tight-lipped on the details; even as normal life appeared to be crumbling and was being left far behind with each passing day, there were still secrets in the darkest shadows.

I replayed the conversation again and again in my mind, but nothing made sense. And now I was too wired to go to sleep, even though I felt as tired as I've ever been.

My uncle had explained that his unit, group or whatever, had been based out of some kind of base near where my folks had lived and that he was testing some new weaponry or something. I never even knew there was a military base near where we lived; it all seemed so suburban. In any case my uncle had said that Dad was involved in testing and analysis of foreign substances and organisms and their application within the military. He didn't and couldn't guess what was meant by 'foreign', only that it was an effort to weaponise something. Uncle Joe didn't know any other details, only that he and his men were meant to be testing whatever it was that was being developed. Apparently it all came to metaphorical blows, which was the root of my uncle falling out with my father. This somehow led to Uncle Joe leaving the military. There was a subtle hint that there was more to it, but Joe wasn't going to tell me, at least not right now.

Why it took this many years for me to find out and why Dad never told me anything about this was a mystery. Uncle Joe tried to help, to explain that my father couldn't have told me anything. Absolute secrecy was demanded and expected. The project, or whatever they were working on, was akin to the Manhattan Project. The analogy troubled me, especially given the current circumstances.

This didn't make any sense; for as long as I remember, Dad was just a biologist working at a local university. Turns out the university might not be as straightforward as I previously thought. I suddenly wanted to talk to Mom and Dad and ask what the hell had been going on. I felt lied to. Deceived. Did Mom even know about this? My uncle couldn't or wouldn't say. He'd left me to process this. He apologised, although I'm not sure what for. And so I sat on my makeshift bed that was now a sort of home and wondered about what the hell I was going to do with all this new information.

Since I couldn't sleep, I went for a walk. I pushed off my duvet, slipped on my sneakers (sorry, trainers), and shuffled outside to get some fresh air. As I stepped outside, the temperature dropped suddenly. The bracing night air filled my lungs with every breath. I walked over to the car park and found a nice kerb to sit on and gaze up at the night sky. More stars than I'd seen before were suspended for all to see. Now that more and more lights had been extinguished, more of the heavens were exposed for all to see. I found it kind of humbling and very hypnotic. I sat for several minutes, taking it all in. I didn't hear anyone approach; I just heard a voice from behind me.

"Hey. Can I join?"

"Sure, Josh. How are things?"

He clumsily sat down next to me and looked up at the sky as well.

"Okay. "Busy," he said. "But I guess you're probably busier than me."

"Couldn't sleep?" I asked

"Something like that," he said with a hint of humour

"Why do I get the feeling that you're up to no good?"

"It's my style."

"You have no style."

We both laughed. Corny as it sounds, I couldn't remember the last time I laughed. Probably with Charlie. I suddenly felt sad. I was aware of a dull, almost stinging sensation at the back of my head. I took a breath and remembered what Uncle Joe had said.

"Listen," said Josh, which was a weird thing the English did. Saying 'listen' while I was already listening. I've since figured out it's when someone wants to tell you something important. They're showing you this is serious without actually saying, 'Hey, I need to talk to you or tell you something, and it's pretty serious to me, so pay attention.' He continued without any more prompting from me.

"You know, if it wasn't for you and Charlie, I wouldn't have survived what happened back at home. I'd probably be..." He trailed off, remembering that one of us didn't make it.

"You saved my life, too," I said. "If it wasn't for you, I'd have stormed in and got myself fucked up when Charlie's truck caught fire."

I turned to Josh.

"I owe you my life."

"I owe you mine. Let's call it quits."

"Even Stevens", I said

He laughed. "Look at you picking up the local colloquiums."

There was another pause; only this time, it was easy, not awkward or tense. Like breathing.

"So how come you're out and about in the middle of the night?" He asked

"Couldn't sleep. Too many thoughts, too many voices."

"I heard a rumour," he started to say

"Please, not an Umbrella Academy reference."

"Hey, I really did hear a rumour that something's afoot."

"Well, that's specific," I said. Hoping the sarcasm wasn't lost on him.

"Specifically, I heard you and Uncle Joe found something that's got everyone in a fluster in Patty's little circle of leadership."

"Please don't call her Patty; you know that's..."

"I know, I know." He said, "Sorry."

There was a slight pause; I could practically hear the gears turning in Josh's head.

"But she is AAAAALLLLLLLL Patty!"

"OH MY GOD," I whispered, realising that other people might be asleep. "Are you doiking her?"

"Doiking?" said Josh, pretending to be shocked. "Such an ungentlemanly concept."

He started putting on a posh British accent to add to the effect.

"I would only consider our union to be a celebration of divine lovemaking."

I fake retched for added effect. Puerile, I know.

"Oh my god. Please don't ever describe it that way again."

"You mean..."

"Stop." I said in hushed tones, "I don't want to know."

Josh sniffed the air, like some kind of weird man-dog

"Jealousy, methinks."

"I'm quite happy keeping to myself, thank you very much."

We laughed a little, and for a moment, it felt like old times. Back at the house. Video games, movies, anime and pizza. Good times. They seemed so far away now. As if it were a different life altogether. I wondered if we'd ever get back to that. To whatever passed as normal. At the time life sometimes felt like a grind, almost oppressive. But now. Now it seemed so easy. I couldn't help but wonder just how much of life we, collectively, had squandered.

"So tell me." said Josh, "What did you find?"

"I have no idea. Freakishly weird. It looks like a living fossil, and the smell is. Indescribable. It's practically panic-inducing."

Josh considered what I'd said for a moment or two.

"Where did you hear the rumours?" I asked

"I overheard Callen talking to a few of the other guys over a few beers. But he was suitably vague. Said he'd be leading the team or something."

I rolled my eyes, although no one could see.

"He sure can talk" was all i could say that was complimentary or at least as positive as I could muster

"So you don't like him?" Asked Josh

I turned to him, my face scrunched up.

"You have a terrible poker face," he said

"Sue me."

Another pause. The chill of the air was starting to nibble at my fingertips.

"What the hell are we doing?" asked Josh. I hopped to the aether because I had no answers. Not anything sensible.

Josh sighed, and I recognised in his demeanour something I'd been struggling with. Adaptation to something new. I wanted to say something, but I could barely find the words for myself, let alone him. Instead, I looked up at the multitude of bright speckles splashed in the night sky and let the universe speak for itself.

"I could murder a pizza right about now."

It was my turn to sigh.

"Meat Feast with Jalapeños and Pineapple," I said

"I can go one better," said Josh, in challenge "Duck and onion".

"Oh shit! With that sweet hoisin sauce."

Involuntarily, I rubbed my hands. Such a silly thing to miss, and I was surprised at how quickly I'd forgotten and how desperately I wanted a pizza right now. Maybe it wasn't the pizza so much, but the connection that came with it. To friends. To memories.

"Maybe one day we'll get to have duck pizza again."

Josh let out a deep exhale.

"I sure hope so," I said

Josh pushed himself up with a slight grunt. He staggered a little at being bent up on the edge of the kerb. He rubbed his hands and coughed a little.

"Well. Duty calls; I've got to make like a mechanic and ser..."

"You can stop right there. I know where this goes, and I don't want to hear it."

Josh shrugged.

"I'll catch you later. Maybe I'll see you tomorrow?"

"Sure. Have yourself a good night."

"Oh, I will," he said with a smile

"Behave yourself."

"Never." he added as he sauntered off.

It was nice to see Josh happy; for far too long he seemed to have a cloud over him. Maybe all this calamity did him some good.

I stayed outside in the cool air, staring at the infinite void above for quite a while. I got lost in the sprawling majesty of it all. When I found my eyes getting heavy, it was a task to get up. My knees ached and complained, and my back felt like someone had stood on it for hours.

I stretched for a moment, easing the aches before heading back inside the center to find my bed and to succumb to the sweet darkness of sleep.

Tomorrow wasn't going to wait.

NINETEEN

My dreams consisted of floating in nothingness, floating in a suffocating black void, devoid of any detail but the shining lighting ahead of me. Somehow I flew, or drifted, towards the light. I sensed that I was going fast and getting faster, but the light never got any larger. I eventually realised the futility and came to a stop, floating in darkness like I was underwater. My movements felt strange, not quite slower but almost smoother. I realised I wasn't breathing in this world. I didn't need to I guess. I spun in place and did somersaults. It soon became apparent that I couldn't move forward or backwards. I felt panicked but for some reason I knew it was a dream. The light was gently pulsing ahead of me. I couldn't perceive the distance, but it seemed both far away and very close at the same time.

I noticed something at the periphery of my vision and turned towards the void. At first I couldn't make anything out, just the dull blackness of space, or whatever this was. My eyes couldn't focus on what it was. All I could see was a glimpse of something. Something large, maybe, or something small, magnified. Shadows, shapes. I peered into the darkness to try and pick out details, but it was useless. I could barely make out the movement. It was almost like several shapes moving together. Like a multitude of writhing worms bundled together. As soon as the thought crossed my mind, the image cleared, and I could suddenly see more, the barest hint of colour. Thin tendrils writhed and tumbled together in the void. A deep, almost brownish, green. I was suddenly aware that they made a noise, like wood slowly breaking. Like a slow snap of a branch under pressure. And then I was falling. My whole body jolted. The light rushed towards me, and I suddenly felt a vice-like grip on my shoulder, and a deep voice was saying my name, over and over.

My eyes opened suddenly. I found myself awake.

"I'm awake; I'm up."

My eyes focused on the figure looming over me. It was Uncle Joe.

"Morning, sleeping beauty. Time to go shopping!"

I have foggy memories of when I was much younger. Maybe five or six, it's difficult to tell, of when Mom and Uncle Joe would take me to the mall. Dad was constantly working. In fact, for the large portion of my developing years, he hardly seemed to be present. Or at least that was my memory of it. In any case, I remember walking around the huge buildings with bright lights and big noises. We'd walk around for what seemed like hours, going to book stores, toy stores and music stores. Everything seemed larger and brighter. I remember laughing lots, and Mom too. In hindsight I can't remember the last time I recalled Dad laughing. He was a serious man doing serious work. He didn't have time for joviality and frivolity. And yet there was a tender, gentler side to him. More than you would expect, or at least from his outward demeanour, would suggest. I remembered the car journeys to and from the mall, Joe's latest muscle car roaring and growling down the highway. I can remember laughing in the backseat and watching the world race by and my mom squeaking as we took corners way too fast for her liking.

I returned to the real world from my daydreams and reminiscing with a jolt. The sunlight of the morning streaming over the lush green landscape. The slow plodding of waking boots on the hard road as our little group outing of five people walked towards Penrith. Aside from myself and my uncle, we had brought three volunteers. Our task today would be to scout out local stores for supplies. This would involve us going near the truck stop where Amos and his folks were camping out, but since they were mostly active towards the end of the day and into the night, we figured we could keep a low profile and keep out of their way, and they wouldn't know any better. For weeks we had kept a distance and stayed out of their way. We'd scrounged as much as we could from smaller shops that were tucked away in tiny villages and raided the houses that were nearby. We'd also stripped the service station down the road and were using it as a makeshift storage area for anything that we didn't have a use for, at least not in the short term. We were becoming hoarders, and anything that might have a use was kept. Valuable items such as tools and food came back to the center with us, along with anything else that we might need: batteries and raw materials for weapons and defence. In terms of weaponry, we had crafted and improvised our own. My uncle was coy about what weaponry he had, and I figured he was keeping a few surprises in the Bronco. Guns and the like weren't our thing. My uncle had surmised that there would be guns in some farmhouses, but until now nothing had turned up. Either the farmers around us didn't have them, had stashed them very safely or the more worrisome theory; someone else had beaten us to them. In hushed whispers, in the quiet moments in small dark corners, speculation grew about what weapons

Amos might have and when he might use them. That whack job would have a field day. I took stock of what we had between us. I had stumbled upon a wooden baseball bat, which I immediately felt at home with. It bounced and jolted a little on my back, reminding me of its weight. I had crafted a pretty sweet sling from bits of an old backpack I had found. I had never been into arts and crafts too much, but I must admit to being proud of my little creation. I had practised taking the bat out quickly from its sling many times. Although not in front of a mirror. I hadn't gone full De Niro just yet. My uncle carried a large knife, strapped to his right leg, a dangerous-looking piece of metal. The other three in our party clasped more homemade and scavenged items, ready to defend themselves if need be. We all had pretty much the same style of weaponry; heavy blunt instruments.

So here we were, a strange band of five people walking in silence, in single file, armed with bats and backpacks, on a mission to see what we could scavenge.

As we crossed over the first roundabout. We all looked up and down, somewhat anxiously, at the M6. Looking for any sign of life or activity. As we crossed, I could see the plane which had brought me and Josh here. It looked remarkably undamaged and intact. I had asked my uncle about seeing what we could scavenge from it, but he waved us on. The little plane would've been too easy a target to booby trap. The logic made sense, but I'd still like to check it out. In any case we pressed on. The traffic lights, which were once working, had now blinked out of existence. They stood now forever dark, waiting for a time when they could once again start and stop the flow of traffic.

We continued down the dual carriageway as if heading away from Penrith. The first left that we could take would take us too close to the truck stop. My uncle didn't want us to tempt fate too much, and so we walked a few minutes down to the next roundabout. A KFC, or what was left of it, stood to the left. The windows had been broken, and there was a whole mess of litter strewn around the small car park. What was once inside was now outside. Boxes of fast food were torn open and strewn around; there was a dim smell of rotting chicken which had been subjected to the outdoor elements, now that they were free of their frozen state. A few crows bounced around and pecked at the odds and ends. A large amount of French fries were littered everywhere, and stacks of paper cups tumbled and rolled around. The group seemed to come to a brief stop and take in the devastation. The whole building had clearly been ransacked. Inside looked worse than the outside. Inventory had been, seemingly, thrown everywhere. Anything that wasn't fixed to a surface looked to have been thrown at a wall or something else. Various red splatters now decorated the walls and one window, which had managed, somehow, to survive.

"I really hope that's ketchup." said one of the guys behind me

No one said anything. My uncle moved forward and followed the road that looked to lead into the town center, and we all followed.

There didn't look to be a soul around as we slowly walked down the street. Even worse, there were no sounds or noises you'd associate with a small town. Where you'd hear the rumble of traffic, the banging and clattering of workers, or maybe machinery working in the distance, there was nothing. Aside from the odd bird chirping.

A set of buildings with slanted rooms lined the road to the right. Signs pointed to Penrith Hospital. One of our group suggested we go look, but Uncle Joe confirmed that the building had been ransacked of supplies; he'd taken other teams inside a few times to see what could be scavenged. Although they did find a few useful supplies, everything was mostly gone. Uncle Joe's real target was the large store and garden centre. Which was hidden behind a row of trees and high vegetation.

Signs pointed to the customer entrance, and we followed

the large opening into the small car park. Litter and other trash lay around. Glass was broken and scattered around a few abandoned cars. As we approached the main entrance, we could see garbage had built up but luckily, however, the glass in the main doors had remained intact. We moved cautiously as a group. My uncle nodded to one of the guys in our team.

"Okay, Sam, get us in."

The blonde-haired and somewhat lanky Sam nodded back and smiled nervously. He shuffled to the nearest window and removed his backpack and pulled out a hammer and a small metal object. He held the long spike-like object at the very corner of the bottom glass pane and gave it a heavy tap with the hammer. The glass cracked in an instant, but didn't shatter. Sam took the hammer and knocked the glass out. It tinkled into the hard ground in a pleasing manner.

"Okay," said Uncle Joe "The clock is ticking. remembered what we talked about, what we trained for. Don't panic and follow my lead."

Everyone nodded.

My uncle nodded towards another member of the team, Daryl, a somewhat overweight individual who was actually slowly losing the weight, what with food being rationed and the extra exercise.

One by one we scrambled into the dark building, with Uncle Joes being the last one in.

Even though there was no light and not that many windows, it was amazing just how much light the building let inside. The hope had been to find a large cache of food, cleaning and hygiene supplies. However, looking at the empty shelves and the strewn packets of random items on the floor, it looked like the large majority of the store had been gone through already. There was still hope as well as they picked through what was left. I found a few useful items, such as bleach and dishwashing liquid, that I could take back with me. Someone had, obviously, found an alternate way in. We stayed together trying to find anything more we could salvage. The further we ventured into the back of the store, the darker it got. I was considering using my head torch, which I had stashed in my pocket, when I heard a sound from behind. The dropping a something heavy on the floor. And then there were more sounds behind us. Footsteps. A gentle sound of metal on metal, maybe, and more footsteps to the left and right. The dim light from the front of the store illuminated the darker rear, but only a little.

"Well! Well! "Well!" said a somewhat raspy voice. "Look what we have here."

"Keep calm," whispered my uncle. "Stay focused; let me do the talking."

No one said anything. I heard one of the other guys breathing heavily. I hoped he wouldn't freeze. I had, at this point, enough experience to know that freezing wasn't going to be an issue for me.

A figure stepped out from the shadows. I could see a few more moving in the darkness behind him. It was difficult to make out just how many there were, but I figured at least five, maybe six. Add another three or four towards our rear, and we'd be outnumbered.

The looming figure in front of us made a tutting sound.

"Well, isn't this a pretty picture!"

The light from the front of the store projected a sort of halo around the figure's body; it was difficult to make out any real detail. Not that it mattered. We weren't here to make friends, and I assumed neither were they.

"I must admit," he continued, "I had my doubts that anyone would show up. But here you are. I guess I should've had more faith in the old coot. I guess he's not as clueless as we thought. And to think you've been sold out by one of your own."

A small ripple of laughs echoed from the small gathering of figures behind the figure and quickly died out and back into silence.

A pregnant pause. The tension was so thick, you could eat it with a spoon.

"What? No snappy comeback?"

"What do you want?" Asked my uncle, in a tone devoid of emotion.

"Want? Want? There is no want. What I need, yes NEEEED..."

Even in the dim light I could see the man's wild, crazed eyes, full of malice.

"Save the melodramatic bullshit," said my uncle, cutting in.

The tall stranger scowled and for a split second looked like he was going to say something.

I don't know what happened in that moment, but there was something in the air, something oppressive. My eyes flitted left and right, trying to keep tabs on who was where. The figures kept on shifting, moving, and relocating. It was like a slow-moving swarm that ever changed. Our little group was the polar opposite. We were akin to statues. I flexed my leg muscles and felt them ache.

"Now, Amos wanted you back at camp. But he never said all of you had to make it and in what condition, neither."

The stranger flashed an evil smile which appeared much larger than normal in the half-light. The tension in the air shifted as the stranger held up some kind of knife. I hadn't seen where it had come from, but that wasn't important right now.

"Go," said Uncle Joe, his voice deep and menacing.

Our small team was a mishmash of people, and to look at us, you'd assume we were exactly what we looked like: a ragtag group trying to survive. Unprepared for this new world. Barely able to function. And to be fair, we were a little like that, but we had become something different over the weeks that had stretched beforehand. We had lived together, trained together, and worked together. Drills, tests, dry runs, more drills. Joe had successfully predicted this exact event. Right now it seemed less of a prediction but more foresight. Even before setting out, he warned us that not only should we be ready for something like this, but also that this was most likely where it would happen. And to our credit, we were ready. My uncle had moulded us from a collection of different parts into something that resembled a whole. We were starting to function like we felt; a proper team.

When we had been pushed into our corner, we knew what to do, lining ourselves up with our opponents, ready, waiting to receive the command from Uncle Joe.

As soon as the words escaped from Uncle Joe's mouth, we sprang into action.

I dashed forward and barrelled into one of the figures and pushed him into another. There was a heavy grunt as the two collided. I reached for my bat, and it slipped quickly from the improvised sling. I drew back and brought the heavy wooden implement down as hard as I could, not really aiming at anything specific. The bat found its target with a heavy crack, and I felt the handle jolt as my weapon bounced against something hard, a kneecap maybe. One of the figures cried out in pain. Confused, one scrambled and pushed against the other trying to get free as I brought the bat around again for another volley and another, and another. Each blow a satisfying thud. Until they ceased to move. I briefly looked around to see blurs of rapid movement. I heard screams, shouts and foul language.

Our would-be captors were seemingly unprepared and taken by surprise.

Looking towards the front entrance, I couldn't see any movement or any signs of what might be reinforcements. I smiled to myself. I looked back towards the chaotic scene and saw a figure lope towards me; my hands tightened on the bat, but I realised it was Daryl, followed by Sam.

"Let's go, like we planned." I said and began moving towards the entrance and the light of the day.

Behind us echoed the sounds of violence. The sounds of

screaming and a whole bunch of swearing, the familiar song of those who were infected. Although unnerving, it was a good sound to hear. It let us know we were winning this little skirmish.

As we exited, we looked around for any other resistance. It was our job to make sure the exit was clear and unobstructed. Sam and Daryl half jogged down the side of the building, back towards the car park, while I monitored the main entrance. After a few moments they waved back, letting me know it was all clear.

I peered towards the dark hole that was the entrance, now silent. I craned my neck trying to make out anything from within until I heard several footsteps. Heavy feet against broken and discarded items. A few seconds later and the remaining member of our team and my uncle emerged. My uncle looked like he'd just been out to buy milk. The other guy looked a bit shocked, breathing heavily. Sam and Daryl had walked back up to join us. Looking around, we didn't look too worse for wear. A few scratches here and there. There were the odd spatters of blood over our clothes and weapons.

"Everyone okay?" asked Uncle Joe

I nodded and took a breath. Collectively we all let out a sigh of relief. The shouts and screams had disappeared. We have literally and figuratively taken no prisoners. I knew this would be seen as escalation. Amos would paint us as the enemy, as we did him.

"Let's get out of here before things get any worse."

We all turned and walked at a brisk pace, heading out of the car park and starting to retrace our route back to the center.

"What happens next?" I asked

But before Uncle Joe could answer, his radio beeped.

He plucked the small unit from his belt and held it to his mouth.

"Go ahead."

A slightly distorted voice, which I couldn't make out who, cracked in response. They sounded flustered, and before they finished their sentence, I knew something was wrong.

"..llen. Double cross..."

"Say again," said my uncle. "You're not coming in clear."

"...aken Vivan."

"Say again!" asked Uncle Joe

My stomach tightened, and I set my jaw. The radio crackled to life again.

"It's Callen," said the scratchy voice. "He's killed sev...." crackles and pops interrupted the transmission before continuing, "...and taken Vivian."

"Copy," said my uncle. "Everyone stay put; I'll be there in ten."

There was no response from the radio.

"Alright, double time."

And with that, we all broke out into a light jog for the rest of the journey back to the center.

No one said anything on the way back. The only sounds were the rhythmic thumping of our feet onto the hard ground and the ragged breaths as we neared our destination. I tried to focus on something, anything to distract my mind, but all I could think of was a perverse sense of satisfaction at being right and all the ways that Callen could and would pay.

TWENTY

The center was a hubbub of activity. A pronounced loud chatter from almost everyone meant you could feel that panic setting in. I saw a few people packing up belongings, stuffing them urgently into their vehicles. It would appear as though some people had had enough and were bailing. I wondered, as my uncle and I picked our way through the car park and headed into the center, where they would go and what they would do. It had only been a few months, and already the vestiges of modern civilisation were starting to erode. Water had stopped running from the mains, and we could see the power grid had largely failed. On a night where once we could see a carpet of lights dotted around the landscape, now there were none. There were a few pinpricks here and there, maybe people like us who had their own generators or some other way of keeping the lights on. I imagine whoever had solar power probably felt vindicated, along with all those preppers in bunkers. Although it seemed that building bunkers was largely an American pastime. I'm sure several home-built ones did exist, but not like back home. Or maybe it was the TV shows that painted a different picture than reality, using it to make fun of those people. To be honest, I made fun of them too. Laughing at how they'd built an airtight underground cellar with goodness knows how much food and water, with generators and all the doodads. I, like many, laughed at the expense and how redundant it was. I guess we're not laughing now.

A serious-looking Patricia greeted us at the meeting area, surrounded by a phalanx of other people. My uncle wasted no time in taking control.

"Bring me up to speed." he said to Patricia, seemingly ignoring everyone else that appeared to be clamouring for some kind of attention. A crowd of people started to gather, interested to see what would happen and how things would go down, I assumed.

"I don't know specifics. What I do know is that Callen, Vivian and two volunteers went to investigate the specimen you found. At some point the two volunteers were killed. Duncan found them down the road after they failed to check in and we couldn't raise them on the radio."

My uncle nodded to Duncan.

"I assume you'd tried to communicate with him?"

"We only go one response," said Duncan "If we wanted to guarantee Vivian's safety, no one should try to follow."

"I guess this confirms our suspicions."

Duncan nodded grimly.

"You knew?" Said Patricia accusingly

"We didn't know anything for sure," said Joe, "but we had an inkling. It's just a shame that Vivian's been caught up in this. I honestly didn't think he'd be this bold. I suspected he'd try to sell us out. But this is next-level scum-baggery."

Someone behind Patricia, looking less than happy, opened their mouth to say something, but my uncle cut them off deftly.

"I can see you're all upset, but if you haven't got any pertinent information, then I'll kindly ask you to remain quiet. We need to resolve this situation quickly, before it escalates."

"There's already two dead," said someone at the periphery

"Like I said. Information and solutions before we turn on

each other. If you want to shout and accuse each other, you can do it later when I'm not here. I'm not interested in anything else, other than getting Vivian back alive and well."

People shifted in the background and grumbled.

"Good. Any other intel I should be aware of?"

No one said anything else, and he nodded.

"First things first. Anyone not directly associated with security or operations beyond the center boundary, please vacate the room."

There was a ripple of muffled dissent, and my uncle, once again, nipped any arguments straight in the bud.

"Time is of the essence, and I need a small, focused team to get Vivian back. The more people that are involved, the greater the risk of failure."

There were nervous glances, but eventually people started filing out.

"Thank you. Patricia will make sure everyone is updated as soon as we're done here."

A few moments later, the room seemed much larger. The echoes of loud chatter were still floating into the room as people, noisily, made their way back outside. A few, overly loud, comments about respect and manners floated in, but Uncle Joe showed no signs of being affected by them.

"Cab, if you can get the door, please."

I nodded and closed the door to the meeting area.

"Which channel is Callen on?" Asked Joe as he plucked his radio from his belt, his rough fingers hovering over the channel selection knob.

"Seven," answered Duncan

My uncle quickly turned the selector, which clicked with each turn.

"Okay," said my uncle, taking a quick glance at everyone. "I guess here goes nothing."

Joe pushed the transmit button and left dead space for a second or two before speaking into the radio.

"Callen, this is Joe. come back."

There was a long pause which stretched into seconds. My uncle pulled the radio back to his face, but the speaker burst into life before he could transmit again.

"Hey Joe, I guess it was only a matter of time before you got caught up."

"What's going on?"

"Oh, you know, the usual. Survival. Husslin'"

"Care to explain?"

"Not really?"

"I find that hard to believe, considering the size of your mouth."

A laugh crackled from the radio.

"Now, now. I thought they trained you not to antagonise whomever you're negotiating with."

"Negotiation? Is that what this is? Besides, I never trained for that sort of thing."

There was another long pause before my uncle pressed the transmit button.

"What is it that you want, Callen?"

"Harsher punishment for parole violators, Stan!"

My uncle looked confused.

There was a distorted laugh from the radio; the idiot was purposely transmitting that.

"Sorry, Joe," said Callen. "I know you don't quite understand, but the reality is. You don't have what I want."

Uncle Joe took a breath.

"I'm sure we can come to some arrangement."

"I'm pretty sure that's not going to work for me."

"Last chance. Let Vivian go, and I can help you figure this out; we can get you what you want."

"You're not the person I need to deal with," said Callen. "You can't help."

"Last chance. You won't get another opportunity. Going down this path doesn't end well for you."

"It's funny, because what you're saying sounds like it should be big and scary, but you sound desperate, Joe. Like I said, you don't have what I need, can't get what I need, and thus, I don't need you. Go fuck yourself, Joe."

My uncle didn't say anything. He calmly got up from the table and clicked the radio off.

"Give me a few minutes," he said and walked out of the room, closing the door behind him.

The few people in the room looked at each other, confused. A few people looked at me, and I had no idea, either. The room was buzzing with a nervous energy. But no one made a move; we all sort of looked at each other and at the clock as the second hand slowly edged forward with each passing second.

Five minutes seemed like half an hour when Uncle Joe returned, with a calm look on his face that I couldn't read. In his hand, another radio. He sat back down at the table and carefully placed the device in front of him.

Everyone looked even more confused.

"Now, we wait," he announced

The clock continued its slow march forwards; seconds drew on into minutes. Everyone seems to be getting more and more uncomfortable in the silence. There were hushed whispers from someone, a few people coughed, and people shuffled in their seats. The tension was starting to get unbearable when all of a sudden the silence was cut as the radio buzzed and clicked a few times, then a soft, quiet, female voice emerged from the speaker of the small radio.

"Southwaite, northbound"

My uncle clicked the transmit button twice and then turned the radio off.

He stood up and slid the radio my way. The room erupted in a deluge of loud questions.

Uncle Joe held his hands out and raised his voice

"Everyone calm down, this is all in hand. Patricia, co-ordinate with Duncan; he already knows what to do."

Without missing a beat, he turned to me.

"Cab, let's go."

The next thing I knew, he was leading me out of the room and through the small gathering of people that were outside and towards the Bronco.

We climbed in and buckled our seat belts.

"This might get a little messy," he said, starting up the vehicle.

The low rumble of the engine vibrating through my seat. He pulled the vehicle around the building and towards the entrance, where already the main "gate" was being pulled back. The gap seemed like it was only just big enough for us to fit through when the Bronco lurched forward, screeching a little as the tyres struggled to find grip as the newer, more powerful engine drove the old vehicle forward. We almost slid around the corner of the entrance onto the main road and tore down the asphalt; the raspy performance engine was pleased to finally be working as designed. We quickly reached the end of the road, and at first I thought we were turning onto the M6, but Uncle Joe turned off before we could reach the roundabout.

The vehicle swung wildly left, and I was shifted abruptly to the right. A funny, almost giggling sound escaped from my mouth.

"Hold on. This might get a little bumpy!"

"Where the hell are we going?" I said, half shouting over the engine as my uncle forced it up through the gears.

"Southwaite services. We're taking the back roads; we don't want to tip Amos or one of his goons who might be looking out for us."

"What's going on?" I asked but didn't get a reply.

I shrugged a little and took a breath and looked out the window. My focus was on the countryside whipping by us at a truly terrifying speed. I was powerless to do anything but to sit and wait for us to arrive at our destination, hopefully intact. The little orange Bronco tore through the scenery. Our path led us down tight country roads and through small villages. We crossed back and forth over the

M6 twice before eventually getting onto a road that was fairly straight and devoid of any harsh turns, which was better for my constitution. I'm normally iron-willed when it comes to crazy driving, but today Uncle Joe was on a different level. There were several times we were sliding around corners, the Bronco seemingly desperate to find traction where it could, the tyres squealing in protest. On the straighter roads I caught glimpses of motorway every so often. It looked like we were following it fairly closely. A few larger houses buzzed by, but these weren't of interest to us.

The road stretched out in front of us, and we could see not only the M6 but also a service station.

"That's it," said Uncle Joe.

In response he seemed to push his foot further to the floor, and the Bronco surged a little more, and then he cut the power. The engine gurgled to a stop, and suddenly we were coasting.

I must've looked confused and maybe a little alarmed.

"Just in case we're not the first ones here." He said with a slight smile.

The Bronco coasted for quite a while, slowly bleeding off speed. A side road, leading right, opened up, and I could see the buildings of the service station clearly as we passed by.

"We'll park somewhere here and keep a low profile."

The Bronco was rapidly running out of momentum. Its weight now working against it.

"Aha!"

Uncle Joe pulled the vehicle to the left and stopped the orange 4x4 in front of a metal gate which appeared to be the entrance to a farmer's field.

Before getting out of the vehicle, he reached behind the passenger seat and fished out a set of binoculars. He reached back again and pulled out a slightly smaller set.

"Here," he said, handing me the smaller set. "They're not great, but they'll do."

"Thanks," which came out more like a question than anything else.

Emerging from the Bronco, we crossed the road and into the field and headed to where we could see the outlines of small details of buildings through a small array of trees. As we got closer we could see there was no real fence; the only hint of a boundary was a line of carefully planted bushes. The going was fairly easy, but the ground was uneven. We passed two trees nestled closely together and made for the line of trees in front of us. As we approached the tree line, we could just about see through and into the large expanse of what would've been the truck park. Our view of the car park was obstructed by another thick expanse of greenery. From our vantage point I could only see a small section of the car park as the bushes gave way to an access road to the left. Various signs appeared to be dotted around the periphery, telling drivers which vehicles were to be parked and where. I scanned around and couldn't see anyone or any sign of activity.

"Doesn't look like anyone is here yet." said uncle Joe

He looked left and right, scanning the surroundings.

"Okay," he said. "stay here; I need to see if there's anyone in the car park."

"Wait," I started to say, but he was off in a low, almost loping, jog before I could add anything else.

All I could do was stand fast, as my uncle would've put it. I saw him run down the length of the tree line where we were hidden. A few places down the tree line were very thin, where there was minimal cover. Where I was hunkered down was fairly thick, dark and secluded. I could make out the shape of Uncle Joe crouching down. He appeared to hold his binos to his face as he looked down the access road to the M6, or at least that's where I thought he was looking.

I looked around myself, trying to see any signs of life or movement of any kind. The whole place was deserted. Something hard and cold formed in the pit of my stomach. I tried not to think of anything else but to watch and wait. To observe only what I saw and not to think or ponder anything else. Especially not getting captured and tortured by Amos and his goons.

'Dammit!'

I had lost myself, temporarily, in those darker thoughts when Uncle Joe returned.

"We're good," he said. "No one else is around."

Joe crouched down beside me and scanned the area, looking left and right. Waiting.

"What are we doing here?" I asked in a low whisper

"Waiting."

"Waiting for what?"

"Waiting to see if I'm an idiot."

"What?"

Uncle Joe chuckled

"We're waiting for the meeting of the great minds."

"This is all very cryptic."

"We're just going to see how this plays out and see if we can't turn it to our advantage."

I sighed. Either I wasn't going to get the full story, or the story wasn't developed enough to tell. For the time being I just sat, observed and waited. I reached into my pocket, hoping to find gum but my hand found a hard plastic shape. Confused, I pulled the object out of my pocket only to come eye to eye with the mocking gaze of a purple-haired troll. Its cute chubby cheeks seemingly mocking me. I rolled my eyes and stuffed the creature back into my pocket.

After a few minutes I heard a dull droning sound. At first it was difficult to pinpoint where it was coming from. The faint sound grew and seemingly disappeared before returning a few minutes later. This time growing louder. Nearer. Both my uncle and I looked left and right. The noise grew louder and became the dull sound of what I thought was a motorcycle, maybe a dirt bike.

It turns out I was only half wrong, as I saw movement to the left. Emerging from behind the fuel station was a small quad bike, pulling a smaller trailer filled with boxes, maybe. A rack on the back of the quad held several large fuel cans, strapped to the machine. I looked closely and could see that the rider was Callen, sans helmet. As he drew parallel with the fuel station, he slowed down and looked around. Both my uncle and I hunkered down. We were confident that we couldn't be seen, but there was no reason not to give any more of a target than we had to. Callen rode the bike around the truck stop and passed us by. The high-pitched ringing of the engine echoed in my ears. He disappeared from view, most likely scoping out the car park before riding back past us. Luckily Callen had decided that it would be best to use the more open truck parking area rather than the more enclosed car park. He turned the quad and trailer around, facing the access road which vehicles would normally come up from the south.

Seconds stretched into minutes, and minutes stretched on and on. Ten minutes ended up feeling like an hour, and a long, gruelling hour at that. I shifted a few times and was worried that I'd snap a twig or sneeze or do something to give away our position. Uncle Joe divided his attention between Callen and the entrance road of the service station. I peered through the dual lenses of the binoculars and watched Callen like a hawk. It was then that something prickled at the back of my neck, something like an uneasy feeling. I glanced around anxiously.

"You good?" Asked Uncle Joe.

"Yeah," I said, although the word didn't sound too confident. "I feel like we're being watched."

"There's no one else but us; stay focused."

I took a breath and pushed the strange feeling down and brought the binos back to my eyes and played with the dial to bring Callen back into focus.

Callen looked at his watch a few times, obviously anxious. I wondered just how long we'd be waiting or if Callen would give up. But it was then I heard the drone of a vehicle approaching from the northbound access ramp that I gave up watching Callen and my head snapped to the right to see a banged-up old Transit van lumbering into view. It was white, or rather had been white and had accumulated so much filth, rust and damage that it looked closer to black than its original colour. Even so, the white peeked through on the top of the van as well as around the edges of the windscreen. I could see, sat in the front passenger seat, the gangly form of Amos. A rando driving. I wondered if it was just the two of them as the van chugged past our position and pulled into the truck parking lot; the exhaust emitted a stream of thick black smoke. The van swung around and parked at the very top of the parking area, leaving a fair distance between them and Callen, who only had eyes for the van. He kept still, perched on top of the quad, his hand at the controls. Maybe ready to bolt at the first sign of trouble or if he felt something wasn't right. The van's engine came to a stop, and Amos lumbered out of the passenger side and stalked slowly towards Callen. The back door of the van popped up, and three people emerged from within. I guess Amos wasn't taking any chances either.

Callen sat up, and I wondered if he thought about running. Either way, he remained seated on the quad as Amos approached and came to a stop about fifteen or so feet from Callen and his steed. The rest of Amos's crew came up behind him and stopped a few feet behind him.

I heard the sound of Callens voice first, but I couldn't make out what was being said.

There appeared to be some kind of exchange which ended in Callen climbing off the quad and approaching Amos. From afar he seemed his usual happy-go-lucky self. I pressed the set of binoculars to my eyes, and it was like I was teleported right there. I could see his smarmy, smiling face as he did his usual 'talk them into submission' thing. I moved from left to right, watching Amos and his crew. I watched as Callen shrugged and gestured his way through some kind of dialogue. Amos hardly moved; he was like stone. Callen was pointing to the trailer with boxes, and he held out his hand. He seemed to want to make a deal.

My uncle breathed deeply.

"I think now looks like a good time to play our hand. Let's see if Plan B is going to work."

"Plan B?"

I had no idea what he meant; he hadn't said anything about a Plan A, let alone a Plan B. I felt like I was just here for the ride. But with all things to do with my uncle, you're never around for a ride or just tagging along. There is always a learning moment to experience. I just had to get out of my own head and observe.

Uncle Joe pulled the radio off his belt, held it to his mouth and pressed the transmit button.

"Channel seven. Go."

There wasn't a reply from the radio, but something happened. Amos turned and barked at his crew; he spat angry words I couldn't quite make out. He then turned to Callen, who now appeared to be gesturing, looking like he was trying to calm the situation down. But I knew from bitter personal experience Amos was not someone who could be calmed down nor, most likely, wanted to be calmed down. The shouting escalated to jostling and pushing. Amos's crew started to spread out and almost surround Callen. Amos stepped forward and shoved Callen to the ground with his long, wiry arms. He stepped back and let his crew do the rest as they descended on him swiftly with a mixture of punches, kicks and assorted weapons. I could hear Callens shouting at first, but this quickly turned to screaming. He tried to fend off the attacks with an arm, but they were too many and too swift. The shouts and screams died, and Called lay on the ground, sprawled out, his face bloody. Amos looked down, seemingly admiring his handiwork, a sickeningly crooked smile on his face. He crouched down and mouthed words that were only possible for Callen to hear. From this distance I couldn't even tell if he was conscious or not, but Amos didn't seem to care either way. He stood up and motioned towards one of the men, who handed him a length of wood which looked like it could've been the handle of an axe. Amos looked at the club and expertly flicked it over length-ways before reaching as far back as he could and bringing the wooden shaft down onto Callens head. He did this several times, smiling as he did, before resorting to just stomping on Callens head, which soon enough looked like a mixed mess of colours and strange, gelatinous shapes. He finally stopped and looked at the mess on the ground and the gore that was left on his boot. He stared for a few seconds, shrugged and spat on the body of Callen. He wiped his boot on the ground a few times before heading back to his vehicle. His small pack followed; one broke rank and jumped on the quad Callen had driven in. The remaining men piled into the van, and they left in convoy, leaving the broken mess that was Callen on the ground.

I let the binos fall to my knees. I could see the truck and quad turning away and heading down what would've been the wrong way onto the motorway. Now it was just the quickest way back down the road.

"What the hell just happened?" I asked, still whispering

"Knowledge, power, influence. Sometimes making the right kind of friends in the wrong places can be a good thing."

"Is this a good thing?" I asked, but I never got an answer.

Uncle Joe was already moving, pushing himself up and heading towards the large parking area.

I followed, lagging behind a few paces as we pushed through the line of trees and bushes. He walked onto and over the dirty and stained tarmac, the years of use and abuse clearly showing. We made our way towards the corpse of Callen. I kept my distance as my uncle approached the body. I looked around, slightly paranoid that Amos and his crew would be back. But I saw and heard nothing. Joe looked down at the broken body before him. He sighed and shook his head, crouched down and went through Callen's pockets. I should've been shocked or at least looked away, but instead the sight of Callen on the floor held a certain fascination. It was almost no longer Callen but something different. Uncle Joe finally stood up and turned in a fluid movement and held up two keys on a keyring.

"What say we get out of here?"

We turned and started walking back, but instead of directly retracing our steps, which would've taken us back through the treeline and across the field which we trekked over, we elected to follow the access road which ran parallel to the field itself. It was the same road we stayed away from in order to keep a low profile. Now, however, it would be the easier and most direct route back to the Bronco. At the top of the road there was a small sign informing people that this was only for guest access to the hotel. I hadn't noticed anything on the way, but I didn't think too much about it; I was too busy trying to erase the image of Callens' head turned into meaty-chunky-jello.

"So what now?" I asked

"We find Vivian, hopefully in one piece, get her and us back to the center, grab some coffee and maybe some shut-eye."

"Sounds like a plan, but do you know where Vivian is?"

"Nope, but I hope she's wherever this is parked," he said, holding up the keys he found on Callen. They jingled ever so slightly.

"What do you think?" He asked

"What do I think? I think it's a small needle in a very big haystack."

We came to the end of the access road, which joined onto the main road; we turned right and saw the bright orange Bronco looking 100% conspicuous.

"Well, I think we can reduce the size of the metaphorical haystack."

"How are we going to do that?"

I paused to think for a few seconds

"Wait," I added. "You already know where to look, don't you?"

"Guilty as charged," he said with a smile.

"Is this where I have to figure this out on my own?"

"You have about a hundred feet to give me a destination."

Then it occurred to me. The quad. The sound was loud, then quiet and then loud again.

"The southbound side of the service station."

Uncle Joe opened the door and climbed into the driver's side of the Bronco. I half jogged around to the passenger side, which would normally be the driver's side in the UK if not for the left-hand drive of the imported vehicle. I jostled into the seat and wrestled the seatbelt on, closing the door with a metallic thunk.

"Tell me how you arrived at your conclusion, Cabbage?"

"The quad bike – I heard it loud, get quieter, and then loud again when it came into the truck stop. I figure it was Callen riding it down the entrance ramp and riding up the motorway before doubling back and coming into the service area from the northbound side."

Uncle Joe nodded and twisted the ignition key. The Bronco thundered into life.

"Not bad," he said

"Is that what you thought, too?"

"I figured it was the closest, easiest place to park a vehicle. Now let's go see if we can find Vivian and figure out what the hell is going on."

It didn't take us long to get to the southbound side of the service station; I suppose we could've walked over the bridge that linked the two, but having the Bronco would provide protection and a quick getaway if we needed it. My uncle elected to follow the same path as Callen, and we doubled back to the services and went into the northbound side of the

M6. We followed the motorway for a few miles before we saw that the guard rail which protected the median between the carriageways was a twisted mess of metal and upturned dirt. A large truck had crashed through, and we could see the wreck of the vehicle on the opposing side, facing the wrong direction.

My uncle slowed the Bronco down as we approached the tangled mess of metal.

"This must be where he crossed over."

Uncle Joe spun the wheel with the heel of his hand, and the Bronco easily handled the rough ground easily. We bumped over the median unceremoniously, and as the Bronco's tyres once again found firm, smooth tarmac, Uncle Joe slowly pressed his foot to the floor, the engine roared into life and pushed us down the road heading southbound.

Within a minute we saw the services and exited the motorway; my uncle eased off the gas pedal, and we almost idled up the ramp towards a large expanse of tarmac which formed the truck parking area. Signs pointed down a small side road to car parking. As we pulled into the truck stop, we noticed two vehicles. A banged-up only Corsa that had seen better days, obviously abandoned; a door was open, leaving the insides of the car exposed to the elements. The other vehicle was a motorhome, or an English equivalent, with a small trailer attached. The van was tall but old. It had a retro vibe to its overall design. The vehicle was filthy, and as we slowly approached, I could see a dingy-looking curtain covering the driver's area. My uncle stopped the Bronco twenty feet from the vehicle, and I could see text on the front grill.

"What the hell is a Bedford?"

"A Bedford," said my uncle, "it's one of those."

Without missing a beat, he applied the parking brake and killed the engine. We both got out of the Bronco and looked around, scanning the periphery for any sign of some kind of attack or ambush. Instinctively I had left my door to the Bronco open, and I had noticed that my uncle had also done the same.

‘Great minds’, I thought to myself, with a slight hint of a smile.

Uncle Joe walked around the entirety of the motorhome from a distance, all the while I kept a lookout. I scanned the fairly dense foliage at the perimeter and kept an eye on the buildings in front of us. The motorhome had been parked to the right-hand side of the truck stop, affording it cover as well as a quick exit to either the north or south. Joe approached the ratty home on wheels and tried to peer in through the windscreen, but it looked like he couldn't see anything through it. I could see that some kind of curtain or blind was blocking the view inside. He turned back to me and shook his head. He knelt down and looked under the vehicle; maybe he was looking for booby traps or something, or maybe he was just checking out the hideous state the chassis was in. In any case, satisfied, he stood up and approached the door built into the body, which served as the main door for the camper itself. He looked at me and nodded; I have no idea what he meant. I simply shrugged back, and he carefully inserted the key into the lock, turned the handle, opened the door and stepped inside. I waited, and seconds stretched by. I nervously looked around, happy that I didn’t hear screaming, shouting or sounds of a struggle. I was considering moving when my uncle appeared at the door and quickly beckoned me to come over.

I quickly looked left and right and then jogged over to the van. I came to a quick walk and instinctively ducked as I entered. The inside was dark, and there was an overpowering smell of damp and old people. It wasn’t entirely unpleasant, but it wouldn’t be my first choice of smells to live with. The van had obviously been well lived in and well loved before Callen had inherited it. The decor was super dated, and everything was cramped; the whole thing looked like it hadn’t been redecorated since its initial manufacture, but even so, there was an ordered chaos to the whole affair. I didn’t have time to take in too many details when my eyes fixed on my uncle and the person sitting on a small bench-style sofa built into the wall.

“Vivian!” I blurted out

“In the flesh,” she replied with a wry smile. She was rubbing her wrists, which I could see, even in the low light, looked red and sore.

“And before you ask, I’ve been better. Although it would appear as if our mutual friend, Callen, is having a worse one, according to your uncle.”

I nodded, not knowing what to say.

"From what I can gather, he was trying to make a deal with Amos. Trade medical supplies for diesel.”

“Medical supplies?” I said, very much surprised

“Check in the cupboards."

I turned and opened one of the cupboards below the small countertop built into the van. It was jam-packed with small boxes of bandages, medicines, wipes and an assortment of all kinds of medical goodies, stuffed in expertly. Callen, it appeared, was a master of Tetris.

I closed the cupboard door and opened another and then another. Each was the same: supplies of all kinds, mostly medical, stuffed carefully into every nook and cranny. He must’ve been funnelling supplies for weeks.

“This begs the question, why?” asked uncle Joe

“According to Callen, there’s some kind of expedition or transport of some kind out of the UK. Something about offshore. We weren’t entirely specific about the details but just mentioned Wick and Elgin.”

“Transport?” I said, “And where the hell is Elgin?”

“It’s about as far north as your can get on the mainland,” said Uncle Joe

“And how do you know that?”

I seemed to be nothing but a question machine at this moment in time.

“The United States Air Force has a base there.”

“Of course they do."

"It does make sense, at least logically. But Callen wasn't military, at least not active. He did talk a big game. Maybe too big."

"So", I said, looking back to Vivian, "how do you figure into this sordid little puzzle?"

"That, I wish I knew."

Uncle Joe sighed.

"We should be getting back. The longer we linger here, the more chance we have at being discovered."

"Cab," he said, "check how much fuel there is in this thing."

I squeezed past my uncle and Vivian; everything was tight, but there was just enough room for it to be on the awkward side of comfortable. I wondered who had lived in here before Callen had claimed ownership. I had visions of an older, retired couple driving around the UK seeing the sights. I didn't want to think about how Callen had gotten the vehicle.

I shuffled through the main vehicle and into the driving area, the curtains still closed. There was just enough room to scootch into the driver's seat.

"Keys!" I half shouted back to the rear of the vehicle

My uncle underhanded them to me, and I managed to just about catch them in one hand. I inserted the key into the ignition and turned it once, and the dash burst into life. Another twist and I'd engage the starter motor, but for now I just wanted the dash working. The fuel gauge barely moved above empty.

"We're almost empty, but not on fumes just yet," I said. "We might have just enough to get back."

"Okay. Cab, you get to drive the piece of shit back to the center with Vivian. I'll take the Bronco. If we're unlucky enough to cross paths with Amos or his crew, I'll run interference. You and Vivian's top priority is to get back to the center and to brief them on what happened here and what we know."

"Got it."

I pulled the curtains around and revealed the outside world, which was suddenly shockingly brighter than I remembered. The dingy inside of the motorhome became slightly more upbeat with the fresh addition of outside light.

"I'll stow the ramp on the trailer. I'll see you back there soon."

"Sure thing."

I heard the side door close and shortly, the bang of metal against metal. Vivian huffed her way up to the passenger side and pulled the rest of the curtain back, letting in more light. I heard my uncle close one door of the Bronco and then another. The throaty engine of the Bronco fired up, and the orange devil pulled up alongside the motorhome. I twisted the key, and the old engine inside the home whined for a good few seconds. There were several coughs, and I pumped the throttle a few times but finally managed to get the old girl going. I could barely hear the home's engine over the Bronco, but I felt the strong vibrations as I sat in the driver's seat. I gave my uncle the thumbs up and he slowly pulled away across the width of the truck park, heading for the road at the far end of the services that would take us towards the motorway. I half expected us to retrace our steps, but I wasn't sure that the old motorhome could traverse the median. I figured Uncle Joe had thought the same as we passed the service station car park and main frontage and headed for the exit ramp that would take us on the southbound portion of the M6. The Bronco pulled away quickly as we headed down the ramp. I tried not to push the motorhome too much, as we needed to conserve fuel. The vehicle felt heavy and unresponsive as I pushed the throttle closer to the floor. The speedometer painfully crept towards forty miles per hour as I reached the bottom of the slip road as we joined the M6. The Bronco slowed down and moved into the middle lane of the M6. I could hear funny knocks and a mysterious squeaking every now and then from the old motorhome. I secretly prayed to the motoring gods to get this bucket of rust and ageing decor back to the center without any trouble. As the speedo reached fifty miles per hour, the Bronco slowed down to match our speed. I made eye contact with my uncle and gave another thumbs up. He nodded and fell back further behind and sat just behind us, keeping a watchful eye.

I fumbled with the steering wheel and looked around the dash but found no evidence of any sort of cruise control. I guess I was having to do this old school.

I flexed my fingers on the steering wheel, which was strangely, and somewhat disturbingly, sticky.

"You seem remarkably calm." I said to Vivian,

"I've been in worse scrapes! All things considered. Callen wasn't all bad; maybe he just had his priorities wrong."

She sounded sad as she watched the landscape go by

"You sound sorry for him."

"In a way I do, or did," Vivian sighed. "In the end he made his choice, and things turned out like they did. But I guess it's not all for nothing."

"What do you mean?"

She turned to me with a smile but said nothing. I heard the ruffling of clothing and saw from the corner of my eye her hand awkwardly searching for something in her jeans pocket, somewhat constricted by the seat belt. A few seconds later she pulled out a small container of some kind. I took a glance or two, keeping my eyes on the road ahead. Something clattered, and I realised that Vivian was shaking the small container which held several small somethings inside. I looked a few times, unable to determine what they were as she held up the container and stared inside.

"What are they?"

"Teeth," she said, looking at me. "Perfect human teeth."

"Where did you get those?"

"Remember the thing you and Joe found?"

"I dug them out of it. These cocoons, or whatever you want to call them, are, or were, human."

Blurting out "What?" Was all I could muster. The shock

must've registered on my face. Mental note. Playing competitive poker isn't going to be a good look for me.

"That's insane," I added.

Vivian shook the container again; the hard enamel nubs rattled against their plastic prison.

"I need more data, but I suspect that I might find a more complete bone structure if I could examine one for an extended period of time."

I couldn't reply. I didn't have the mental capacity. All I could do was drive. But my thoughts raced at the prospect. Could these things really be human? What was going on? How could this happen? I opened my mouth as I formulated a barrage of questions, but it appeared that Vivian had anticipated this.

"Before you ask. I have no idea as to the who, what, why or even how this is possible. All I know is that I pried these teeth out of what looked to be a jawbone that was lodged in the thing you and your uncle found. It might be a stretch to say it was human. We probably should find more."

I nodded. We were in strange times. And it would appear as though things would be getting a little more stranger.

When we arrived back at the center Vivian was greeted with enthusiastic hellos, hugs and a barrage of questions. I held back, not wanting to get pulled into the vortex of chaos that appeared to be forming. My uncle stepped in; almost as suddenly as it started, the vortex fell apart, and people returned to their normal duties looking a little happier. I noticed a few of the stragglers that had opted to leave were looking at each other and started talking in low tones. Where once their actions had been quick and deliberate as they packed up their belongings into whatever little car they had, they were now slowing down and becoming almost laboured. I smiled.

"Fair-weather friends," I said under my breath and followed the contingent of Vivian, my uncle and Patricia into the center for the inevitable meeting that was about to take place.

The area was a buzz of activity, and the room was filled with an excited energy. My uncle spoke first, giving a brief explanation of what we had seen. He did a good job of leaving out the gory details of Callens' demise and expertly glossed over and sidestepped the method of how we received the location of Southwaite services. Vivian stepped in and gave her calm and very detailed testimony of what she had seen, experienced and gone through. She covered how Callen had let her start her examination and kept out of her way. But it was obvious half an hour later when he returned that this was just a ruse to get rid of the other two people in the escort group. Vivian went into detail about what Callen had told her about the transport and military-style bases in the North, at Wick and Elgin. There was an obvious shift as she told the story. People looked at each other, and a few leaned in and whispered. I could almost see the division that was starting to form. I half expected Patricia to step in, but it was Vivian that broke the chattering.

It was then that she dealt the coup de grace as she pulled out the small container and rolled it across the table and explained her preliminary findings from the examination of the cocoon, as she called it. Eyes went wide and mouths were agape. Patricia carefully looked at the contents of the plastic, cylindrical container. She almost seemed transfixed by it as she rolled it around in her hand. She eventually placed it gently on the table. A few other people stared at it, yet didn't yield totally to their curiosity and left the small container where it sat.

"I'd like," said Vivian, "to have another crack at the cocoon. To take a deeper look and try and find out what's going on here."

"If I may," interjected Uncle Joe, "we need to assess our most obvious threat."

"Amos?"

He nodded.

"I think it's safe to say we can expect more trouble from him at some point in the future. He's already stretched, in terms of available resources, and he's bound to be looking for more. I would assume it's safe to say he probably sees us as an easy target. And after today he's only going to be more paranoid and eventually more violent. The only variable he doesn't know is what we have and how much of a hassle it will be obtaining them."

"What are you saying?" asked Patricia

"We're going to have to decide if we stand and fight or if we talk about taking a risk."

"A risk?"

My uncle nodded.

"What Callen told Vivian. This transport, whatever it is. Even if that doesn't exist, the base does. So we choose; do we relocate on a chance or attempt to hold our ground here? Either way, sooner or later we're going to have to make a decision. Or it'll be made for us."

Patricia nodded. A few other people, who I have no idea were, looked nervous. Vivian had settled back into her chair, and for the first time since we picked her up, I saw that she looked tired.

"It's clear we have much to discuss and debate," said Patricia. "For now I think Vivian, Joe and his team need some much-needed rest. Over the coming hours we'll evaluate what we know and move forward with a clear plan. It's clear we need to understand what's going on as well as protect ourselves."

It didn't seem too definitive, but then I guess this was new information. I, too, suddenly felt very tired. It'd been a busy day full of confrontation, and the images of Callens's abused face suddenly floated into my mind. I sighed and waited for people to filter out of the room before I attempted to find coffee and somewhere quiet to sit for a while.

My uncle walked over to me.

"You did well today."

I smiled, somewhat awkwardly.

"But the real test is coming," he said, looking around the room as the last few people filed out.

"Remember what I said. Survive. Because this is just the start."

THREE MONTHS LATER

My uncle was right. I had to survive. No. I wanted to survive. No. I would survive.

I looked at my face in the mirror. The still red, although now fading, scars serving as a reminder of how fragile everything was, the body included. Nothing was or is permanent, and while it would probably put fear into some people, it gave me focus. Because it meant I could tear down anything or anyone in my way. I stared at myself in the mirror. Things had changed and would continue to change. More than anything, I felt I had changed. In the months that had passed I felt very different. Physically and mentally. Now that the world, or at least our part of the world, had somehow devolved into a simpler life. Time passed quickly. Survival was everyone's goal. Although to others, power and domination still called. Violence would be met with violence, and in this new world I had to make changes too. What's a girl to do?

The answer, of course, would be to rip every fucker's head off that threatened our community. Although my anger still raged, I had developed a more subtle control. I had moments, small slips every now and then. I would add a new scar maybe, too. But there was something else that nagged at me, from the deeper depths of my consciousness. It would plague me at nights, waking me up every now and then, cold and sweaty. There was a rage, a thirst for vengeance. It required sating. And maybe it wouldn't be sooner. But maybe later. But eventually, that thirst would be sated, and I could put the voices to rest. Or rather the voice. That one voice which haunts me to this day. The one voice who I can never forget. Charlie.

In the still hours of the early morning I can sometimes hear his mocking laughter on the wind. I am ashamed of myself, torn by the illusion that I could've done something. But maybe something, anything, would've helped. I try to move on, to try and let the dead rest. But there's that monster inside, deep down, that lets me know there's a score to settle. It doesn't matter who or when. All that matters is that someday, somehow I WILL settle my debt to my friend. And I'll burn everything to do it. So help me, or my name isn't...

A knock on the door interrupted my thought process. I was jolted back into reality. The door opened, and a head popped around the edge; it was Ellen, one of the newer members of the community. Someone else that had made it this far that we managed to keep out of Amos' grasp.

"Hey Pu..." she started

"What's up?" I asked with some level of abruptness. I didn't have too much alone time, especially with the growing number of residents here, so maybe it was a little rude of me. But damn. I needed my own space.

I was suddenly aware of commotion behind her. I saw shapes darting left and right, and I heard a higher level of noise and excitement emanating from the center. More than usual. The confusion must've shown on my face because Ellen didn't beat around the bush as I refocused on her slender, yet moonlike, face.

"Amos is coming!"

I nodded, and she withdrew her head, and the door closed behind her with a slight bump. So it had finally come to pass. Between the small victory that Amos had gained against

Callen and with my uncle secretly ferrying supplies into Amos' encampment, we'd managed to stave off the inevitable. But like my uncle had warned, these were only temporary measures. And now it looked like we were in for a fight, and a big one, too.

I leaned against the edge of the basin and took a deep breath and looked at myself in the mirror. I tied up my now long hair in a ponytail. Gone was the short bob I had previously cultivated. I pushed away from the sink and stalked across the room and put a hand on the handle. I paused, knowing that as soon as I opened and passed through the door, I would be like a leaf on the stream, taken by the current, a passenger to the wild unrelenting flow. Sink or swim. It was all down to me.

"Survive," I said and opened the door.

EPILOGUE

A figure. A shambling mess of a human, wrapped in found clothing, huffed and puffed through the undergrowth. Howls and screams echoed behind the man, now caked in dirt, grime and dried blood. He moved with a pronounced limp, but there was a determination in him. Driven by something deep. Something almost alien. His limbs worked robotically; he moved without thought but with purpose. The figure navigated through trees and moved around them in a haphazard way, stumbling from one to the next. Sometimes flailing. But always moving. An animalistic growl erupted from his throat as he emerged from the woods. Behind him he heard others. His face set into a snarl of pain and frustration. His eyes narrowed, and he set his sights beyond the field in front of him. He shambled forward, slowly at first but then hobbling and almost skipping a few steps when he got up to a brisk pace, at least in his physical condition. More calls and shouts echoed behind him. He had a decent lead on his competition, but they would be faster, nimbler, and in better condition. But he was more dogged, more wily. He had previously, successfully, deceived those behind him. Pretending to go one way, then going another. A wild goose chase. A gamble that had paid off. The underdog had gained the upper hand, but only for a short period of time. That's how this new world would work. No rules. Anything by any means. It wasn't just about being the strongest but about being smarter and more devious than the competition. And in this new world, competition was everywhere. The figure lopped on through a field of grass-like crops. He made a 'shushing' noise as he moved through the waist-high flora. Halfway over the field he heard them behind him. They howled and screamed. Mad things. Angry things. Gaining ground rapidly. Even the most devious couldn't outrun the strongest and more physically capable forever. The figure paused for a few seconds, seemingly taking in the scene of other shambling and striding figures, his heart threatening to beat out of his chest. The figure turned and pushed himself on. His arms working hard, as if to make up for the lack of movement in the stiff, almost unmoving right leg, which dragged, at times, on the ground.

The figure grunted in pain; teeth gritted, he pushed himself on. He wouldn't be denied this victory. As he came to the edge of the field, approaching the tall hedge in front of him, he glanced behind and saw the others in pursuit. A figure fell to the ground; their foot had found a rabbit hole or some other defect in the ground. The figure smiled before turning to the hedge and stepping forward. He was aware of a dull droning from beyond the hedge and an almost strange mechanical slapping sound. His eyes widened, and he turned back to the hedge and started to push through, almost in panic. His motions uncalculated. His arm caught on something sharp and prickly. The droning somehow grew louder and fainter at the same time. The figure stumbled through the hedge and pushed out the other side. He sprawled on the soft grass. His limbs were exhausted and screaming in pain. He pushed himself up, the bright sun beating down, and saw it in flight. A small, white plane lifting into the sky. He lunged forward as he watched it turn around. Desperation overwhelmed him as he hobbled forward and reached for the object, waving frantically, hoping those onboard would see him. He shouted and screamed for them to see him. To come back. He stumbled forward as he did. Continuing to watch the object as it circled. For one desperate moment it seemed like they could see him and would return. But as his gaze followed the craft, it turned towards the sun and moved away. He fell to the ground. Exhausted. He rolled onto his back and gazed up at the sky.

Then he heard the sound. The screaming and shouting from beyond the hedge. He knew he had no time. He thought of just lying there, letting them do what they will. But that would be quitting. And he didn't like to quit.

"No fucking way," he said out loud in a rasping wheeze. He rolled over and pushed himself to his knees and awkwardly got to his feet and stumbled forward. His leg was stiff again, but he forced himself to move. His gaze automatically found the nearest small building, and he hobbled forward in a skipping run. Figures burst through the hedge immediately spotting their prey. The figure swore and doubled down, calling on all his reserves of energy. He screamed himself. And surged on. The grass was easygoing, and he banged against the closed door to the building. He fumbled with the handle and, at first, thought it was locked until he twisted the dirty knob the other way. He burst through the door and closed it behind him. There was a small catch to lock the door, which he turned. The muffled voices and noises of the chasing pack were almost at the door. He looked around, taking in his surroundings. He quickly saw an old wooden table. He wrestled it into position against the door as he heard the first impact from outside. He quickly found smaller, heavier objects to build a makeshift barricade. A small filing cabinet, with not very much inside. Several fire extinguishers. A random box of junk, which was way heavier than he expected. Other small bits and pieces were thrown here and there to provide support. By now the banging and scratching behind the door grew louder. He almost expected the door to splinter and give way, like he'd seen in the movies, but it held strong.

He looked around for another door or window through which they could get in. But the barricaded door appeared to be the only way in and out. Satisfied the door would hold, he turned to survey his surroundings. A large area that appeared to be a sort of weird hybrid of office and lounge. Maps were mounted on the walls, along with pictures of various planes throughout the years. Another photograph, which was really two pictures joined together, adorned the wall, which was of the area which appeared to be taken from the air; one image was dated a few years ago, and another from fifty years previous. There were a number of boxes dotted here and there; contents had been scattered about them. The previous visitors had gone through them. Maybe trying to find something of value or use. The man limped across the room and eyed the large couch which adorned a nearby wall. He glanced towards the door, the banging still consistent. He didn't know how long they would keep at it. He knew he was in for a long wait. The couch called to him. He thought he might sleep for a week, even with the banging. He turned from the couch and shuffled into a small kitchen area. Licking his lips, which were now dry and peeling, he turned the cold water tap. A steady stream of water started to flow. He thrust an eager hand under the stream, which was cool and soothing. The scratches on his hands smarted. He splashed water onto his face and felt immediately refreshed. He drank for another handful and then turned the tap off. Conserve. How long the water would last would be an unknown. Growing ever tired, he opened the cupboards and searched for anything to eat. It looked like someone had gone through and taken everything.

"Rats!" he thought

He looked down and saw a small bucket that had been used as a rubbish bin, filled with several chocolate bar wrappers and other packaging from biscuits and small savoury snacks. His stomach grumbled. He noticed the fridge. Walked over and pulled the door open.

To his surprise, it wasn't completely empty. A crooked

smile crept along his dirt-stained face. He hurriedly reached inside and pulled out a can of coke, a packet of biscuits and a single lemon curd bun.

"Fuck yes." he said, placing everything on the countertop.

Happy that he now had something to put in his stomach, he turned the water back on. He rinsed his hands and let the dirt run off. He splashed water onto his face and rubbed what he could off. He scooped several handfuls of water over his head and through his hair. Water dribbled down his face and onto his ratty clothing and onto the floor. He took another scoop of water and rubbed his face for the last time before turning off the tap. He found an old, stained tea towel, but the stains didn't matter. He rubbed his face, neck and head. He finished by wiping his hands as dry as he could and then stretched the now damp towel over an empty space on the countertop.

He took the food and drink from the counter and hobbled back into the main office area and collapsed onto the couch. His leg sang out in pain, and he winced. He sat back and let out a ragged breath of air.

The banging at the door annoyed him, but there was little to do about it, other than try and ignore it. The man took a deep breath and wriggled out of the makeshift poncho he had fashioned from the things he had found. The improvised apparel was dirty and bloodstained and smelled less than desirable. He threw it to the ground before taking off his own filthy jacket. He kicked off one shoe and then another. His right foot ached and had been bleeding. He dreaded to think what it looked like under the bloody sock. He wiggled his feet; it wasn't too painful. Electing to take care of that issue at a later date, he left the sock on. He pitched the jacket into the air, and it fell to the floor several feet away. He reached for a can of coke and cracked the tab. The can made a quick fizz. A small rivulet of coke erupted from the top and dribbled onto his well-worn jeans. Only a few days earlier he would've cared. He would've cursed himself, but now he was just happy to have something sweet and tasty to drink. He slurped deeply, finishing the can in short order. Gasping for air, he crumpled the can and let it fall to the floor. He tore open the packet of chocolate digestives and pushed one into his mouth and chewed. Crumbs fell onto the couch, and he gorged himself on three before he stopped. He sat back and was happy for a few moments. He felt very tired, even with the banging and occasional screaming at the door. This was life now. This was how things would work. Run. Hide. Survive.

He sighed and pushed himself up, hopping around on his good leg before gently applying weight to his right. He hobbled past the kitchen, hoping to find a toilet. He saw the door, labelled as such, and pushed into the small, functional room. A small, rectangular window was open. He looked into the stall and saw there was toilet paper. Life was getting a little easier, it seemed.

He walked to the urinal and, for the first time in what felt like a long time, took a pee with little to no trepidation. He finished and washed his hands at the nearby basin. Using a generous amount of soap to further clean his hands, which, even when finished, were still stained with dirt and filth.

We wondered if they'd ever be truly clean again. Both physically and metaphorically.

He looked at himself in the mirror. He'd picked up a few extra cuts and bruises to get here. He thought this would be the end of the line. This would be his goal, that when he got here, everything would be okay and that things would be like they were before. How wrong he'd been. He chastised himself. If he were quicker, if he hadn't been injured...

It was useless to think this way. At least he tried to tell himself that, but he knew he'd think about this for a long time to come. His attention shifted to the steady banging and scratching at the door. They wouldn't tire for a long time, and, worse, they knew he was inside. Their bloodlust seemingly giving them superhuman stamina. Desperate for a thrill kill they knew was so close, but just untouchable. It spurred them on and made the pounding, scratching and wailing more intense.

The man laughed and shook his head, almost in resignation. But a glimmer of hope still flickered at the edge of his consciousness. That quiet little wolf still growled and made him push on. Made him survive. Even so, the enormity of what he faced was still daunting. Goodness knows how many dark figures were after him, fuelled by their need. A severe lack of food and no clear plan or destination made the man dizzy. He settled his hands on the side of the basin in front of him, trying to drown out the awful sounds of the murder pack outside. He looked up and stared at his own filthy reflection; he locked eyes with the doppelgänger in the mirror.

"How the hell are you going to get out of this, Charlie?"

A MESSAGE FROM THE AUTHOR

Thank you, mysterious reader, for taking a chance on a complete unknown especially when there are much better and well known authors out there for you to spend your hard earned money on. Your support through the purchase of the paperback edition means that I can continue to write more (which may or may not be a good thing depending on your point of view!)

I hope you enjoyed this opening salvo into what I've called "The Weird World Saga". As you might have guessed I have plans and ideas to take this further as well as to tell other, unrelated, stories. But let's not get too ahead of ourselves here!

Thank you, once again. Your support means everything

www.ingramcontent.com/pod-product-compliance
Ingram Content Group UK Ltd.
Pitfield, Milton Keynes, MK11 3LW, UK
UKHW012123101125
464927UK00001B/2

9 781919 323305